A.E.W. Mason can be credited with novel of the 20th century – notably filmed seven times.

He was born in 1865 and educated at Dulwich College before going up to Trinity College, Oxford. Once his formal education was completed, Mason went on to become an actor, which had been an ambition since schooldays. He appeared on the London stage a few times in the latter part of the nineteenth century.

He began his writing part-time, commencing with historical fiction and romance, but his first novel was a commercial failure. His second, however, '*The Courtship of Maurice Buckler*', written in 1896 was a success, and this persuaded him to write full time. Several more followed before '*The Four Feathers*' in 1902. There was also an adaptation of one of his works for the New York stage at this time.

In 1906 he moved into the arena of politics, becoming a Liberal Member of Parliament for Coventry. Writing became secondary for a while, although '*The Broken Road*' was published. But Mason's love of writing carried on and he left politics in 1910 to resume it full time. He developed his style to incorporate detective fiction, introducing one of the earliest fictional detectives, Inspector Hanaud in '*At the Villa Rose*', being the Gallic counterpart to Sherlock Holmes. His detective fiction contains material clues and spontaneity which readers continue to find extremely satisfying.

During World War I, Mason served in the Royal Marine Light Infantry, but subsequently transferred to the Admiralty, where he worked in intelligence and set up counter-espionage networks, serving also in Spain and Mexico.

After the war his success continued and he became prolific in output, later counting his friend King George V amongst many avid readers. He also enjoyed considerable success through stage and screen both sides of the Atlantic and received regular positive reviews in UK newspapers and the likes of '*The New York Times*'. There are numerous films and productions, many still extant, of his work.

By the mid-1930's he turned increasingly towards non-fiction and '*The Life of Sir Francis Drake*' was published in 1941 to great critical acclaim. He died in 1948, at the age of 83.

Musk and Amber

A E W MASON

HOUSE OF
STRATUS

This edition published in 2012 by House of Stratus, an imprint of Stratus Books Ltd., Lisandra House, Fore St., Looe, Cornwall, PL13 1AD, UK.

www.houseofstratus.com

Typeset, printed and bound by House of Stratus.

A catalogue record for this book is available from the British Library and the Library of Congress.

ISBN 0-7551-1749-2
EAN 978-07551--1749-9

Contents

Contents (contd)

Too many there be to whom a dead Enemy smells well, and who find Musk and Amber in Revenge.

"Christian Morals"
by Sir THOMAS BROWNE

Chapter One

AT GREST PARK

Mr James Elliot reached Grest Park in his coach at half-past seven of the evening. He was not an assiduous visitor of country houses, for he preferred the artistic society of Continental cities. But Grest held a special place in his affections. It was not a castle, frowning from the top of a rock over a country of serfs; nor a Tudor Palace of dark panels and diamond-paned windows; but a mansion of his own eighteenth century, spacious and light, and, whilst reserving its own privileges, paternal. A great Whig house in fact. Wide corridors with white walls ornamented with plaster plaques by Adam led to long oblong rooms lit by high rounded windows. Big mirrors in gilded frames of Chinese Chippendale hung on the walls between the windows. Lofty ceilings, barrel-shaped and painted, spread a panoply above the head. Nothing frowned. There was a suggestion of humanity. One moved in a world of white and gold, of space and grace and high colonnades. Yet comfort was not lacking. Deep carpets of soft patterns made walking a caress. There were small rooms where one could be private, with open fireplaces and sweet smelling logs burning in the iron baskets.

Three years had passed since Mr Elliot's last visit. Philip, the owner and builder of Grest, had died a year before after a long illness, and Elliot wondered with some trepidations what changes had been made in this lordly pleasure-house. But after he had driven past the great stables and up the wide avenue to the west front his trepidations diminished. For an old friend in a butler, growing grey now and stooping under his long years of service, welcomed him with a smile.

"Gurton, I am delighted to see you again," said Mr Elliot handsomely.

"You are very kind, Sir."

Gurton led the way across the vestibule and up the stairs to the bedroom over the great south portico which Elliot had occupied before. A footman and Elliot's own servant followed with the travelling bags.

"Her Ladyship fancied that you would like your old room, Sir," said Gurton.

That would be Lady Frances Scoble, daughter by the first wife, of course.

"Her Ladyship is most thoughtful," said Elliot. He went across to the central window and, as he looked out, he sighed with enjoyment. The Italian garden behind its wrought-iron gates stretched out in front of him, an oblong of grass paths and glowing flowerbeds, of box trees and hedges, of stone seats at the sides and in one corner, a ridiculous charming little temple with open pillars and a roof of green and gold. Beyond the garden, lawns like velvet shaded here and there by a big cedar sloped gently to a lake. The east side of the lake was guarded by a ridge with a coppice of trees to crown it; and straight ahead a wide country of fields and villages melted into a blue distance where round smooth downs rolled upwards and closed it in.

Mr Elliot enjoyed the familiar view and still more he enjoyed his enjoyment of it. He was a man of forty years now and had begun consciously to make much of each little sensuous pleasure, recording it carefully in his memory.

"There have been, I suppose, many changes and surprises, Gurton, since I was here," he said sympathetically, "though, upon my word, I have seen no sign of them yet."

Gurton, however, was not to be led to talk.

"Surprises, Sir, must be expected," he answered, a little formally. "Supper will be at nine."

"Thank you, Gurton."

Left to himself, Mr Elliot was conscious of a change. A gentle melancholy stole over him; and in spite of the beauty of the scene before him he almost regretted that he had come to Grest. He was going to miss the long intimate conversations with his former host, pacing the gardens or sitting over their wine with the candlesticks pushed aside so that they might argue the better; he, the dilettante, the idler, and the other, the great nobleman who by some miracle of industry managed his estates, made a speech of some wisdom in the House of Lords from time to time, and yet lived magnificently for months on end in some great villa in Rome or Naples or the Apennines. James Elliot was not a parasite, but he was something of a snob; and with the death of his friend there was an emptiness in the year's progress which he could not hope to fill. How they had talked, the two of them, and from whatever point the conversation had started, how surely it always came round to the same subject – Italy and the development in Italy of that new, odd, artificial art, the opera! Romanina, the young Farinelli, Domenico Scarlatti, the poet Metastasio, the triumphs of Handel in London.

Mr Elliot flung up the windows. A cascade of rooks had just burst out from a grove and the birds were wheeling about the sky with loud cries, as though they were sorting themselves out before they went to bed. Then they were hushed and the world was given over to the evening hymns of blackbird and thrush. And whilst he listened and looked, the air noisy with melody and the fresh earthy scents of young summer mounting to his nostrils, a note was struck upon a harpsichord in a room opening on to the portico below him. Mr Elliot turned his head sharply. Of all the things in the world, music was the most real to him. He waited, his body and his mind tense. What was to follow upon that note? One never knew – one always hoped. Mr Elliot in the matter of music was at one with Gurton. Surprises were to be expected; and one leaped at Mr Elliot now. Through an open window in the room below him a young clear voice, with such an appeal as had never moved him in all his wanderings, poured out melody upon the air.

"Young Cupid with the bandaged eyes
Draws tight his bow of pearl and jade.
Swift from the string the arrow flies
To wound the heart of youth and maid.

But in this odd world of sevens and sixes
Nothing is quite as it ought to be.
It's only my heart that the arrow transfixes
And never the maid's that was made for me."

Mr Elliot sat down in a chair before the open window. The song couldn't end there. He was thinking not of the song nor the singer. He was wrapt in delight. Changes were to be expected, Gurton had said. Here were changes indeed, but Mr Elliot was insensible of them. He waited, expectant, his ears ravished, and the voice rose again on a lilt of pleasure:

> "I have her picture carved upon crystal,
> Painted in exquisite colours and rare.
> A pledge? If a pledge, it's a pledge that the tryst'll
> Only be kept by one of the pair.
>
> She has eyes that are deeper and kinder than sapphires;
> Her lips' dark velvet defies the rose.
> Oh, I can't believe that other lads have fires
> Fierce as the one which destroys my repose."

Every word was clear, every note true and effortless. It rose and swooped and fell, a boy's voice, fresh and pure as a bird's, but with a throb of passion, an infinity of delicate cadences which no bird ever had. It rose – no – it poured itself out again like water sparkling from a glass ewer.

> "And so I wander by forest and boulder
> Hoping that one day in spite of my fears
> I shall wake with a golden head at my shoulder
> Instead of a pillow wet with my tears."

The last two lines were repeated with a change in the melody, so that the joyous eagerness of the first ending declined in a curve of disappointment and died away in unhappiness. But so the musician intended. There was no faltering in the voice which sang the music. When it died away upon the air, it died in a sigh.

Mr Elliot sat without moving in an enchantment. The garden, the lake beyond, the summer evening, to his eyes had suffered the same change as he and lay hushed under the same spell. He almost expected the blue downs in the far distance to melt and reveal some exquisite glimpse of a world unknown. He was brought back into the life of things as they were by the entrance of Gurton, who had come up to see that one of his favourite guests lacked nothing for his change of dress.

"I'll send up your man to you, Sir. It is now twenty minutes past eight."

"Thank you," said Elliot, and after a pause, "I suppose that was his Lordship singing?"

Gurton smiled with a smile of real pleasure.

"Yes, Sir. His Lordship has a very fine voice they tell me. His Lordship's father thought very highly of it and had great teachers down from London to advise him. A Mr Handel came once."

That of course was the explanation why Elliot had never heard the boy before. Mr Elliot nodded his head. It was a matter of training. He had not been allowed to sing even before the small public of a country drawing-room. It had all been scales and scales, and one simple phrase repeated and repeated until the last drip of music had been extracted – Porpora's way, Jommelli's way, the way of all the great teachers.

"So Mr Handel came to Grest, did he?" Elliot mused. "Let me see! His Lordship will be twelve now?"

"Twelve last month, Sir."

Gurton might be reluctant to discuss the changes which the last years had brought about at Grest, but he was prepared to make speeches about his young master.

"Of course he is not so given to his singing as he was. It's a sort of gift with him. If he comes across a song he likes, he'll sit down and sing it. But all those trills and roulades and shakes which seem so popular, he's weary of them, one might say."

"A pity," said Mr Elliot.

But Gurton would not listen to any reproach of his idol, however mild.

"His Lordship's a proper boy, Sir. His heart is set on the sea, as a boy's should be. He sees himself an Admiral in a blue coat, commanding a fleet against the parlez-vous, or stumping with a wooden leg up and down his quarter-deck."

"And Grest?" Mr Elliot asked. "What of Grest meanwhile?"

"Grest won't run away, Sir," said Gurton dryly and he departed.

Mr Elliot smiled ruefully. He repeated to himself two lines of the song which he had heard.

"In this odd world of sevens and sixes
Nothing is quite as it ought to be."

Here was a voice which from the throat of some surpliced chorister should be beating against the roof of the Sistine Chapel like a bird seeking its freedom; and it belonged to Julian John Philip Challoner. Carolus Scoble, Earl of Linchcombe, Viscount Terceira – there had been a Scoble who had sailed with Drake to the Azores and very likely that fact accounted for the boy's present ambition – Baron Hardley, owner of Grest, a seat in the House of Lords and half a dozen pocket boroughs! He didn't want to waste any more time over shakes and trills. Not he! He had a divine gift, the rarest sweetest gift made to one single person in a century, that he might entrance the world, and he wanted to be Old Timbertoes on his quarter-deck. Mr Elliot was annoyed with Julian John Philip Challoner and the rest of it. He flung the clothes he was taking off about in a pet. None the less at ten minutes to nine, groomed and spruce, from his powdered wig to his ruffles, as one of the box trees in the Italian garden, he descended into the great drawing-room. A wood fire was burning cheerfully in the grate and a young woman in a dress of flowered satin was standing in front of it with a hand upon the marble mantelpiece. Elliot saw her face reflected in the mirror with its curious frame of gilt birds and human figures before she turned to him. She wore her brown hair unpowdered and arranged in a simple coiffure which gave her an appearance of early youth. She was, as Elliot knew, twenty-seven and had always been handsome rather than pretty. But tonight she had a colour in her cheeks and a light in her brown eyes and a smile upon her lips, which made him forget the strong features. Before, it had been the bone-structure which had been noticeable. "She's a demned fine gel," her father used to say of her, "but, by Gad, she'll look like a horse by the time she's forty!" Well, forty was still a long way off and it was the warmth and softness of her flesh which now caught and held the eye.

"Mr Elliot," she said as she gave him her hand, "we have no company for you except our poor selves. You are our first visitor and we treat you as one of the family."

"Lady Frances," Elliot answered, very much flattered as he bowed over her hand, "you could do nothing more gracious."

"And Julian," she continued, "insisted on staying up beyond his bed time specially to welcome you."

Rather shyly the boy who had sung came forward from the embrasure of the high round-headed window. Mr Elliot would not have known him again, so great a difference the three years had made. He had been small then, and though he had not really outgrown his age, the slenderness of his figure and his long, straight legs gave to him a greater look of height than he possessed. Moreover he had grown beautiful. Mr Elliot could think of no other word. He had the beauty of a Greek statue – a broad forehead; a nose straight with nostrils which a sculptor might have carved, ran down from it without a notch at the root to the short upper lip; a mouth wide enough to show an unspoilt range of white teeth; and a jaw with the clean curve of the moon's sickle. It would have been a face too regular but for its lively expression and the eyes, which were at the first view enormous. They were of a deep violet and set wide apart between dark lashes as long and silky as a girl's.

"The boy Paris on Mount Ida," Mr Elliot said to himself. "Well, his voice will crack like a tin kettle, but he'll still be able to toss the apple to whatever goddess he approves."

If there was a fault, it was to be found in a delicacy too fine for the world's rough and tumble. Certainly his dress set him off to advantage. A wealth of brown hair, not as yet tied back by any riband, flowed down to a white collar hemmed with lace and a shirt of white lawn open at the throat. He wore a coat and breeches of black velvet with buttons of cut jet, black silk stockings and shoes with black jet buckles, as though he still was dressed in mourning for his father.

"I was very glad," he said, "when my sister told me that you were coming to Grest," and he held out his hand and clasped his visitor's in a firm grasp. "I wonder if when my lessons are done tomorrow, I might ride with you for an hour?"

He looked towards Lady Frances for permission and Mr Elliot wondered whether the boy's father would not have found this docility a trifle spiritless. Were Admirals made of quite this stuff? Mr Elliot doubted.

Lady Frances was in something of a hurry to reply; and again Mr Elliot wondered. Had his own face been a trifle too easy to read?

"Why, of course, Julian. You will have finished by twelve. At half-past twelve, Mr Elliot, if that is agreeable to you, Julian will be free."

"It will be very agreeable to me," said Mr Elliot and Julian thanked him, bade his half-sister good night and went out of the room. Mr Elliot was inclined to modify his censure. There was something very winning in the boy's manner, a modesty, a courtesy, and perhaps a quiet will lying undisclosed behind them.

Mr Elliot, however, was given no time to pursue his reflections. A step sounded on the gravel path and a young man in a coat of brown cloth embroidered with silver passed the window on his way to the door.

"My cousin Henry," said Frances. "You know him, I think."

Mr Elliot didn't know him from Adam. He saw a tall, strong, handsome animal of a man, with the dark blue eyes of the Scobles, only harder than he remembered in any other of them, and a jaw rather more pronounced and rather redder – a Scoble, he would have said, who never left the table until the bottle of port was tucked away under his waistcoat.

"No, we have never met," said Henry with a nod which suggested that indeed there was no particular reason why they should have met this evening. And as Gurton announced that supper was ready and Frances led them into the small dining-room, Mr Elliot began to wonder why after all they were meeting.

"Yes, why was I invited, the first guest of all after the year of mourning was completed?" he pondered. He could imagine no point of sympathy with Henry, and though Frances Scoble had directed the household and sat at the head of the table ever since her father's second wife had died, he had never been on more than formal terms with her. Undoubtedly the invitation to him was odd and he determined to keep an ear open on the chance of intercepting a reason for it.

But it was his eye which first warned him that there was a reason. For they had no sooner taken their seats at the small, round table than he caught across the candles a slight glance and a little nod made by Henry to Frances. His cousin, however, was less crude in taking up her cue, and she began with a polite question or two to Mr Elliot on the

8

discomforts of his journey from London and whether he was well rested and what new fashions he could describe to country mice like herself. Mr Elliot made the proper gallant replies, but Henry broke in upon them impatiently.

"The fashions, my dear coz, which Mr. Elliot noticed in the Mall two days ago are to be sure altogether démodé today."

"He's a bear, Mr Elliot," said Lady Frances laughing very prettily. "I wonder I put up with him. I lent him the Dower House and I vow there's only one reason which stops me from taking it away again."

"And that reason, Madam, so that I may make the most of it?" said Henry with a mocking humility.

"Julian," said Lady Frances, and with the name both of them put away their frivolity. Lady Frances sighed.

"I am the boy's guardian. I must do my best. But he's a heavy charge for an ignorant body like me. He will go to Eton in due course and he has tutors, but how to direct the tutors? I should be in a sad quandary but for my bear of a cousin."

Mr Elliot started. It was as much as he could do not to gasp. He certainly stared beyond the time limit of good manners. In the use of a gun, in the training of a dog, in the schooling of a horse, Henry Scoble would no doubt be an admirable director of tutors. But for Julian, with the wide opportunities awaiting him, someone of a finer culture was required. Mr Elliot, however, managed to keep his tongue still. He recognised that the boy's possession of a rare voice and his exquisite use of it had, so far as he himself was concerned, clothed him with a glamour for which there might not be the least justification. Choristers abounded who, once they had slipped out of their cassocks, were just snotty-nosed little ruffians with minds as foul as their voices were divine. No one knew it better than Mr Elliot who had more than once wasted his charity, beguiled by an anthem. But he was still under the spell of the voice and the gracious manner of Julian Linchcombe. The country should be combed for tutors to educate this paragon. He stammered out: "Choosing teachers for a lad with a future so important is of course a most delicate matter. One cannot exercise too much care, or seek too experienced advice."

Mr Henry Scoble lolled back in his chair and laughed – with enjoyment rather than annoyance.

"Mr Elliot, my dear cousin," he said easily to Frances, "does not know that though I hunt four days a week through the winter, I am none the less a Fellow of Oriel and a scholar. Yes, Mr Elliot, a scholar. If your attention had ever turned to the poet, Propertius – is it too much to suggest that it never has? – you would have found your way made easier by some trumpery notes of mine. I was glad therefore to offer some suggestions for the direction of my young relative's studies."

Mr Elliot was staggered.

"I hadn't an idea," he mumbled. "You must forgive me if I seemed, to hint that any other advice should be sought; and so—" all his admiration for cultured accomplishment showed in his face—"and so you actually lecture at Oriel?"

Mr Henry Scoble shrugged his shoulders.

"I do, Mr Elliot. I am a poor man," and then he leaned forward and his manner changed altogether.

"But my fortunes are a very small matter compared with those of the boy we are talking about. Latin, Mr Elliot! You shall give me your opinion upon that in a minute." It was quite obvious that he would not have given an old frying-pan for Mr Elliot's opinion. "In the education of a gentleman, Latin is the first necessity. And not only because Latin makes good tags to a speech, or because the language has a sonority and rhythm which cannot but be of value to one occupying a great position. But above all, because there is a sobriety in Latin authors. Observe that word, if you please, Mr Elliot. Sobriety! Isn't it the watchword of the Whigs? And we are a great Whig family, looking forward to the leadership of our chief-to-be, Julian Linchcombe."

Henry Scoble spoke without bluster but forcibly, leaning forward with his elbows folded upon the mahogany table. There was no longer any indifference in his face or his eyes; and Mr Elliot, looking round the room where family portraits were framed in the white panels of the walls, understood, or thought that he understood, the spirit in which Henry Scoble spoke.

"For myself," he said, "I remember that Gaul was divided into three parts and that Virgil sang of arms and the man. And there my Latin comes to a full stop, and, to be honest, I don't feel a penny the worse for it. But then I don't belong to a great Whig family."

"To be sure you don't," Henry agreed heartily, and Mr Elliot was a trifle nettled at being taken up so readily. He was spurred on to put in a word for a subject much nearer to his heart than Latin.

"We ought perhaps not to forget that Julian has a rare and lovely voice."

Did he notice a sharp flash in the lady's eyes? A curious hint of a smile, at once amused and disdainful upon her lips? But Mr Elliot stuck to his point.

"Julian's father certainly recognised its beauty. He was having it trained under the best advice. Was not Dr Handel of the Royal Music himself brought down to Grest? And ought you – I have no right of course, beyond what my old friendship with his father gives me, to interfere – ought you not to continue as the father began?"

Frances Scoble tossed her head back impatiently. "His voice! Not so great a thing perhaps as teachers in want of a fee are inclined to make out, Mr Elliot," she cried with, surely, a spice of venom in the words.

Henry slipped swiftly and smoothly in.

"What my cousin means is that the mere graces of life, music, singing, are at this moment not so important. We shall not neglect them. You may be assured of that, Mr Elliot. But—well—let me put it in a sentence—" and he smiled: he had when he chose the charming smile of the Linchcombe family. "We don't want a troubadour in the family, do we? So," and he waved his hands, "the sobriety of the Latins! More of Horace than of the Odyssey. For to tell you the truth—" He broke off and turned to his cousin. "My dear cousin, I think we ought to take Mr Elliot fully into our confidence, since we are fortunate enough to have him with us."

Frances nodded her head very definitely. A conjecture flashed in and out of Mr Elliot's thoughts. Were these two coming by a devious way to whatever strange cause it was which had prompted their invitation.

"Julian is nervous for his age," Henry continued. "He has odd fancies. He's a dreamer of queer, outlandish dreams. He is a little more sensitive to impressions perhaps than he should be." Mr Elliot could not find in this farrago of words amongst which Henry was treading, as it were on tiptoe, anything very alarming. "In fact we are rather disturbed," Henry declared and he turned to his cousin. "Frances, tell Mr Elliot what happens."

Lady Frances Scoble threw a glance towards the little ormolu clock which stood on the marble mantelpiece in front of a Hondecoeter picture of a peacock and hens with a stately mansion in the distance.

"Yes," she answered quickly. "It is almost ten."

"Oh, of course, I didn't mean that ..." Henry began, and his voice trailed away.

"I shall have to go in any case," said Frances.

"Well, of course, I am merely the tutor," observed Mr Henry. "It's for you, my dear, altogether."

Whatever it was, it seemed to James Elliot that they were making a great to-do before they let him into the secret. But for their very manifest concern, he would have believed that they were deliberately engaged in fomenting in him a condition of excitement and expectation.

"At ten, or a little after, every night," Frances explained, "Julian is seized in his sleep by some sort of horror. If he is alone, he wakens with a scream, a scream of sheer terror. If I am with him in time – and I make it a rule to be – and hold him close and comfort him – it's the sound of the words as much as their meaning which soothes and quiets him," she explained with a smile, "why then he never really wakes up at all. He lies back upon his pillow, the fear dies out of his face and he sleeps till morning."

"Does he never say what waked him – what terrified him?" asked Elliot.

"He remembers nothing the next morning."

"Not even when you are not at his side, when he wakes screaming?"

"Not even then."

Mr Elliot, in his turn, was disturbed. Hysteria? But the boy wasn't hysterical. Mr Elliot was indignant that so outrageous an idea should have occurred to him.

Frances Scoble got up from her chair.

"You are going up to him?" Elliot asked.

"Yes. Will you come with me?"

"I was going to ask for your consent."

Chapter Two

MR ELLIOT IS PUZZLED

Mr Elliot followed her along a corridor towards the east side of the house. Ever since Grest had been built there had been a great bedroom and a dressing-room on the ground floor which had been used by the owner of the house. It was Julian's room by right of birth; but when the lights were all out, and servants and guests were all comfortably bedded on the upper floor, it was a lonely part of the house, given over to echoes and all those sly, menacing, mysterious sounds which emanate when darkness and silence brings furniture to life.

"Julian is alone down here amongst these big black empty rooms?" Elliot asked in a low voice.

"Gurton sleeps in the dressing-room."

That was all very well. But a boy of twelve? Imaginative too. Wouldn't a woman have been more desirable?

"His old nurse for instance?" Mr Elliot asked.

"Old nurses are difficult to please when the tutors come," said Frances Scoble, and Elliot had no answer. She put her finger to her lips as she stopped at a high pedimented door. She opened it gently and looked in. Then she turned her head and nodded to Mr Elliot. He followed her into a dark room, big as a wilderness. The walls were hung with brown silk, the windows shuttered and curtained. A door at the side led into the dressing-room and far away, in a great bed of blue and gold with a shaded night light on a stand at the side, the boy was lost. He was asleep. They could just hear him breathing regularly, normally. Frances Scoble picked up her skirt so that it should not rustle. As they approached the bed, Mr Elliot upon his tip-toes, they could see Julian. The bedclothes were tucked up under his chin, his mouth was open just enough to show the gleam of his teeth, the dark eyelashes lay quiet upon his cheeks. There was colour in his face. Except for the lift and fall of his chest, he lay without movement, untroubled by dark dreams, a boy just stoking himself with sleep to seize his handfuls of the glory and wonder of the next day. Mr Elliot could hardly refrain from a chuckle of sheer pleasure.

But Frances Scoble was not satisfied. She lifted a hand to ensure Mr Elliot's silence. She drew up a chair to the side of the bed without a sound; she sat down, she drew out her watch from her bosom, looked at it with a shake of the head and held the face of it towards Elliot. The time was still two minutes short of ten. She replaced the watch and leaned forward, watching Julian, her face above and near to his. The nightlight burned on the stand beyond her. Elliot could only see the dark side of her profile. It was set like ivory, the eyes open and steady like the eyes of an image. Of the two, Elliot would have said that the boy lived, the woman had ceased. But the change came.

Julian stirred. He frowned, his eyelids tightened over his eyes, his face puckered and creased until it was the face of a little old man; and a cry like an old man's whimper broke from his lips. He pushed the bedclothes down from his chin, but before he could struggle up, Frances had slipped her hands behind his shoulder blades and lifted him against her breast. For a moment or two he fluttered in her arms, his head thrown back, his mouth working and such small sobs bursting from his throat as a boy makes who for his boyhood's sake will not, though he wants to, give way and weep.

For a little while – about a minute Mr Elliot reckoned – this agitation continued. Then the whimpering ceased, the small body grew still and Frances Scoble laid him gently back upon his pillow and drew up the clothes to his chin. His breath was as easy, his face as composed as when she and Elliot had first entered the room. Elliot, who had been closely watching the boy with a trouble at his heart which quite surprised him, turned towards the young woman and was startled. Her gaze was fixed upon his face with an extraordinary intensity. Her eyes stared, not at Julian but at him. In the dim gleam of the candle under the shade, they seemed to him black as night – and as unfathomable. Elliot actually recoiled a step as they watched him. Then with a sign to him she rose. He followed her to the door of the big, long room.

"In the morning," she said in a whisper, "he will not remember one thing about this troubled dream of his."

"And you of course do not remind him?"

"Never," she agreed. "Come!"

She opened the door silently and went out. Again Mr Elliot followed her, but as he was carefully drawing the door shut, he looked back to the bed and now he was more than startled, he was shocked. The boy's eyes were wide open. They looked to him enormous. They were watching him as he went. Julian lay quite still; not a hand fluttered outside the sheet. But he was awake, completely awake, and Elliot read in those wide, staring eyes – or seemed to read, he could not be sure whether his imagination played him tricks – a warning, a prayer not to betray him. Elliot nodded his head to reassure him and silently latched the door. Frances was waiting for him in the passage and together they went back to the dining-room where Henry was sitting over his port. Henry half rose from his chair as he saw Elliot's face.

"Here, sit down!" he cried. "You look a bit white. You are fond of the boy, eh? Like the rest of us, yes!" and as Elliot sat down a trifle heavily and wiped his face with his handkerchief, he passed the decanter across the table to him.

"Try a glass of that! It'll renew the blood in you. So you saw, eh, you saw?"

Elliot filled his glass with a shaking hand.

"Yes, I saw."

But what he had seen he did not say. With another glance at him Henry turned a little anxiously to Frances.

"Something new?"

"No," she answered.

Henry leaned back. He was undoubtedly easier in his mind. "But disturbing." He sat pursing his lips and nodding his head thoughtfully. "You'll have to call in the doctors, coz. Though we know what they'll say." He laughed contemptuously. "They'll suck the gold heads of their canes and look as wise as owls and say in a chorus, 'A change of

15

Scene'. I can hear 'em. There's some little trouble deeper than that will reach. But that's what they'll say, my dear, and you'll have to try it. A change of scene!"

Mr Elliot had by this time recovered sufficiently from his shock to wonder whether the half-sister and her cousin were not making too much of this nightly interruption of the boy's placid sleep. Queer little things which they themselves forgot entered the minds of children and remained somehow to come to life again in their dreams; and they grew out of them, as Julian would. Only – and he pondered a good deal over that word – "only", as he went to bed – only, Julian woke and wanted his waking not to be known. Why? Fear could not be the reason. Yet Mr Elliot slept ill with the vision of the boy staring at him with open eyes across the room.

"But in this odd world of sevens and sixes
Nothing is quite as it ought to be."

Chapter Three

TWO TRUANTS

The words of the song jingled in Elliot's brain until he fell asleep, but in the morning, when the sun slanted across the garden, he took a more cheerful view. He rode with Julian at half-past twelve, he on a quiet cob, Julian on a pony, and could hardly believe that the boy at his side was the same who had whimpered in his sleep and then opened his tragic eyes upon him the night before. For all the boy's talk was of ships and great seamen and great victories upon the waters. He was full to the brim of Commodore Anson who had captured the great galleon *Acapulco* and just lately brought his ship, the *Centurion*, back to Spithead after circumnavigating the world in the wake of Francis Drake. All his conversation was in terms of the sea. They never moved to the right or to the left, but always to starboard or to port. However, Julian was very gentle with Mr Elliot, when owing to his ignorance he made a mistake and Mr Elliot enjoyed himself immensely. They came out from a ride, cut through a wood on to a high knoll where the fields of grass and plough were spread below them, and in the distance the great house overlooked its Italian garden and its lake.

"So you are going to be an Admiral, Julian," said Elliot. "And what of Grest?"

The boy looked across the country to his house and said with a smile: "I shall always come back to Grest."

"You are fond of it?"

"It's my home."

He looked up at Elliot.

"I am not a politician, you see."

Mr Elliot nodded gravely.

"No?"

"No. But my wife and children will be there. Between voyages I shall always come back to Grest, and when I'm old I shall stump about looking after it."

"Oh, yes. Old Timbertoes. I had forgotten you were going to lose a leg," said Mr Elliot.

Julian laughed and they rode homewards. Neither had mentioned the ominous little moment of the night before. In the clear daylight with the countryside laughing to the sun and the blood brisk in their veins, night and its terrors were very far away. This was the real Julian Linchcombe, the Admiral to be, who was not a politician but would stump happily about his garden on his wooden leg with his wife and his children and manage his affairs in the quarter-deck style, gruff and kindly, masterful and wise. There was nothing amiss with Julian, Mr Elliot thought comfortably; and a small incident later confirmed him in his belief.

It happened on the Monday morning. The vicar of the parish church which stood in the park under the east side of the house, had come in to supper after his last service on the Sunday evening. One or two neighbours were present and Julian, who had been allowed to sit up, had thrown off his mourning and appeared resplendent in a pink silk suit with an embroidered waistcoat of white satin. The hour of ten had struck whilst they were all still at the table and the dreaded moment had passed unnoticed. At eleven on Monday morning Mr Elliot had made his adieux, his chaise was waiting at the door to drive him away and he went up to his room to make sure that none of his belongings had been left behind. Satisfied upon that point he came out into the long corridor, just as Julian ran quickly up the stairs with a book under his arm. He did not notice Mr Elliot at the, first, for he was continually looking over his shoulder as if he feared, to be pursued. He opened a door and slipped through the doorway. At that moment the boy's tutor, a short-sighted old scholar in horn-rimmed spectacles, called out from the vestibule below.

"Julian! Julian!"

Mr Elliot followed Julian, thinking that the cry had not reached him. He found himself in a short passage from which a narrow staircase climbed to a great attic hidden away in the roof. Elliot remembered it as a lumber room full of old furniture and cabinets, pictures and big, disused mirrors. On the bottom step stood Julian. When he saw his friend Mr Elliot, the look of concern upon his face changed to an impish grin. He flourished the book he was carrying, a volume of Hakluyt's Principal Navigations, and then, laying a finger on his lips, scuttled upstairs as quickly and silently as he could.

Meanwhile the tutor's voice continued to call upon his pupil from the vestibule. Mr Elliot went back into the long corridor, carefully closing the door behind him, and saw the tutor panting up the stairs with a hand heavy upon the banisters. He stopped when he saw Mr Elliot.

"Have you seen Julian, Mr Elliot?"

Mr Elliot lied regrettably without the least hesitation.

"No, Sir! I said goodbye to him in the portico."

"Dear! Dear!" cried the tutor with a groan. "I am sure that he has gone up to the attic. But I can never find him there. He has some hiding-place." The tutor wiped his forehead with his handkerchief. "There's a morning wasted, Mr Elliot! And I was going to introduce him to Cicero's *De Senectute!*"

"Very appropriate to be sure," said Mr Elliot with a chuckle.

"Boys!" cried the tutor throwing up his hands in despair and turning down the stairs again.

"Yes, boys are the very devil," said Mr Elliot, and five minutes later he drove away from the door with a pleasant feeling that he too had been playing truant from his lessons.

"Just the young imp a boy of his age should be," he reflected and laughed aloud. But he was to remember that little narrow staircase and Julian with his grin and his finger on his lips at a time when no laughter was possible.

Chapter Four

ON A BALCONY

A year later, almost to the day, Mr Elliot drove away from Rome by the gate of St. John de Lateran. He had a tedious journey ahead of him which he might have beguiled by comparing it with the description written of it by Horace to his friend Lollius, had he possessed that knowledge of Latin which Henry Scoble thought the necessary accomplishment of a gentleman. But Mr Elliot was not distressed by the dreariness of the scenery or its ruined towers. For every step of it, along the Appian Way, the by-pass round the Pontine marshes, the Appian Way again to Capua of the mild air and fertile soil, brought him nearer to the home of Italian music and his journey's end – Naples. Elliot passed through the gate of San Januarius as the evening fell and drove to the great inn on the Corso between the Castel dell'Ovo and Posilippo where he was accustomed to stay. Mr Elliot was happy. The air was scented with lemons and oranges and all the fragrance of the Campagna Felice. The moon was rising and the great bay curved within its horns like a sheet of silver with the riding lights of the fishing boats gleaming like topazes upon its surface. The streets were crowded and noisy with laughter and talk. The day was the first Saturday of the month of May. That the dark flower of tragedy was opening amidst all the fragrance of this beloved city on this very evening, Mr Elliot would never have believed.

There was always, he remembered, a small throng of curious idlers about this famous inn "The Golden Ox", but tonight it was larger than he had ever known it to be, and, marvellously, it was silent. Up and down the Corso, voices chattered and clacked. A little way off someone was thrumming a two-stringed guitar. But here under the windows of "The Golden Ox" there was a crowded patch of silence. The little throng gave way politely as the carriage with its four horses dashed up to the inn door, but it closed in again round the equipage and Mr Elliot noticed that all the faces, so white in the gloom of the night, were turned upwards and that from a suite of rooms upon the first floor the lights blazed out above their heads. For a moment Mr Elliot conjectured that some great "milor" had suddenly arrived and astounded Naples by the magnificence of his retinue. But a phrase or two spoken by one of the crowd corrected him. A woman's voice first. She threw back her hood and cried: "Cristo Benedetto! Let him sing again."

And a man answered her.

"Where's the use if you squeal?"

Mr Elliot was delighted. He understood now the reason for all this to-do. One of the great ones, one of the soprani, as famous for their vanity Sand parade as for their matchless voices, was giving his birth-town a free performance to celebrate his return. Farinelli perhaps from Madrid? No! One heard strange tales of his modesty. Senesino then? Certainly it would be Senesino, back from a season at the London Opera House in the Haymarket – Senesino, one pocket heavy with good gold English guineas and the other stuffed, strangely enough, with *billets doux* from the ladies.

But again Mr Elliot was wrong. For the singer did sing again and he knew the song and the singer too well to remain in any doubt, even though he had heard the song but the once.

"She has eyes that are deeper and kinder than sapphires,
Her lips' dark velvet defies the rose.
Oh, I can't believe that other lads have fires
Fierce as the one which destroys my repose.

And so I wander by forest and boulder
Hoping that one day in spite of my fears
I shall wake with a golden head at my shoulder,
Instead of a pillow wet with my tears."

Again the magic of the notes twisted Elliot's heart and brought a lump into his throat – the high lift and throb of passion snatching at happiness beyond reach and then declining in a long sustained curve upon a grief which the exquisite purity of the voice made at once intolerable and yet left an urgent longing that it should be repeated. The crowd in the street broke into cries of delight. It clapped its hands, it brandished its arms, it did not go so far as was the fashion in a theatre at Rome where enthusiastic youth was wont to take its shoes off and toss them over its shoulders, because most of it had no shoes upon its feet at all. But it clamoured for more and uttered one loud groan when swiftly the curtains were drawn across the windows and the light streaming out above its heads was darkened.

Mr Elliot turned into his hotel. His bedroom had been reserved for him and whilst his landlord showed him into it and lit the candles, he ordered his supper.

"You have a great deal of company tonight," he said.

The landlord smiled happily.

"The Feast of San Januarius always brings us company. There are great and splendid processions and the miracle of the blood to end the day. It is a very curious miracle, as your Excellency doubtless remembers."

The landlord shrugged his shoulders and laughed rather sceptically.

"Yes, I do remember it now," said Elliot, who up to this moment had not given a thought to it. "The first Sunday in May to be sure."

"A very important day for Naples, illustrious one! Were the miracle not to repeat itself, the lazzaroni would expect misfortunes and disasters. The Saint is their patron as your Excellency knows. They would look for a reason for his anger; an Archbishop of whom he did not approve; a heretic on a balcony over the square or in the crowd who had laughed – ah, ah, it might not be pretty that scene. But then," and the sceptical landlord shrugged his shoulders, "the miracle never does fail – even with a new Archbishop as we shall have tomorrow."

Mr Elliot was only listening with half an ear. He did not believe at all in violences and outrage by the lazzaroni – those thirty thousand homeless, ragged, good-tempered vagabonds who roamed the city by day, cuffed out of the road by running footmen, willing to run an errand for a few soldi, picking up a living somehow and sleeping on doorsills by night. He took no interest in the miracle of the blood of San Januarius at the moment. But he knew his landlord, Gasparo Rossi, of old. He must have an excitement if he could whip it up, and he must be allowed to run on, until he ran down. So Elliot answered: "You have a new Archbishop then?"

"His Grace, Signor Giovanni Rondella, a man of great holiness. Oh, the blood, my nobleman, will melt under his fingers, be assured." After all it never paid to frighten your guests out of the town. "All will be well."

Elliot saw a chance of asking his question at last. "You have amongst your guests, Gasparo, old friends of mine, I think?"

Gasparo nodded his head vigorously.

"You were often here, my magnificence, with the old Earl of Linchcombe. We have now his daughter, the Lady Francesca, the Lord and his tutor, a Lady Fritton, the Lord's great-aunt, maids, valets, a courier and a doctor."

"Ah! A doctor?" said Elliot.

"A doctor," Gasparo repeated admiringly.

So Lady Frances had called in the doctors. And they had recommended, as Henry Scoble had prophesied, a change of scene and a jaunt to Naples for one of them, with a nice fat fee no doubt to complete his enjoyment.

"Only the English milords travel in such state," Gasparo added, wishing the world was full of them.

Mr Elliot shrugged his shoulders. Well, if they could afford it, why not! He could not bring himself to believe that there was much wrong with the health of the boy Julian Linchcombe. The clear sound of his voice denied it. But at the same time he felt grateful to Frances for the loving care she was bestowing upon him; and he took his supper up there in his bedroom with a glow of friendship for her; of which he would give some little proof to her in the morning. But not tonight. Elliot was never in a hurry to exhaust a pleasure. Naples now! He had travelled in his coach throughout a long day. He was not going to spoil his first visit to an old friend or a theatre or a popular booth where a new farce was being staged by carrying his fatigue with him. He supped slowly, undressed with indolence, dismissed his servant and went sensibly to bed. But after he had extinguished his candles, he found by one of the contrarieties of nature that although he was tired, he was very wide awake. His windows were open, the curtains withdrawn, and the moonlight and the hum and chatter of the streets poured into the room. But the noise gradually died away and he was just turning over on to the other side, with the first languors of sleep descending delightfully upon him, when two voices speaking in low tones and speaking English rose to his ears.

Elliot's room was on the second floor. These voices were rising from the balcony below it, the one of a woman in a panic, the other of a man trying to compose her, but none the less puzzled; and Elliot could not, after the first moment, doubt to whom the voices belonged. Nor could he help but overhear them.

It was Frances Scoble who began.

"I thought I would never live through this evening! Henry, we should have travelled under false names. Lots of people do. Incognito!"

"But, my dear, that could only have meant more trouble. Worse than trouble, questions. Worse than questions, suspicions. Once start people wondering, who knows what guess won't hit the truth and the guesser thereafter know that he has hit it? But we have thought everything out – how often, you and I? Gone over every point. Made it all smooth and open and public and natural! You are overstrung tonight, Franky. So near – the last step to be taken – as easy and simple as the rest we have taken."

"I know," she broke in, and there was a pause. Elliot imagined her clinging desperately to her companion's arm. Companion's? No, lover's, and smoothing her face against the breast of his coat. "Oh, I know, Henry, but tonight I am afraid."

"Why?"

"I don't know. All those people standing beneath the window – listening whilst he sang."

"But that was good."

"It seemed to me that all Naples was listening."

"Alas, all Naples will have forgotten it tomorrow. A pity! Such a picture! The family group by Kneller. The boy singing at the harpsichord – the admiring relations – the old lady beating time with her hands – the doctor trying to keep awake! My dear, we wanted a pet spaniel or two to make a picture for the great drawing-room at Grest."

And now Mr Elliot was sitting up in his bed, his nightcap all awry, his ears strained. A love affair between Henry and Frances? Certainly he had not guessed it on his one visit to Grest since Frances Scoble had held authority there. But why shouldn't it be? There was no obstacle to prevent it, no reason for secret plans – unless there was some provision in the daughter's jointure of which he knew nothing. But even so? A clandestine arrangement between them – could it need all these wild fears of hers, and all these reassurances of his?

But she pushed aside his rallyings.

"Henry," she cried in a low, urgent voice. "All this evening the thought's been growing – wouldn't it be better if we waited—?" and there followed a pause as though he turned to her and her voice trailed away to silence.

"Not unless," he said quietly but firmly, "there is something you have planned of which you have never told me."

"No!" she exclaimed. "Henry! How could there be anything?"

"I don't know," he answered, half in rough jest and half in all seriousness. "You are a crafty little piece, my dear. I am not sure that I trust you, once you're t'other side of the hedge."

"Henry!" and her voice was all reproach.

"Swear it!"

"Oh! You hurt me!"

"Swear it, my pretty bird!"

"Henry, of course, nothing that you don't know. I swear."

It seemed that he let her go.

"Very well!" he said. "Now listen. There never will be, if we live till we're a hundred, an opportunity so well prepared, so sure of its result. If we don't take it now, I have done."

Again a silence followed upon his words. And after it, she spoke in a small and humble voice, as though she was once more at his side.

"It shall be as you say. I know your last word, my dear."

Her skirt rustled, she laughed and had gone. For a little while Henry Scoble stayed where she had left him. Did he doubt her? Mr Elliot neither knew nor cared. He had a little scheme in his mind but he dared not put it into action until Henry Scoble had left the balcony and he began to wonder whether the fellow wasn't going to stand on watch there till the morning broke. Henry went in the end, walking slowly and heavily, a man dissatisfied.

Elliot lit his candles and, after slipping on his dressing-gown, sat down at a writing-table between the windows. His writing case was already laid out for his use. He wrote down on a fair sheet of paper word for word the conversation to which he had listened. He read it through when he had finished.

He too was dissatisfied.

Some words were missing. Of importance? He did not know. It was no business of his, of course, if a pair of lovers chose to discuss – an elopement perhaps – some unravelling of a tangle in which they were caught. But he felt an imperative demand upon him to put down in black, undeniable ink, an exact copy; and reading and re-reading he discovered the missing phrases.

"Not unless there is something you have planned of which you have never told me."

"No! Henry. How could there be anything?"

He inserted them in their proper place, locked the paper away in a secret drawer of his writing case and returned to his bed. He was perplexed and uneasy but he fell asleep at last; and when he awakened and saw the sunlight playing upon the bay and his morning chocolate at his elbow and felt his body rested, he was like a man who wakes with the meaningless fringes of a nightmare still not quite faded from his recollections. Against them he set a memory, vivid and pleasant – the memory of a woman holding a sleeping boy against her breast and trying by her warm, firm clasp and her will to drive out from him, whilst he still slept, some haunting and troubled dream. That was the Frances Scoble he remembered on this friendly morning and he took himself to task.

"James, this will never do. You are Paul Pry. You are Tom-the-butler-at-the-keyhole. I shall hear of you next as a romantic."

Mr Elliot rose and dressed. He sauntered out along the Via Chiaia, he bought a great many flowers and he sent them with a note to Frances Scoble, praying that he might be allowed to wait upon her at a convenient hour. The streets were crowded with processions of monks bearing their great silver crosses and the banners of their Order, all on their way to do homage to San Januarius at the Duomo.

Mr Elliot sauntered up the great Via di Toledo, listening to the chants of the monks and admiring the splendour of their appurtenances, deafened and jostled and thoroughly happy. When he got back to the inn, he found that his messenger had brought him back a charming letter from Frances Scoble inviting him to dine with her at three that afternoon. He presented himself at her apartment to accept the invitation and found that all of her party were taking the air. His young Lordship? His young Lordship was sailing out in the bay with his tutor and the courier. Mr Elliot watched the boats swooping over the water in the sunlight. A change of air. There was a good deal to be said for the prescription.

Chapter Five

MR ELLIOT GIVES AN OPINION WITH CONSEQUENCES OF WHICH HE IS UNAWARE

At three o'clock Mr Elliot, his wig powdered to the last curl, his ruffles frothing to his knuckles, presented himself at Lady Frances' apartment. One didn't dine in linsey-woolsey at Naples halfway through the eighteenth century. Already the guests were assembling. Elliot heard Princes announced. He saw an ecclesiastic of the most distinguished appearance, with a scarlet sash about his waist, and to his astonishment, his hostess leave that ecclesiastic in the middle of a sentence and hurry to greet him, as if he were the oldest of her friends.

"It is the most fortunate circumstance that we should meet again in Naples," she said as he bowed over her hand. "I have been reproaching myself and you, I think, might perhaps set me at my ease one way or the other. My cousin Henry – well, no doubt you remember him and his ideas?"

She looked around her. Her guests were talking. No new ones were arriving.

"We have a moment perhaps," she led the way through a glass doorway on to a wide balcony and continued: "It is about Julian. His father, as you no doubt know, gave what seemed to us in England, too much of the boy's time to his musical education. Henry of course had little sympathy with it, but since I have been once more in Naples, where music is in the air, I have been wondering whether Henry was right."

Mr Elliot bowed. It seemed to him that he was listening to a carefully conned speech. This was the preamble. She motioned him to a chair and herself took one at her side.

"Will you tell me, Mr Elliot, for you, I know, have knowledge where I have not, would you say that Julian had a remarkable voice?"

Mr Elliot sat back in his chair. To him music was almost a religion. He could not talk of it lightly. He must weigh his words. He must speak only what he believed.

"Julian has a remarkable voice for an Earl of Linchcombe," he replied. "It is pure, it is clear, it has a moving note like a bird's. But whether it would be a remarkable voice, singing behind a screen the Miserere on Good Friday at St Peter's, that, Madam, is a thing which I am not qualified to say."

"It is not trained, you mean?"

What Elliot meant was that it never would be trained, Julian being not a chorister, but Lord Linchcombe.

"I am a mere dilettante, Madam," said Elliot, "and I speak without authority."

But dilettantes are of two kinds. One kind believes that the amateur, free from the necessity to practise the tricks of the trade, has thereby a superiority with which the professional cannot cope; the other that the pursuit of perfect command can only be obtained by the incessant concentration of the professional. Mr Elliot belonged to the latter kind.

"Julian has a lovely voice. It is moving. In a room it can provoke tears. Believe me who have heard it! But of course it has not the volume of the great singers, it cannot swell and diminish on a sustained note like an organ; and of course in a few years it may be nothing at all – a pleasant compliment to his guests at an evening assembly in his house."

Lady Frances was listening carefully to his words. It seemed to Elliot that she was in some way relieved by them. He understood hers too, or thought that he did. Julian would have work for which he must fit himself, sterner work, work dealing with the management of estates and the government of the realm. Music, singing? So many decorations, charming, enervating, perhaps, ample enough to occupy the life of Mr James Elliot, but pure waste for the chief of a great Whig family with – how many was it? – a dozen, pocket boroughs to echo his politics. Lady Frances nodded her head.

"I am glad to hear you say so. I had a fear last night that I had left a great gift to tend itself more than Julian's father would have done, a plant unwatered, as no doubt our good vicar would have said. For Julian sang last night and in this town, where the best singers in the world are familiar to the ear, and a crowd gathered."

"Madam, you could gather a crowd in Naples with a cracked accordion."

"But it would laugh and go on. It would not stay, planted there," and she pointed her finger to the roadway beneath them. "It would not demand an encore."

"And yet, Madam," said Elliot with a laugh, "not one of that crowd today would do more than say, 'Last night I heard a pretty voice from the first floor apartment of the Inn of "The Golden Ox", and tomorrow it would not even be remembered.'"

He heard his companion draw a long breath. For these words then she had waited. So great was her relief that she must needs hear them again. With a bubble of joy she cried: "It would not be remembered?"

"Neither the song nor the singer."

"It would not," and she sought for a word, "it would not be recognised – after a time – as something once heard from the first floor of …" and she stopped rather suddenly as though some new question had slipped in amongst the others to trouble her.

"No, indeed," said Mr Elliot a little puzzled by the lady's insistence. "It would be lost amongst the recollections of a thousand voices."

"You speak as if you yourself had heard Julian last night," she said rather sharply.

"But I did. My carriage, I am afraid, for a moment scattered his audience."

Lady Frances recoiled. Elliot could think of no other word for that swift startled movement. Uneasiness began once more to take hold of him. He looked forward over the Bay, trying, to set a cause to it; and he heard her asking him in a voice he hardly recognised, and with an effort at carelessness which he did.

"So you are staying at "The Golden Ox"? I imagined, that you kept always an apartment in the town."

"Oh, no, Lady Frances," he answered with a smile, still occupied with his puzzle, "I am lodged above you. See!" and he turned and pointed upwards to the windows of his room.

"There?"

Some queer sound as though the little trivial word was strangled in her throat made Mr Elliot turn his head quickly towards her. He met the same bleak, hard indecipherable stare which had once before startled him at Grest. But it did more than startle him now. It frightened him and he had a suspicion now that it was really fear which he had felt at Grest. So utterly did that look change her, make a stranger of her, strip her of all her friendliness, of the polite and engaging ways which went with her dress and the tiring of her hair. She was plucked out of her century, she became – primeval. Just for a flash it lasted. She rose and as she rose, Elliot remembered, without so far as he could see any reason why he should remember, the omitted lines which he had restored to his written account of the dialogue exchanged on this balcony the night before.

"Not unless there is something you have planned of which you have never told me."

"No! Henry! How could there be anything?" It was Henry who brought the conversation to an end. He came out upon the balcony looking for Lady Frances.

"You are there?" His eyes lit upon Mr Elliot none too pleasantly; and he glanced from him to his cousin.

"My dear," he said reproachfully, "your guests are waiting."

She followed Henry back into the room and made her apologies. Mr Elliot saw Julian in front of him, rather shy and very dignified.

"I have grown?" Julian confided hopefully as he shook Elliot by the hand.

"A young giant."

The boy had grown, certainly, and he blushed with pleasure at its recognition. He was dressed, too, to make the most of his new inches. His brown hair was drawn back with a blue ribbon. He wore a great cambric bow at his throat and lace ruffles at his wrists. A coat of navy blue embroidered with gold and a white satin waistcoat set off his figure.

"Admiral Timbertoes, bless me if it isn't," said Elliot shaking the boy's hand, "but I see you haven't lost it yet." He looked down upon a slim pair of legs as straight as the box trees in his garden at Grest, sheathed in white satin breeches and silk stockings and finished off with small polished shoes with red heels and gold buckles.

"I hear, Sir, that you were sailing your frigate in the bay this morning."

Julian laughed delightedly.

"I held the rudder. It jumped against me. It was glorious."

Folding doors were thrown back. A major-domo appeared with a gold aiguillette across his chest.

"Your Ladyship is served."

A look of disappointment clouded the boy's face.

"You are not hungry?" cried Mr Elliot in alarm. "That will never do. You must go to bed."

Julian laughed.

"Oh, I'm hungry. I could eat a sheep. But I wanted to sit next to you."

"That was charming of you," Elliot returned. "But the ladies have a prior claim upon your society."

The cloud of disappointment still remained.

"To tell you the truth, Mr Elliot," Julian said gravely, "I am not very interested in ladies."

"No?"

"No."

"Well, take heart! That will come later on and, let us hope, before the wooden leg."

"You see, they talk of such silly things."

"Not ships, for instance?" said Mr Elliot.

"No, nor of miracles," and the boy's face lit up. His eyes danced. "I am going to see the miracle at the Duomo."

"San Januarius?"

"Yes. I hoped that you would tell me all about it first. I am going with our courier Domenico." And he added, "I do hope we shan't sit long over dinner."

"It doesn't happen 'till the evening," said Elliot.

"I know. But I want to get close. I want to see it really happen."

But at that moment the party began to move in due order into the dining-room and no more was said between them. In any case,

Mr Elliot reflected, he could never have hoped to dissuade an eager boy from the spectacle of an actual miracle to take place before his eyes. But wasn't there some risk? Rossi, the innkeeper, had hinted that there might be, if the miracle were delayed. And Julian meant to get close in the forefront of the crowd. It was true that the courier would be with him, and no doubt Lady Frances had assured herself that there was no ground for any fear. Still Mr Elliot was troubled. But he saw the scarlet sash of the Monsignor in front of him. Perhaps if he were near enough, the Monsignor might have a word to say.

As it happened, the Monsignor had a good deal to say but it was not all in the vein which Mr Elliot expected or hoped for. Julian was placed at the far end of the table between one woman, fat and maternal, whom Elliot put down as his great-aunt, Lady Fritton, and a pretty Italian woman who had eyes only for Henry. A question asked by the tutor with the horn-rimmed glasses set off the ecclesiastic.

Chapter Six

DISQUIETUDE

"We should consider San Januarius the spiritual descendant of Virgil," Monsignor Vitello Lappa began. "Virgil at Posilippo set up on a rock a bronze archer with the shaft of his arrow drawn back to his ear and the barb pointed at Vesuvius. I need hardly apprise you that the threat of that archer kept the volcano quiet through many generations."

There were some present at the table who knew Monsignor Lappa to be a distinguished member of the Arcadian Academy who could turn an elegant sonnet and by the easy standard of that institution passed as a wit. The rest merely stared, thinking the statement unusual and still more unusual as coming from a cleric.

"Unfortunately, a peasant," Lappa continued, without a twitch diminishing the thin severity of his lips, "with the sense of humour so indigenous amongst Neapolitans of the lower kind, one day flighted the arrow and hit the mountain."

"But—but—Monsignor!"

It was Julian's tutor who, with a face behind his big spectacles puckered with bewilderment, and an accent you could cut with a knife, interrupted.

"Yes?" Lappa asked.

"A bronze arrow—" stammered the tutor.

"Its weight no doubt kept its direction straight," said the ecclesiastic.

"And it struck the mountain, shot from Posilippo?"

"And the impact was at once followed by an eruption of the most terrible character."

"But surely that was—" the tutor's manners forbade him to contradict a dignitary of the Church with a red sash about his waist. He caught himself up—"that was—remarkable."

"Very, very remarkable," Monsignor Lappa agreed gravely. "But, my dear Doctor, was it any more remarkable than the miracle which our young friend there—" and he waved a shapely white hand towards Julian—"is going to watch this afternoon?"

Doctor Lanford, the tutor, was silenced.

"Obviously," Lappa resumed, "something had got to be done about it. Virgil was long since dead. No new archer made any difference at all. Not one could quell the angry mountain. The black pall hung over the peak. Molten lava burnt up the fields upon the slopes. Vast masses of stones, causing a great mortality, were flung into the air. Archers were under a cloud, the Vesuvius cloud. Oh, clearly something had to be done. And in the great amphitheatre of Pozzuoli – the Virgil country as you will notice – something was done. San Januarius, during the persecutions of Diocletian, was there thrown to the lions – who at once laid down at his feet."

"Really! Really!" exclaimed Dr Lanford, helping himself to a pinch of snuff.

"This pleasant variation from those animals' usual behaviour in an arena," Monsignor Lappa continued smoothly, "marked out San Januarius as Virgil's successor. A Bishop – for San Januarius was a Bishop – at whose feet lions ceased in a moment to feel hunger, was obviously the man to quell the anger of Vesuvius. None the less, the savage Pretorian Timotheus, who had learned no compassion from the lions, cut his head off. A saintly woman happened to be present and in more senses than one kept her head."

Henry Scoble chuckled, one or two devout ladies looked shocked, and the rest, who had no doubt met other clerics of the same sceptical character, were amused. The one man who neither smiled nor relaxed the austerity of his face was the Monsignor.

"She collected some of the martyr's blood in a phial. His head was retrieved and encased in a silver bust of the Saint which is kept in a press in the Cathedral. From that point of vantage San Januarius watches over the city. Now it is common for foolish people to ask for a proof; and three times a year, the first Sunday in May being one of the times, the proof is given. The silver bust is brought out on to the porch and at the end of the day, after all the communities have made their processions, the Archbishop leads his. He carries the phial containing the congealed blood of the martyr, and as he holds it on high in the crowded square before the bust, the blood within the phial is seen to melt."

"And if it didn't, Monsignor Lappa?" Henry Scoble asked.

Monsignor Lappa's face assumed an expression of despair.

"We should have to expect calamities such as waited upon Rome when Julius Caesar fell."

He recovered himself with a jerk and turning to Henry smiled benevolently.

"But it always does."

"There have been delays, Monsignor," said Elliot, speaking for the first time.

"No doubt," replied Lappa. "A little suspense, a little fear that Naples may have to pay for its sins, may not after all be harmful. In the square before the Duomo, you may see perhaps the women in tears, the men praying fervently and, alas! some of the lazzaroni undutifully abusing the Saint as a yellow-faced old rogue who doesn't deserve their veneration. But in the end the Saint relents, the congealed blood liquefies, the Archbishop, in the gathering darkness holds the phial aloft, the banners are raised, the trumpets roll, the people fall upon their knees, the tears of woe become tears of joy."

"But before that happy moment, Monsignor," Elliot persisted, "is there not an interval of danger?"

"Of danger?" Lappa answered with a hint of disdain in his voice.

"A boy, for instance," Mr Elliot stuck to his objection, "probably of another faith and certainly of gentle birth, might he not in an angry and frightened mob run a grave risk?"

Mr Elliot looked towards Julian as he spoke and met his eyes. They were watching him, wide open and big as on the night at Grest when they had watched him from the bed; and with just the same prayer darkening their blue, as all emotion did, and asking for his silence. It struck Mr Elliot suddenly as extraordinary that the boy should set such store on witnessing the miracle.

"I shall be so quiet that no one will notice me," said Julian eagerly. "Besides, I shall have Domenico the courier with me. Oh, I shall be safe!"

Julian spoke in Italian with a purity of accent which quite surprised Monsignor Vitello.

"Nay," he said with a smile, "if your Lordship speaks so, not the angriest lazzarone amongst the lot will take you for a foreign heretic. You will be not a son of our brown Naples, to be sure, but of some castle in the Apennines."

"Besides," Frances Scoble added, "our minister, Sir Edward Place, has written to me that he has a room opposite to the Duomo overlooking the square where Julian will be welcome. So if there is any sign of trouble coming, he has a refuge there."

Mr Elliot had no more to say. Certainly Julian spoke the Italian tongue like a native. His father had been particular upon that point as upon no other, so deep had been his love for Italy. At the end of the meal the company returned to the drawing-room in the foreign way. There was no drive today for the fine people of Naples in their painted carriages with the running footmen. The processions, which were now returning to their monasteries by other roads than those by which they came, occupied the streets. But on the other hand there was music in the drawing-room with the balcony which overlooked the bay. Barbella, Naples' most finished violinist, Orgitano at the harpsichord, a mandolin, a French horn and a violoncello made a quintet which for one of that company, at all events, caused time to cease and the world to vanish beyond a golden mist of melody. The shadows indeed were beginning to fall when Mr Elliot came out from his dreams. He was in the mood to expect visions and marvels. Music half opened a door and raised the edge of a curtain for him upon an unknown, entrancing world, so unearthly that he could never describe it, never be more than exquisitely aware of it waiting, a world of delicate, lucent air and colours more lovely than eyes have ever seen. The door was slowly shutting upon him now, the edge of the curtain swinging slowly back into its place, when he saw across the room in that magic doorway the boy Julian Linchcombe standing like some beautiful page who held the keys of entrance.

Julian was standing actually in the doorway of the room with a cloak across his arm and his three-cornered hat under it. A concerto by

Niccolo Jommelli was being played and as the boy stood listening with a smile of expectation upon his parted lips, it seemed to Elliot that the melody, which now soared into a cry of passion, now swooned through cadences of moving appeal, was trying to tell him of great overwhelming changes impending over him, as though for him too the doorway was to lead into a new world where all was strange, and whence he was never to return.

But although this message was loud to Elliot's ears, not a whisper of it, clearly, had reached Julian. He was waiting for the concerto to end, and as soon as the applause died away he crossed the room to his half-sister.

"I am going," he said. "Domenico is waiting for me downstairs."

"Very well."

Frances Scoble walked with the boy to the door. He was to be careful in what he said, not to laugh, and at the first sign of any trouble to seek the shelter of the Minister's room over the square.

"And wear your cloak, Julian," Elliot heard her say at the doorway. "It will hide your dress and at the same time protect your throat. Let me see you put it on!"

Could anyone have been more thoughtful, more kind? Frances was outside the door now, but Elliot could see her and Julian. He swung the cloak over his shoulders. It hung down to his ankles and he hooked it across his chest with a chain. But Frances was not satisfied. She drew the edges close beneath his chin and taking a brooch from her dress pinned them together. The brooch flashed and sparkled as she pinned it and Elliot wished that it had been less noticeable and costly. But they made a pretty picture framed in the doorway, the young guardian fussing over her ward, lest he should catch some trumpery cold, and the young ward eager to be off upon his adventure. Mr Elliot sauntered out on to the balcony a minute afterwards and watched Julian and the courier walk away from the inn. He remembered Domenico, a sleek, smooth fellow and competent, who had been courier to the boy's father before him. That recollection pleased Elliot. Domenico would have a sort of lineal interest in his charge; and suddenly Elliot asked himself a question.

"Why shouldn't I go and watch this regularly recurring miracle? I need not push myself on to anyone's attention. But I never have seen the blood of San Januarius melt amidst the tears and blessings of the populace. It seems foolish to be in Naples on the first Sunday in May and not to see it. There are not so many miracles happening about the world that I can afford to miss one within a stone's throw.

Thus arguing, he made his bow to his hostess. He too feared the chill of sunset. He went up to his room, slung a cloak over his shoulders and in front of a mirror settled his gold-trimmed hat upon his curls. "You're a romantic," he said, rebuking himself with a forefinger. "You find fears in dark corners."

In the streets all Naples was loitering, chattering, singing, laughing and standing – mostly standing. Elliot dodged up the Via di Toledo and along the narrow Tribunali until he reached the Duomo. Here, although a goodly number of people of all kinds, from lazzaroni in their rags, to shopkeepers, lawyers and nobles, stood in groups, there was quiet. The silver bust gleamed upon a stand in the portico. The smaller processions had made their reverences and gone back to their monasteries. The great culmination of the day was awaited in a suspense, whilst the dusk gathered. "All the better for the miracle," thought Mr Elliot; and suddenly a cry was raised. "They are coming!" and suddenly the open space was flooded with such a concourse of men and women, gesticulating and shouting, that except on the outer edges not a stone of the pavement was visible. Mr Elliot was jostled back against the wall of a house just opposite to the portico, as a way was made for the Archbishop. At this moment, a lackey in a red livery forced his way to Elliot's side.

"It is Mr Elliot?"

"Yes."

"His Excellency, the English Minister, will be glad if Mr Elliot will make use of his room. The door is close by."

Elliot followed the man with relief, climbed a stair and found himself in a great room upon the first floor amongst many guests. The Minister, famous for his kindness, his hospitality and his love of the arts, came forward with an outstretched hand.

"I recognised you below where you can see little. You have become a stranger to Naples these last three years, but you will find many friends whom you will remember."

Mr Elliot, indeed, was warmly greeted and then a hush fell upon the crowd in the square and all turned to the windows. The Archbishop in

his stateliest robes with his mitre on his head led forward the great
army of his clergy. He carried the sacred phial, held aloft and enclosed
within the palm of his hand. He stopped as he drew near, and an
attendant in the portico draped the shoulders of the silver bust in an
embroidered robe of purple velvet and crowned it with a mitre which
blazed with jewels. Then the Archbishop stepped forward again and,
bending low before the image of the Saint, prayed him in the humblest
voice to favour his faithful votaries by the melting of his blood; and in
that prayer all joined, the women with upturned faces and clasped
hands, the men staring at their feet, so that a hum of innumerable bees
filled the air. And the hum continued – and in a little while it swelled,
and into a sound more urgent. The Archbishop was chafing the phial in
his hands. An old monk took it from him, rubbing it himself and gave
it back. A few cries rose. "It is hard as a stone!" And the women began
to wail with the tears pouring down their faces. If their own Saint
turned against them, what disasters might not be looming for the people
of Naples?

A few minutes more and another note was heard, perhaps the most
frightening of all sounds in the world, the mutterings of anger spreading
through a crowd. Sir Edward Place understood the note. He bent
forward anxiously over the sill of the window.

"He's new to it," he said under his breath. "He's himself terrified. He
should be quick."

Mr Elliot caught the words. The Archbishop was fumbling the phial,
chafing it so that his shoulders and elbows moved in jerks like a man
who works a machine. Bees? Yes, but not bees humming drowsily
within the cups of flowers, bees angry, deadly. Elliot looked round the
room. He caught the Minister by the elbow.

"Julian?" he cried. "Julian Linchcombe?"

For a moment Edward Place stared at Elliot. Then his eyes swept the
room.

"He should be here! He was here!" he cried and then, shouldering his
guests aside with a violence which surprised them, he craned his head
out of the window.

The cries of anger were mounting. It was almost dark now in the
square below. Amidst the passionate appeals of the women words of
abuse rang fiercely. "You old yellow-faced rascal! A fine Saint you

are!" Was there ever such an ungrateful old rogue? Funny? Amusing?
To Mr Elliot it was sinister. A people turning on its Gods, but not
disbelieving their power to hurt and destroy and maim, turning in a
blind, impotent rage. Woe upon any victim who stood near! A heretic
– perhaps – perhaps a boy who laughed. Sir Edward Place turned back
to Elliot, his face white and disordered.

"He slipped away down the stairs. I didn't see. I can't see him now,"
and as he spoke the sullen, angry roar of the crowd suddenly rose like
a black pall lifted in a wind. It was blown away. The fury changed to
anthems; hysterical screams of delight took the place of prayers. The
Minister turned back with a cry to the windows. Banners were waving,
trumpets blowing, men were shaking hands, people pranced; and above
their heads the Archbishop was waving the phial from side to side.

The evening was so dark now that no one six yards away from him
could see whether the blood had melted or was still congealed. But it
flashed like a liquid in the light of a hundred torches and as the
Archbishop dropped upon his knees, a Te Deum rolled out from the
Cathedral organ through the open doors.

Sir Edward Place drew a breath of relief.

"He won't make that mistake a second time," he said grimly,
nodding his head towards the Archbishop. "The old fool! There will be
no trouble now."

And there was none. The Saint's blood had melted. The archer still
aimed his bronze shaft at Vesuvius. For four months at all events, from
visitations of evil, from plagues, from eruptions, Naples was safe.
Elliot watched the crowd disperse in groups, the big flagstones glimmer
white like a chequer-board. He listened for footsteps underneath the
window, but all the footsteps which he heard were receding. The guests
began to take their leave. In the smaller by-streets the little cabriolets,
gilded sedan-chairs with a horse instead of porters and a driver with a
whip, perched up aloft like the hansom cabman of a later century, were
not allowed to ply their trade.

"Julian will find his way back," said Place. Elliot and he were alone
now and the Minister's voice shook a little as he spoke. His face against
the darkness of the room shone as white as wax. "Domenico was with
him and Domenico served his father. A man to be trusted, I think."
He was talking to keep off from him a whole swarm of reproaches for

his inattention. Once Domenico had delivered the lad into this room, he should have seen to it that he didn't escape again until the miracle was satisfactorily accomplished.

"But boys!" he cried, "they slip out of your hands like fish … We will give him a little time. He may have been carried away in the crowd." The square was quite empty now. Under the portico the two men could see the silver bust glint palely as the ushers locked it away in its press.

Suddenly Sir Edward said with a catch of hopefulness in his voice: "He may have gone straight back to the Inn with the courier. Oh yes! He probably has."

But Mr Elliot remained quite still, quite silent.

"You don't believe that?" the Minister asked sharply.

"No, Sir Edward."

"Why?"

"He has the good manners of his father. He would have guessed that you might be anxious. He would have come back to thank you for your hospitality." Elliot stretched out his hand towards the square. "Nor would he have laughed down there."

He was leaning on the sill and stood up.

"But there is something we might do. He might not be sure of the house. If we set a candle in the window for a sign?"

"To be sure."

Something to do at all events. Sir Edward found a tinder-box and lit a taper. There were a couple of candles in candlesticks of the Capodimonte porcelain upon the mantelpiece. He lit them and, as he carried them towards the window, a knock sounded upon the door.

"Come in!" he cried eagerly.

But it was Domenico who came in and he came in alone. His broad, fleshy face was shaking, his eyes distraught with terror.

"His Lordship?" Sir Edward shouted at the man. But Domenico could not answer. He choked, he swallowed and his hands fluttered at the end of his arms, as though they must speak for him instead of his mouth. Place set down the candles on a table against the wall, poured from a decanter a brimming glass of hock and thrust it into Domenico's hands. The courier drained it at a single gulp.

"Now speak!"

42

"I stood by the door, Excellency, on guard. He slipped down the staircase and was past me as I clutched at him. I called to him. I followed. He was an eel, Excellency. And then the Archbishop came – and in a second one was drowned in the crowd. I shouted 'Milord! Milord!' and everyone hooted. I knew that his Lordship wanted to be close to the miracle—"

"Yes, that's true," Elliot interrupted suddenly.

Domenico uttered a cry and let the glass in his hand fall and splinter upon the floor. Far a few seconds he was again silent. Then: "I had not seen you, Signor."

"What does that matter?"

"Yes, continue," said the Minister savagely.

"Excellency," and Domenico turned back again to Sir Edward. Elliot had never seen a man so frightened. His teeth rattled, his body shivered, his eyes glanced from one to the other extraordinarily bright. "I tried to thrust myself to the front too. But a boy can dive under elbows, make a tunnel–" and suddenly he broke off and began to sob. Elliot could see the tears running down his face.

"What will become of me? I shall be blamed, suspected, ruined," and he wrung his hands together.

"You!" cried the Minister in a voice of scorn, and the man stopped crying.

"I will tell you what I think," he said in a quieter voice. "When his Lordship got near in the thick of the crowd and the blood in the phial would not melt – he laughed."

"No!" Elliot interrupted again and violently. "That's a lie."

Domenico cringed as though the words were the lash of a whip across his shoulders.

"Your Excellency knows best. I am at your feet. It's no doubt as you say."

He stood up again.

"Then I am more afraid."

"Why?"

"His Lordship's cloak was fastened at the throat by a big diamond brooch."

The Minister turned with an exclamation towards Elliot.

"Is that true?"

43

"Yes," Elliot returned. "His guardian, Lady Frances – so that he shouldn't catch cold in the night air – yes, at the last moment, outside the door of her drawing-room, she took a big jewelled brooch from her breast and drew the cloak tight about his throat."

"Madness!" cried Place.

"No one thought …" Elliot began lamentably, but no one was listening.

"It may be that he has gone back to 'The Golden Ox'", Place continued with a wry smile. "For once his good manners may have failed him. You, Domenico, run to the Inn. Mr Elliot, my carriage is waiting in the street at the back of this house. If you will honour me—"

He ran down the stairs with Elliot at his heels. They drove as fast as the loiterers would allow them, through this and that narrow passage. They broke out at last upon the open shore. The serenity of the moonlit bay appeased them both.

"All's well, I am sure," said Mr Elliot.

In the windows of "The Golden Ox" the lights were golden.

Chapter Seven

A CHANGE IN THE PEERAGE

Julian had not returned; and the Inn which had but that afternoon been gay with music was given over to consternation and dismay. Sir Edward Place used all his great prestige with the police. Domenico was taken to the guard and questioned and held in custody. A search of the city was begun. Twice during the night Sir Edward drove back to the Inn, only to find Frances Scoble, now blaming herself for neglect, now dissolved in tears, whilst Henry paced the room and rushed to the window at every sound. Mr Elliot, too, passed a disordered night. He was not welcome in the apartment on the first floor, being outside the family and of no help; and he could not sit or lie in his room upon the second. He paced the streets, imagining in every sleeping figure in a portico or on a doorstep the truant Julian.

He went back to "The Golden Ox" at four o'clock in the morning as the sun was rising in a stainless sky and met the minister, pale and haggard in the doorway.

"I shall see King Charles this morning. No one will be more distressed. His affection for the English … the good name of Naples … nothing, you may be sure, will be left undone."

As he got into his carriage, he added: "The boy may be held to ransom. We must tread gingerly," and he flung himself back unhappily against the cushions.

On the first floor landing two chambermaids were crying with stifled murmurs of "Pobrecito!" and their aprons to their eyes. All next day the search went on.

"Julian went for a sail in the morning of yesterday," said Elliot hopefully.

"With Bortolo Scalfi and his two sons," Henry returned at once. Mr Elliot had sought news of him and Lady Frances at noon. "I engaged them myself after I had taken the best advice. They have been questioned by the Police. They were all three last night at their home at Santa Lucia."

Santa Lucia, just to the east of the Castel dell'Ovo, was the quarter where most of the fishermen lived.

Mr Elliot's sudden hope died away.

"It's my fault," Frances Scoble broke in with a tragic air like a Queen on the stage. "I fastened the diamond brooch in his cloak. I was afraid of the night air – and its danger for his voice. I alone am guilty."

Mr Elliot would have been inclined to look upon such an outburst as acting and not very good acting. But he knew the world too well to make that assumption. People under the attack of extreme emotions, despair, grief, even joy, did behave in the most absurd theatrical manner, even the sedatest of them. They leaned against walls and buried their faces in their arms, they blubbered and beat their breasts, so that not an actor at the Lane was a match for them. Lady Frances, who had held the boy so tenderly to her breast, lest he wake in some convulsion of terror, might well be breaking her heart over her careless folly.

"Sir Edward knows this country better than we, Madam," he said in a desire to console her. "It may well be that Julian is held to ransom. At any moment some ragged paper may be left by a boy quick as an eel to disappear …" and he stopped short, realising in a horror that he was using the very words in which Domenico described how Julian had escaped from him.

But no ragged paper was left, and as the days piled themselves one upon the other, Henry Scoble grew more gloomy and restless, Frances more distraught.

"How will it end?" she cried in an odd kind of passion, her voice breaking as though she were at the end of her strength. "And when— when?"

"Nay, my dear coz," said Henry, laying his hand tenderly upon her shoulder, "the time has not come for despair. There will be time and to spare, if grief must come. Never run halfway to meet it."

The Queen, Maria Amalia Walburga, received Frances Scoble, dismissing all her own attendants, and kept her by her side for an hour. Frances returned to the Inn, a little comforted by that great lady's condescension; but on the next morning all fears were confirmed.

Thirteen days had passed since the festival of San Januarius. Mr Elliot remembered the moment to the end of his life. The hooded band of the Misericordia, the stretcher they carried with the little shrouded body upon it – a package wrapped in a cloth – hardly more. They carried it up the hill to the Carthusian Monastery of San Martino; and thither Henry and the doctor were summoned. Fishermen working out in the Bay over towards Vesuvius had felt a weight in their net as they drew it in. The weight was a boy of the height and size of Julian, but he had been in the water too long for any recognition. He wore the clothes, however, in which Julian had left the Inn, even to the dark cloak which was drawn tight about his body with a cord. But the brooch, the buckles from his knees and shoes, the jewelled pin in his cravat had all been wrenched brutally off. Moreover, a broken cord was twisted about his waist as though a heavy stone had been tied to it to keep the body deep. Frances refused to accept the evidence. She called upon the doctor from London to support her. But the sea and the fish had worked their will. She gave in at the end. Two days later the boy was buried in the Protestant corner of the Campo Santo on the hill. Both Henry and Frances had wished the ceremony to be as private as possible, and they were helped in that the Neapolitans wished the slur of this death upon their hospitality to be removed from sight and recollection as soon as might be. None the less there were many present, representatives of the King, and the whole retinue of Lady Frances.

"With rich flames and hired tears they solemnised their obsequies," Elliot quoted to himself as he heard the lamentations about him. He returned to "The Golden Ox" and asked whether he could be of service.

Frances smiled with a wan gratitude.

"Nothing. I should call on you without hesitation if there were. You were a friend of—" but she couldn't speak the name. "I am going tomorrow," and in a sudden outburst, "I never wish to see this town again as long as I live."

Mr Elliot bent over her hand. He was himself deeply moved. That dreadful little package on the stretcher between the shrouded servants of the Misericordia – Julian Linchcombe – old Admiral Timbertoes stumping in the Italian garden amongst his children. He murmured a broken word or two of farewell. As he stood erect again, the doctor and the tutor entered the room together.

"I asked for you, gentlemen," said Henry, "to announce that we shall leave at seven in the morning. So if you have farewells to make, they should be made this afternoon. I shall ask you to be precise to the minute."

There was a noticeable new stateliness in Henry's address which took Mr Elliot by surprise. The tutor, whose eyes were swollen and red behind his horn-rimmed spectacles, could only sniff and nod his head. The physician was calm as became his profession and his experience.

"You can count upon our punctuality, my Lord," he said, and with a cry Henry covered his face with his hands.

"Oh, no! Please!"

Then he lifted a face twisted with pain.

"Not yet! Let us go back as we came!"

The physician bowed with discreet and silent sympathy. Mr Elliot was almost startled out of his skin. "My Lord" – Henry Scoble! He had not given a thought to this change in Henry's fortunes. Henry Scoble, the son of Philip's younger brother, a mere tutor at an Oxford College with a cottage in the Park was now Henry Scoble, Earl of Linchcombe, Viscount Terceira, Baron Hardley, the owner of Grest and all its wide acres, its appurtenances, its pocket-boroughs, its power.

He had disclaimed the title almost with horror, certainly with distress. That was much in his favour – yes – he earned the best marks for his revulsion from the title. Yet – yet – was there more than an unusually dramatic "*nolo episcopari*" in his outcry? There had been undoubtedly a new stateliness and authority in his injunctions to the two doctors … Mr Elliot wondered. Henry was dressing himself in the robes, whilst rejecting, or at all events deferring, the style.

Chapter Eight

A SONG IS SUNG TOO WELL

Julian waked for a few moments. He was conscious of an unendurable agony in his head where a hammer was pounding with the regularity of the ormolu clock on the mantelpiece in front of the bird-mirror in the great drawing-room of Grest; and of a throat like nothing at Grest – parched and black and leathery – like something – like a black octopus on a beach in the sun. Then in a whirl of pain he fell down through darkness into oblivion. When he waked again, the hammer was lighter in its strokes. It had not the sharp clang of iron. They had muffled it. It fell with a thud – almost endurably, if it hadn't been for the great log which crackled and threw out sparks. For each crackle was the thrust of a penknife into his head, and each spark passed through his eyes, searing the brain behind them. A cry, weak as a little child's, struggled from his throat, and a woman rose. She lifted his shoulders and he moaned. She held a cup of goat's milk to his mouth and turned it up until he had swallowed the last drop. Then she laid him down again and fastened a damp cloth about his forehead. His body beneath its rough covering relaxed and now he slept. The woman squatted at his side until his eyelids closed and his breathing grew regular. Then she moved away and said in a low voice: "*Guappo il ragazzo.*"

A grunt answered her. Julian waked the next day and though he neither looked nor felt festive, as she described him, he was able to notice that he lay upon an old pallet in a hovel full of smoke. A man bent over him – Julian knew his face again – a man of middle age in the clothes of a peasant – and drew the mattress out into the open air and left it under the shadow of the eaves. A young woman brought out to him some spaghetti and a glass of a rough red wine which set his throat tingling. She was not ill-looking, with a broad, dark face and a wide mouth, and her voice was kindly.

"Lie still," she said. "No one will hurt you."

Julian looked at her with big, solemn eyes and said nothing. The woman went back into the hut. Julian heard her say:

"That boy frightens me," and an older woman – or so it seemed to the boy – cackled suddenly.

"That atom of white flesh?"

Julian lay back; a rough sack supported his head, a goatskin covered his body; he was lying high up on a slope of the hills. Bells, little pleasant musical bells were rattling and stopping and rattling again. He saw a herd of goats against a sky line and to the sound of those bells he slept. As the sun sank behind the hills, he was taken again into the hut. In the morning they told him to get up and dress. He was given a shirt of flax, a rough jerkin and breeches and a pair of sandals for his bare feet. He went out into the sunlight. A youth – Julian had seen him before, too – drove a herd of goats out from a pen. He grinned at Julian.

"Good fishing in the bay!" he said and laughed as though he had uttered the finest witticism. The man came out of the hut with the mother and the girl; and the three of them looked Julian over.

"He's fine," said the man.

"He's ready," said the woman. She was probably of no greater age than the man, but she was wizened and wrinkled like an old apple.

"Tomorrow then," said the man.

But the girl stuck her hands upon her hips and objected.

"No! It is too soon, Father. He must get stronger. In a day or two perhaps."

Julian drew back until his shoulders rested against the wall of the hut. The three of them were watching him brightly, curiously. He shivered suddenly and sheer terror stared out of his eyes. To the girl they seemed to grow enormous and with their beauty obscure all the beauty of his face.

"Poor child!" she murmured with a helpless little movement of her hands. Then her face lightened.

"You are hungry?"

Julian was in terror and doubt of many things, but of one he was sure.

"Yes," he said eagerly.

"Wait," said she, and she ran back into the hovel. The man turned away with a grunt and a shrug of the shoulders. The older woman turned back into the hovel. In a little while the girl brought out to him a steaming bowl of *zuppa di vongole – frutta di mare* the dish was elegantly named, but it was nothing but limpets stewed to a broth. Julian, however, was not in a critical mood. There was nothing left in the bowl when he had done, even the wooden spoon was licked clean. And to round off the meal she brought him a platter of dried apricots. The boy's face lit up with pleasure when he saw them.

"Eat your fill, child! They are good."

Julian was too busy to spare words. He grunted, only with more good-will than the man had put into his grunts. He sat back at last and wiped his hands upon the turf at his side.

"What is your name?" he asked.

"Costanza."

He repeated it gently.

"You are kind."

"Boys need kind people."

He moved a little nearer to her and caught her arm.

The terror was back in his eyes now. He dropped his voice to a whisper.

For a little while Costanza was silent. Once or twice she looked at him and looked away again. Then she said: "Sing to me!"

Julian frowned. He could not follow her thought. It was no answer to his question.

"Sing to me," she repeated with a touch of impatience in her voice which still more frightened the boy. Sing! He was never less inclined to sing in his life, but he could not afford to lose the friendliness of the only person in this family who had a care for him.

"I'll sing."

He thought for a minute or two, searching for some air which might please her. He must choose one which would show off his voice at its freshest and sweetest, one which made a demand or two upon his management of his throat and was difficult to sing without even a "serpent" to lend him any support. For her friendship's sake and the promise of help which he read into her gentleness, he gathered his strength about him to give her such pleasure as he had never given, to sing as he had never sung. And it was his fatality that he succeeded.

One song, partly for its own loveliness and still more because of its supreme associations, stood quite by itself in Julian's memories. On that most memorable day when Handel had come to Grest, he had given the boy in the morning the score of a song from his opera *Poro*, with the words by the Italian poet Metastasio; and after dinner he had seated himself at the harpsichord in the great drawing-room and, setting Julian beside him, had made him sing the aria to his accompaniment. "*Se possono tanto*," it began, a song for a soprano which fitted Julian's treble very well, and for a few moments after he had finished, Handel had continued to play, running his fingers over the keys and striking a chord or two very gently. Julian had stood by the great musician's side, feeling that he had fallen below expectations, but suddenly Handel had looked up. There were tears in his eyes and he laid his hand on the boy's shoulder and said: "I thank you for discovering for me what I made."

Julian had practised that song again and again with his master after Handel had gone. It burst from him now in a torrent of sweet melody made passionate by a sudden longing for Grest and all the grace of its life. It soared up above those upland pastures and – lost him Grest for ever.

For as he sang, bewilderment showed itself in Costanza's face.

"*Gesù Cristo!*" she murmured.

The bewilderment changed to admiration and that again into delight. There was a movement inside the hovel and the older woman shuffled to the door and stood listening. Julian was away by then on his own wings and they had carried him back to the great drawing-room and Handel at the harpsichord. He did not notice the look of greed which began to fight with the delight in Costanza's face and, in the end, conquered it all. She looked at her mother, nodding significantly and smiling, but with as mean a smile as ever disfigured a comely face. She could hardly wait for Julian to finish his song. She sprang up and drew her mother into the hut. She left him sitting with his back against the wall, without a word.

"Marvellous," she said in an eager, excited voice. "They said it was nothing. A voice which would do very well for a choir-boy in an unimportant church and come down in a year or two to a guitar twanging in a back street for enough farthings to buy a plate of beans. What nonsense! It's not to be understood …" and indeed it was not to be understood for years, and then not by Costanza. "It's a voice in thousands. One of the great ones!"

And she had been thinking of helping him to escape! – yes, actually, in the kindness of her foolish heart it had crossed her mind to open the door when all were asleep, whisper to him the path to take and give him food to carry him down to the sea. Luckily she had asked him to sing. Music was good, but music which meant money was ever so much better. There was money paid already which soon they would begin to spend. But with this voice, there would be more, wouldn't there? Lots and lots more. Bargains would be made – surely. Costanza plunged her hands into imaginary bags of money and dripped gold between her fingers.

"But you mustn't catch cold, child," she cried, coming quickly to the boy and trying to repeat the compassion of half an hour ago. "Come in! The evening air is dangerous. Come in!"

Julian rose at her bidding. He no longer made any appeal to her. Once he had made it, and then something had happened, and he had lost somehow the charity of the one compassionate being he had found amongst his rough captors. It was not within his nature, even at his age, to plead twice. As he sat, whilst the two women planned his future within the hovel, he began to collect in a sequence for the first time all that he knew of what had happened to him, in the hope that he would find in it some outlet by which his small body might escape.

On the morning of the festival of San Januarius, he had gone sailing. His uncle Henry had arranged the expedition for him with Bortolo Scalfi, the fisherman. Domenico the courier, Dr Lanford and himself made the water-party, and Scalfi was to bring his two sons to help with the big, heavy lateen sail. But Scalfi had not brought his two sons. He had brought one and besides the one, the youth who drove the goats up the hill in the morning, Tonio – yes Tonio Traetta.

For a time, under the guidance of Bortolo, he had steered the boat. But the boat was heavy, and though he adored steering it, he had grown tired and wanted a rest.

"I gave up the tiller and crawled forward under the big sail and lay on some fishing nets in the bows, with my head over the rim of the boat, watching the water divide, and seeing little fish darting about deep down. It was adorable. Then Tonio began to talk to me."

Yes, Tonio had crept forward too under the big sail and he talked about sailing and what fun was to be got at night when in the darkness you suddenly flashed a bright light close down over the water and the fish rushed into it, so that you could net them by the hundred. To the boy the scene which he imagined, rather than Tonio described, seemed pure magic. He looked with a sharp envy on the youth who spent his life doing such lovely things. The stars, the cool night, the boat swishing through the water, the bright lamp hung over the bows and then the fish streaming like flecks of fire towards it!

"Oh, if I could only come!" he had cried; and in front of the big sail, what with the breeze and the rush of water, he must have made a louder outcry for a word of it to have been heard in the stern.

"Why shouldn't you?"

Julian shook his head wistfully.

"I am only a boy. I have lessons to do. I have a doctor besides," and he grinned with amusement at this absurd appendage of the Linchcombe retinue.

Tonio wrinkled up his face in contempt of such maidenly doings.

"It is a pity. There will be no moon until ten. We shall go out early as soon as it is dark for an hour." Julian sat up on the nets, all the imp in him lighting up his face.

"For an hour?"

"Yes."

"As soon as it's dark?"

"Yes."

"You and your father?"

Tonio nodded vigorously and laughed – laughed mirthfully, but with something secret in his mirth. Julian, up on the hillside, remembered that for a few seconds he had been puzzled and uneasy.

"We should have this, boat?"

"This or another like it," said Tonio with a shrug of the shoulders. Tonio was cunning. His fish was already on the hook. Why pull at it and see it break away? He turned on his back and drew a battered broad-brimmed hat over his face.

Julian in a little while laughed and glanced guiltily back under the sail. His old tutor was fast asleep with his mouth open in the shadow of the sail, dreaming no doubt of Aeneas and post-pluperfects.

"I am to see the miracle of San Januarius in the Duomo square," he, resumed. "It takes place in the evening when it's getting dark. The square will be crowded. I could slip away."

But from the Duomo to Santa Lucia where the fishermen lived was too far. He could never wriggle through the crowds in time. It was disappointing and no doubt his face grew cloudy.

"It's no good, Tonio," he said, and the name startled his companion. He sat up and asked fiercely: "How do you know my name?"

"I heard your father call you by it."

"My father's an old yellow-faced fool," Tonio grumbled and he leaned towards Julian. "No, it can't be managed. You see, we shan't start from Santa Lucia. We shall get better fishing on the other side of the Bay." They would push off from the beach below the Largo del Mercato.

"Is that far from the Duomo?" Julian asked.

Tonio shrugged his shoulders.

"Five, ten minutes."

Julian grew excited.

"And you come back – where?"

"To Santa Lucia, of course."

"When?"

"Eight, half-past eight."

"Oh!"

At once this expedition became possible. He could slip away from the room hired by Sir Edward Place – that would be easy – and pass through the crowd. What did the miracle matter compared with this wonderful sail? Perhaps he would be allowed to hold the tiller whilst the others were forward hauling in the net! He alone at the stern, steering the boat in the darkness over the Bay of Naples – something to remember all his life! And he would be back at the Inn before anyone could wonder.

"I'll speak to Domenico. If he will come too, it will be splendid."

The boy could not believe that Domenico or anyone in full possession of his wits would not grasp at such a glorious excursion. Tonio was indifferent.

"It is as you wish. We shall not wait."

Then he appeared to think for a moment.

"You know the Head of Naples?"

"No," answered Julian.

"It is the great head by the Church of St Eligio, close to the Mercato – in any case Domenico knows it. I'll be there, under the head, at half-past six. If you and Domenico meet me, well, we'll go."

Julian called Domenico forward into the bows. Would he come? Oh surely! It would be a night of nights. And only for an hour. No one need know. Domenico would not hear of this truancy. Domenico relented. Before the boat reached Santa Lucia and Dr Lanford waked up and readjusted his spectacles, Domenico had agreed.

Julian passed an afternoon which was almost unendurable in its delicious anticipation. But everything happened as it had been planned. Domenico and Julian escaped from the Duomo square whilst the Archbishop was still making his supplications to the Saint. They went as swiftly as they could through a maze of intricate narrow streets and met Tonio under the great Head by the Church of St Eligio. Together the three went down to the dark and deserted beach.

It was at this point that Julian, sitting with his back against the hovel, found that his memory was playing him false. He remembered a strange man – not Bortolo Scalfi, but one whom he now knew to be the older Traetta – who had risen up from the stern of the boat. Had he been struck down by a blow on the head? He could not remember. He had recovered his wits to find himself lying at the bottom of the boat unable to move, with his mouth gagged. He remembered the sail like a black wing of death swinging across above his head as the boat went about, and then he lost consciousness again. He waked once more in dreadful pain, shut up in some stifling sack and jostled and flung and bumped on the back of a mule. Then he had gradually struggled back to life and perception and pain in this hovel in a cup of the hills. Where he was he did not know. No one had come to rescue him and take him home. And there was something this family meant to do to him – something which would need his strength – something horrible then. The boy shivered again in a panic. He must escape before they did it. He must! But he had sung his sweet song too well. They did not let him go out and two days later the barber came up the hill from Naples.

Chapter Nine

JULIAN'S CHOICE

"So! What is your name?"

Julian was sitting in his old place with his back against the hovel wail in the rough dress he had been given to wear. It was on an afternoon when the sun was hot and the grass brown and only the temperate air of these uplands mitigated the oppression of that cup of metal which was the sky. For eight weeks had passed since the barber had come up the hill from Naples. Julian was white and frail now, with that unmistakable strain and fatigue in his eyes which is left over from long-borne pain. But there was defiance in them too, as he sat up facing his enemies. They were there, squatting on the grass in front of him, like people at a show waiting for the entertainment to begin.

"So! What is your name, boy?" Traetta the father asked.

"Julian, John, Philip, Challoner, Carolus, Scoble, Earl of Linchcombe, Viscount Terceira and Baron Hardley," answered Julian and his audience received the answer with a great gust of laughter which an expected jest arouses. The old woman cackled, shaking her head, Tonio rocked from side to side, crying "*Viva, il Maestro, il Conte,*" and beating the ground with his stick, Costanza clapped her hands, "*Bravo quaglio! Bravo il guapo!*" but she was watching the boy shrewdly. As for the father Traetta, he laughed too, but not with any heartiness. He was a thickset fellow with a curiously sharp face and a pair of small eyes hard as buttons. He had slung a coat over his shoulders; otherwise he was naked to the waist with a fell of black hair upon his chest on which drops of sweat shone and ran.

"Come!" he said. "A joke is a joke. Let us be serious, Giovanni! Tell your good friends your name."

His voice was wheedling, yet as hard as his eyes; but Julian answered: "Julian John Philip Challoner—" but that was as far as he got in the list, for old Traetta with a sudden brutal sweep of his hands cried: "Stop!"

He felt in the pocket of his coat and pulled out a newssheet creased and grimy.

"You can read?"

"Yes."

It was more than Traetta could do, but in one corner was printed the image of a coffin, with a paragraph in a black rim beneath it.

"Read, then!" he said, and tossed the sheet on to the boy's lap. Julian closed his fingers on the paper, but he did not lift it to his eyes, he did not even glance down at it.

"Read!" Traetta repeated violently.

"When I am alone," Julian answered.

Traetta raised his hands in imprecation. He was holding out against them – this wisp of flesh and bone! Costanza got up from the ground.

"Let us leave him to read it," she said, aware that the boy was at the end of his strength.

Grumbling they obeyed her and disappeared through the doorway of the hut. Costanza went last and stood watching the boy secretly from the threshold. But even when he was alone Julian did not read the newssheet. His eyelids closed over his eyes, but from want of strength to continue in this abominable world rather than any desire of sleep.

Costanza turned back into the hut.

"That boy will die on our hands," she said quietly. "He has no heart to live."

"The man wished him to die," said Traetta sullenly. "But the woman did not. It was the woman who paid. She wanted him to live very miserably quite a long time, begging for a bowl of soup at the convents and then to die at last under a barrow. *O Dio!* but that woman can hate! Brrrh!"

"But she has paid and gone," said the older woman shrilly. "She'll not come back."

Costanza stamped her foot in the most unfilial scorn. "But are you all little children? Did you not hear him sing? That good woman was deaf through her hatred. A few years at the Conservatory and he will have a name like Senesino and money like Senesino and, if he likes it, a Dukedom like Caffarelli. And wouldn't there be some of it for us? Die under a barrow! Bah, he will die in a Palace, and" – she laughed brutally – "since there will be no wife to drive us off or children to inherit – eh, it is worth while to look beyond the nose."

Of the four brutes, she was the only one with intelligence. The others had only cunning for the day.

"You go," she ordered the two men, "and you, mother, sit here very quietly. I will talk in my own way to the boy."

Tonio went up the hill to his goats. Traetta, the father, walked out of eight to the shade of a rock.

"Why should I listen to her?" he growled. "Isn't she my daughter? Why don't I take a stick to her shoulders?"

He appealed to the universe and the universe gave him no explanation. So he lay down in the shade and slept, and dreamt no doubt of the pleasant little farm which he would have, where the women did all the work, as soon as this accursed boy with the big, still eyes was dead or in some way off his hands.

Costanza, meanwhile, returned to Julian and squatted at his side. But there was a change in him. The languor, the indifference had gone from his face. It was quietly alert. His eyes were open, but they kept as ever his secrets.

"You have read?" she asked, looking about him for the paper.

"It is in my pocket," said Julian.

"But you have read it?"

"Yes."

"You saw then there is another who has all these fine titles?"

"Yes."

Costanza felt uneasy. He was always reticent. He had never burst into torrents of abuse of them for their cruelty. They had done him the irretrievable wrong and hurt him terribly and he had screamed a little, more than a little, but from pain, from humiliation, not from anger; and then when he ought to be well, he went on slowly dying. But he certainly was not as far now on the death-road as he had been an hour ago.

"Yes," he repeated the word. "I see that there is another who has my title and Grest too."

He lingered gently over the name Grest as he spoke it. He saw something more too which he was going to keep to himself. Had he been kidnapped, the Traettas would have asked a ransom for him. There would not have been a boy's body retrieved from the Bay and buried. There would have been a payment and he would have been restored. Or there would have been a hue-and-cry. But he was not to be restored. It was never wished that he should be.

"Who is it that I am?" he asked without the slightest sign of irony.

"Giovanni Ferrer."

He repeated the name to himself, looking down at his body and his limbs. He seemed to be trying it on as if it were a new suit of clothes.

"Yes. Oh, you are more sensible. That is good," said Costanza cheerfully. "Now listen to me with both your little ears. You cannot stay here. For you will die if you stay."

"Yes, I shall die if I stay."

"But you can be a great singer, little boy," she said shifting herself nearer to him. "A few years at a Conservatorio under a great teacher, and with your beauty and your voice you will have the world at your feet."

"The woman's world," said the extraordinary boy, and Costanza swung away from him.

"But that's all the world there is—for you," she cried in exasperation. "You'll find that out in time," and she caught herself up sharply. Her business at that moment was to persuade, not to jeer. "You will be rich, Giovanni. You will have jewels. You will live in your own world amongst high-born gentlemen and elegant ladies," and she kissed the palm of her hand towards the high Heavens. "Titles? Pah! You can be a Duke of Naples with a fine, great house on the hill of Capodimonte. It is understood?"

For a full minute Julian remained silent, staring out in front of him. Then he turned to her and smiled.

"It is understood. I am Giovanni Ferrer and I shall sing."

"Good!" and she sprang to her feet. "You must eat and get strong. And then—" she made a gesture to pile all the riches of the world into his lap.

"Costanza," he called as she turned towards the door. "Yes," she answered, stopping. What now had this uncomfortable child to say to her?

"I suppose that Giovanni Ferrer lies in my grave?"

"Will you be quiet?" she cried. "*You* are Giovanni Ferrer."

Julian nodded his head solemnly.

"And I shall sing. And I shall be rich and a Duke of Naples?"

Was he laughing at her, the incomprehensible one, she wondered? But Julian was not laughing at all. Old Timbertoes would never stump about the Italian garden with his wife on his arm and his children's cries filling the air with their shrill and lovely cacophonies. Grest had gone, its gracious rooms and long corridors. But something else was replacing in his breast that exquisite vision – something dark and grim and yet engrossing – something which already began to have a pleasant savour in his nostrils – the musk and amber of revenge.

Chapter Ten

A PRESENT IS GIVEN AND A DEBUT MADE

Thus in a month's time the Conservatorio di St Onofrio opened its doors to a new soprano. The Maestro di Capella, Signor Durante, successor to the famous Porpora, passed the boy in upon one audition. He was bound for a term of six to eight years, variable for any special reason by either side. The lower floor of the school was occupied by the instrumentalists who practised their different instruments at the same time and filled the air with the ear-splitting roar of their discords. Julian, however, was taken to the upper storeys, which were kept warm and quiet and consonant with these hothouse flowers. He was dressed in the uniform of Saint Onofrio's Conservatory, a jacket and breeches of white cloth, white stockings, with a black sash about the waist. There, under a strict regime, with every now and then a procession to a church upon a Saint's day, when the pupils were allowed to try their voices in a great choral celebration, he remained until the day he was eighteen.

On that morning the Maestro Durante made him repeat over and over again one series of notes. It seemed that Durante would never be content and the harassed student began to wonder whether his five years of intense application were to end with the Maestro's disapproval and his own dismissal from the Conservatorio. His heart sank when Durante leaned back in his chair and cried: "So, my boy! I have nothing more to teach you."

He did indeed begin to think that he was the world's worst football, when Durante sprang up and clapped him on the shoulder.

"Nay, never look so miserable! I shall take you after dinner to the house of Sir Edward Place. You jump a little? Yes, it is to be understood. Sir Edward is the kindest and most generous patron of the art of music and my very good friend. It is not every pupil of St. Onofrio's whom I ask him to help. Please him, Giovanni, this afternoon and your fortune is in your own hands. Meanwhile I shall give you a little book," and the Maestro took a small, slim volume from a drawer in his bureau.

He opened the pages at one place and another and chuckled over the passages which met his eyes.

"It is by Benedetto Marcello, a great musician and a great patrician of Venice. I wrap it up, for you will not read it yet," and whilst he talked, Durante folded a paper about the book and tied it with tape. He lit a taper upon his table and sealed the book with his seal and wrote on the envelope in his minute hand, "From Durante to his pupil, Giovanni Ferrer."

"There! On the night when you have made your debut and the candles of the Opera House are all extinguished and you are back in your lodging, with the 'Vivas' still ringing in your ears, you will light a candle and sit down to read Marcello's book. You will laugh, as you heard me laugh, but since you are intelligent, you will also learn a great lesson." He handed the book to Julian. "So! Tie back your hair with a ribbon, polish your shoes, and sing your best this afternoon."

Julian, when he had left the room, leaned against the wall of the corridor and his face went white. He had travelled the first stage of his journey and now that he had come to the successful end of it, he was suddenly surprised by an overwhelming fatigue. All the anxiety and labour of the last five years swept over his head like a tidal wave and left him as weak and unsteady as an invalid. He went on slowly, clutching in his hand Durante's gift, to the dormitory which he shared with seven others of his kind and lay for a little while upon his bed, reflecting bitterly: "Yes, it is, so. Where anyone else would be throwing his cap in the air, I am swooning like a girl at the sign of a mouse."

But there was no sign of that discouragement when he followed Durante that afternoon into Sir Edward Place's music-room and was greeted for the second time in his life by the English Minister.

"You will sing to us, Signor Ferrer?" the Minister said courteously. "There are but the five of us here, my wife, the Princess Iacci, Lord Fortrose, a compatriot of mine and Signor Durante, five of us who are very fond of music, and sympathetic with young people starting out upon their careers. You will feel yourself at home with us."

It was a speech to set a novice at his ease and Julian was grateful for it. There had not been a spark of recognition or surprise in Sir Edward's eyes. And indeed there could hardly have been. He had seen a boy once for a few seconds in a motley of guests. He saw now a youth, fairly tall, slender, gracious in his bearing and of a beauty which seemed to have as its particular quality a modesty and diffidence in its appeal – a broad rather than high forehead, a nose which a Greek sculptor might have chiselled, an honest mouth, teeth white and even, a chin rounded and firm, a clean curve of jaw and a pair of big long-lashed violet eyes for which women would have pledged their souls.

Durante, with a superb confidence in his pupil, had chosen for his very first display that song by Hasse with which the famous Farinelli had for twenty years conjured the melancholy of Philip the Fifth at Aranjuez. Julian stood up before his tiny audience and sang. The years of training had given a great volume to his voice, a power of swelling out and holding and slowly diminishing the note without a breath, which was of the rarest. They had increased its compass so that he could reach F in altissimo without effort, and that moving sweetness which it had always possessed was clearer than it had ever been. He sang with feeling and a throb of passion, forgetting himself as it seemed, but controlling his voice with the reticence and taste which were a part of his nature. His audience, which had expected much from the pains the Maestro had taken to bring him to their notice, was startled. Little exclamations of delight escaped from them as song followed song, and the two women were in tears. He avoided the gross sort of ornamentation with which so many singers were accustomed to overgild their performances. There was a delicacy even in the strongest passages; and the effect was indescribably helped by the beauty of his appearance and a certain loneliness which hung about him like a charm. Sir Edward Place was not content until he had taken Durante's seat at the harpsichord and had made Julian sing an aria of his own composition. Then he presented the lad with a silver snuff-box in which there were twenty guineas, thanked him for the great enjoyment he had received and promised him all the help he could give in launching him on his career.

"We make our séjour for the summer at the Villa Angelica by Vesuvius," he continued, "and there, once a week, we have an accademia."

The musical evenings of Sir Edward Place gathered together not only the devotees but the potentates, the men who held the keys of the outer doors. Durante came near to a frank gasp of relief. A debut for his favourite pupil at the Villa Angelica was the hope which he had been cherishing.

"Shall we say then next Thursday?" said Sir Edward with a smile. He was all that was gracious and condescending and kind.

"Thursday," Durante agreed warmly. "Giovanni will be grateful to you all his life."

But the ladies would have none of so early a date. They had dried their tears. They uttered little screams of horror.

"Thursday?"

"Impossible!"

"Ridiculous, my dear!"

"The boy wants clothes."

"Well," said Edward, "he has three days to get them in."

But again the screams cluttered the air. Sir Edward was a monster.

"A barbarian, Etta," cried Lady Place to her friend.

"Giovanni must cut a figure to match his voice."

"A voice in slops! Not a soul will listen to it."

"Besides he's too pretty a boy to be negligently presented."

"It would be to set a fine play in a miserable decor."

The men meekly bowed before the storm. The debut was postponed to the second accademia and the ladies went into committee upon this important matter of his dress. Giovanni stood apart whilst their eyes measured him and coloured him and he ruffled him, as if he were a girl to be decked out for a Court Ball. Once a wisp of a smile curved his lips when Lady Place suggested that black would suit him, and the Princess, rather shocked, replied that black was the patrician colour and not for Giovanni Ferrer. In the end agreement was reached. Giovanni was to wear a velvet coat of a deep rose colour, a white satin waistcoat and breeches and white silk stockings. He was to go to Sir Edward's tailor to be fitted. The Princess was to provide the lace ruffles for his wrists, Lady Place had a set of paste buckles for his knees and his insteps. Red heels he must have to his shoes, but there was a great debate whether he should have a wig with a bag, or his own hair powdered. Giovanni had a mass of brown hair shot with gold curling about his face, and it was decided that it would give him a more fresh and ethereal look, if he wore his own hair powdered rather than a modish peruke. Lady Place would send her hairdresser on the morning of the performance to dress it for him. Thus it was arranged. Julian had not a word to say. He stood apart – it would have been against all etiquette to invite him to sit and not even Sir Edward thought of doing so – quite silent and indeed grateful, and keeping his secrets as always to himself. Like any other novice to whom a great opportunity was granted, he dutifully thanked his patrons.

He made his début ten days later before an audience which filled the great music-room of the Villa Angelica. He repeated "*Pallido il sole*", and an air of bravura from the same opera of *Artaxerxes*, which was composed to show the compass and the control of a great soprano voice – "*Son Qual Nave*", a solo from Jommelli's *Demophoon*, and another from the *Achilles in Scyros*. He made, not a success, but a triumph. Standing up on the dais before an audience for the first time, his voice for the first few notes had trembled and quavered, but the music had mastered him then and, though his audience still existed in front of him, it existed as something dead into which his voice and his melodies were to breathe life. And his audience was inspired. This was no longer the pretty boy in the pretty clothes, this was a singer who could lift you into azure dreams or drop you into a swooning sadness. When he finished, the *Evvivas* rang loud, fans tapped the palms of hands in applause, flowers were thrown at his feet – and in the midst of these extravagant favours, he saw on the outer edge of the chairs, Lady Place standing beside a Captain of the Royal Navy in his blue coat with a string of glistening medals across his chest. The Captain was applauding, but whilst he applauded, he spoke under his breath to Lady Place, and Lady Place agreed with a nod – and Julian on the dais receiving the ovations of his audience burst into tears.

He couldn't help it. He felt the bitterest shame. "I'm womanish, but not a woman. I'm a man and less than a man. I'm a doll with a voice, and he's telling her so, and she is agreeing." The fact that the man wore the blue of the Navy made that moment doubly bitter for Julian Linchcombe. "And now I am crying like a girl," Julian said to himself. "Before all these people. And I meant to be an Admiral."

But he was wrong. What the Captain had said was simply, "That boy is about as English as a good foreigner can be," and Lady Place had answered, "He has the Englishman's reticence." But the audience took his exhibition as no more than an emotional tribute to its applause; and as he descended from the dais one great lady threw her fur coat about his shoulders and hooked it across his throat.

"Poor boy! It is charming that you should weep. So many only return us insolence for our applause."

Julian saw himself in a long mirror with this fur-coat about his shoulders; he who had meant to stump his quarter-deck with a wooden leg, whilst his wife and children waited for him at Grest, was petted as a girl, and looked like a girl in the Villa Angelica at the foot of Vesuvius.

"It is arranged," said Durante as he and his pupil drove back to Naples. "You will make your appearance as Megacles in the opera of *Olympiade* by Metastasio in a month's time."

"Where, Sir?"

"Why, at the great Teatro San Carlo."

For a few moments Julian was silent. Then he said: "I shall owe you, Signor, a great deal more than I can ever repay."

"Then let me hope that you will remember it," replied Durante. "Most of my pupils do not. But there is still a fault to be found, Giovanni," and his enthusiasm for his art overcame his resentment against the indifference of his old pupils. He criticised the division of an aria here, the portamento there. He forgot himself in his minute directions, until they had reached the doors of the Conservatorio.

"But do not fear, Giovanni," he cried as the lad got out of the coach. "You will go far. Beyond Naples you will make yourself known."

"That, Sir, is also my wish," said Giovanni Ferrer. Yes, one of these days, a long way from Naples he would make himself known. All the more because he had behaved like a whimpering schoolgirl tonight. The scent of musk and amber was stronger in his nostrils than that of the lemon trees of Naples.

Chapter Eleven

THE NEW BARONET SUFFERS
A SHOCK AT VENICE

Whilst Julian sang in the Villa Angelica, Mr James Elliot's father lay dying in London. He was an East India merchant of advanced years and great wealth who, for reasons which no doubt Sir Robert Walpole could have explained, had been made a baronet. He died before Durante and his pupil had reached Naples. "A little more embroidery, more shakes – the public adores them," said Durante with a shrug of the shoulders, and the aged Baronet in Kensington Square drifted placidly into another world. James Elliot, already comfortably furnished by his mother's bequest, now became Sir James and a man of wealth.

The incident would be of no importance whatever, had not Sir James, after the sixteen tedious months occupied in the transfer of the estate, determined to give his title an airing in his favourite Italy. So many Dukes, Earls, Barons, Baronets and Knights had lived and travelled and scattered their gold sovereigns from Turin down to the heel of Calabria that English titles were held throughout that country in the highest esteem. The degrees were hardly recognised. They were all English Milords, imperious in their demands and fabulous in their generosity. Thus Sir James was not surprised, nor indeed was he displeased, to find himself presented with a bill by the landlord of the Lobster Inn at Milan addressed to "Milord, the Right Honourable Sir James Elliot, Bart" Sir James was on his way to Venice, where he proposed to stay for some weeks, and being fastidious about his comforts, he had commissioned a friend of his at the English Ministry to secure an apartment for him and the necessary service.

Elliot reached the little town of Mestre on the mainland late in the afternoon, and found his friend waiting for him with a boat large enough to hold all his baggage and his servant. Elliot took off his hat and breathed the cool air with delight as the magical city grew across the level water of the lagoon.

"Yes, yes," said his friend Charles Williams, with a laugh. Williams' duties at the Ministry were very light. He had been appointed to Venice years before for a brief holiday. He had refused promotion which would remove him to another capital. He had friends in every circle in that city of many circles each new Minister found in him a walking encyclopaedia. "The Ministry without Charles Williams would be Venice without the Campanile," had said one of them. "Yes, yes," said Williams, smiling contentedly, "we middle-aged fellows no longer take things as if they were dropped there for us to cast a momentary glance at and pass on. With all its gaiety and its grim dark background ..." Perhaps Sir James looked a little surprised at the application of such heavy words to what he knew as a city of pleasure and the arts—" Oh, yes, it has a dark background, my friend, though English Milords do not often see the shadow of its shadow – it is the Venus of cities."

It took them two hours to cross the lagoon and descend the Grand Canal between the Palaces. At a corner between the Rialto and the Rezzonico Palace where the Rio San Polo debouches upon the canal, Williams gave an order to the boatmen. The boat was turned and brought to a stop at the steps of an entrance just within the Rio.

"Your apartment is on the top floor of this Palace," said Williams, "and you have your own staircase leading up to it."

Sir James Elliot's new servants were waiting for him at the steps.

"By the way, your servants will sleep at their homes. You will have your own man with you at night."

"Nothing could be better," said Sir James. He was in the mood to be satisfied with all the arrangements. And indeed when he had mounted to his eyrie, he had reason to be more than contented. The long windows of his rooms opened on to a great balcony. A stone parapet protected it and, looking down from the parapet, Sir James saw the waters of the Canal washing against the walls of the Palace. No building overlooked him and the Canal ran in so twisted a course to the sea that the Campanile and the Piazza of San Marco were directly opposite to his windows. He had the most complete privacy and the most wonderful view for a man who did not pine for green trees and the songs of birds.

"I cannot thank you enough, my dear Williams," cried the Baronet and perhaps there was just an unnecessary flavour of his Baronetcy in the manner of his address. But Williams, radiant with the knowledge that he had given pleasure to a friend, did not notice it.

"Now you have dined?" he said.

"At Treviso," said Sir James, "and not too well."

"We shall make our amends at supper at the Caffè Grimani," said Williams. "You have just time to change your dress. We shall be late but that will not matter."

Sir James, who had looked forward to an idle, busy evening, setting out in his rooms those little personal ornaments and commodities without which no one is ever quite at home, was a trifle ruffled.

"You have made plans for me?" he asked. "None that you cannot disregard," replied Charles Williams. "But tonight the Opera House of San Benedetto re-opens; and you have a box there on the first tier, next to the stage, reserved for you for the season."

"Oh, I have?" exclaimed Elliot, turning about. The first tier, next to the stage, were his favourite positions.

"I saw to it," answered Williams.

"I am grateful."

"But of course you need not go at all. Or you can go for half an hour," said Williams.

Sir James smiled.

"I perceive that you want me to go." Charles Williams nodded his head. "For you can hardly avoid inviting me to go with you."

Elliot laughed.

"And the evening promises to be agreeable?"

"Hooked!" thought Williams. But he flourished his hands and made a show of declining responsibility.

"You might not think so who come from London."

"I might guess whether I would, if I were told what opera was to be given."

"*Achilles in Scyros*," said Williams.

"Ah! Metastasio!"

"With a new score by Baldissare Galuppi," Williams added indifferently.

"Indeed! The Maestro of the Incurabili?"

"A Venetian and therefore a favourite in Venice."

"But a great composer," Elliot added with a touch of rebuke in his voice. "I am tempted. One should spend one's first evening in Venice worthily," and he bowed over the balustrade his duty to the city.

"Played," Mr Williams said to himself. Aloud he continued: "Maria Baretti will sing the part of Deidamia."

Sir James swung round again delightedly.

"I have heard her in Milan. She has a strong voice with a good shake."

"Also ..." said Williams and paused.

"Yes, also ..." Elliot repeated impatiently.

"A new soprano will take the part of Achilles."

"His name, Charles! His name."

"Much is expected of him."

"You are outrageously annoying! His name."

"Marelli."

"Marelli?" Elliot shook his head. "Marelli?"

"He came out of the sea, it is said, a year or so ago. Hence his name. He took Naples by storm. Last season he was the idol of Florence. He is young, a mere boy with a powerful, sweet and most appealing voice, so they say, and charms all by his modesty."

"What!" cried the Baronet. "A soprano who is modest? A paragon then! A second Farinelli!"

"Well, there will be a crowded house at the San Benedetto," said Williams. "So we shall hear tomorrow."

"Tomorrow!" Sir James stared indignantly at his friend. Had he lived so long in Venice that there was now only fish-blood in his veins? Tonight there would be suspense, excitement, the whole theatre a-tingle, perhaps a resounding triumph with men throwing their shoes about and women sobbing, perhaps – and equally not to be missed – a formidable fiasco.

"I will change my dress and we shall hear tonight," he said firmly, and, calling to his man for a hot bath and more suitable clothes, he hurried towards the door of his bedroom.

"Landed!" said Mr Williams.

Elliot halted at the door.

"We shall need a gondola in half an hour," he said.

"It shall be at your steps," replied Williams.

In fact it was already there with two gondoliers to man it, already attired in the Baronet's livery. Williams used it to carry him to his own lodging on the Rio Polo where he made some changes in his dress. But he was back before the half-hour had elapsed and a magnificent Baronet, jewelled and rosy, appeared upon the steps.

"My dear Charles," said Sir James, as he took his seat in the gondola, "my livery! What forethought and kindness! How shall I repay you?"

Williams smiled contentedly.

"I got your colours from your servant in London. I wanted you to cut a proper figure in Venice."

They were rowed across the Grand Canal and along the Rio di Santa Luca to the theatre of San Benedetto which they reached some minutes after the curtain had risen upon the second act.

Metastasio's operas have been dead these many years. But they were very much alive in those days. They were more than librettos. They were dramatic plays with the dialogue pruned and compressed, and songs to stress the poignancy of the scenes. The dialogue was spoken in recitative, sometimes but not always to music, and in the songs the composer had his way. Wherever opera was sung, Metastasio's were being produced with new scores, *Achilles in Scyros* especially, since the very theme made it suitable to those bygone victims of a barbarous custom, the sopranos, the *musici* as they were called.

Sir James was thus at no loss to pick up the threads of the old legend. How Thetis was terrified by the declaration of the oracle that Troy would never fall unless her young son Achilles, famed alike for his valour and his beauty, led the Greeks; how she packed him off disguised as a girl in the charge of his Governor Nearchus, disguised as his father, to the Court of Lycomedes, King of Scyros; how he was placed amongst the hand-maidens of the Princess Deidamia; how he fell in love with her and she with him; and how the wise Ulysses coming to Scyros with his ships, discovered Achilles and by cunning devices sought to force him to fling off his disguise; and how the youth's love for his Princess fought a battle with his manliness until a middle way was found. Elliot knew the book so well that the first words he heard, as he followed Williams into the box, evoked the scene upon the stage – Ulysses in the Hall of Statues, reproaching the image of Hercules for sheltering in women's clothes beside his favourite Iole, and Achilles in just that travesty secretly overhearing him.

"Alcides here, alas! excites our pity
No more Alcides son of thundering Jove …"

As Ulysses spoke these lines in the dark and crowded house, Williams took his seat in the front of the box and Elliot unslung his cloak from about his shoulders, slowly and indifferently with his back to the auditorium, as though he had more than enough time to hear and see all that he wanted of the play. But here Achilles must speak and as his voice wailed,

"It is the truth. Oh, my eternal shame!"

Williams saw his companion stiffen. Then Elliot turned not so much his hand as his ear towards the stage and stood listening with so complete a concentration of his senses that his body seemed to have no more life than the statues on the lighted stage. The scene was broken off, Achilles rejected his governor and, falling under his passion again, sang of his love for Deidamia. Elliot shivered, to Williams' thinking, just like a man suddenly stricken, and then as the voice died away he slowly folded his cloak with a care which he had certainly never shown before and laid it on the couch. But he did not yet turn towards the stage. He is incredulous, Williams reflected and changed the word.

"No, he's afraid. He is not sure. He is waiting to be made sure."

"There can't be two voices so alike," Elliot murmured.

His thoughts flashed back to the night in Naples when a throng had gathered under the windows of the Inn and Julian had sung. Had he been kidnapped because of that song, by some who heard him, from the square of the Duomo on the day of San Januarius?

"I grow fanciful," Sir James thought, but he did not dare to turn round lest his fancies should be established as the sober, horrible truth. A moment was coming when he could not fail to know. He would wait until that moment before he looked.

It was here – the great banquet in the Hall, when Ulysses brought forward his presents, the golden armour, the shield, the sword and once more "Pyrrha" sang of love and then dashed the lyre upon the ground. It was a song of many verses demanding all the delicacy, all the sweetness which music could give and rising to a passionate outcry. Once that moment was reached, he would know – he could make no mistake – and God forbid that he should know what he feared to know.

"Marelli! The boy who came out of the sea!" – he remembered those words with which Williams had described the singer. And as he remembered them, old Lycomedes spoke. His daughter was to bid "Pyrrha" take her lyre and sing.

There was an unendurable pause whilst a page brought the lyre and "Pyrrha" tightened the strings; and then the singer's voice rose again in an indictment of love's tyranny. Baldissare Galuppi had excelled his high talent in the composition of this aria. There was revolt and helplessness, anger and defeat. The voice rose and throbbed and fell. It was a wounded bird which soared in a desperate effort to vanquish and annul its hurt and fell broken-winged to earth. To Elliot the aria chimed too exquisitely with his fears. It was the boy's own soul which he was pouring out in an intolerable longing and in a poignant despair. The crowded house was held in an enchantment, hanging upon each note and clasping its clear truth. But Elliot had but one thought. "It must stop! It must stop!"

He swung round violently to the ledge of the box, he leaned forward over its ledge and his eyes met the eyes of the singer on the stage. He had no doubt now. It wasn't that the lad was startled by this one swift movement when all the rest of the house was still. It wasn't that he himself knew the features of Julian Linchcombe and the big eyes which lit his face. There was recognition in those eyes and upon the recognition the voice faltered. A woman in the pit cried out as though she swooned in pain. But that faltering was in the pattern of the scene. Achilles flung the lyre upon the floor, seized the golden shield, drew the sword from its golden scabbard and holding it high, seemed to challenge all the world.

"Ah, now I know myself Achilles."

And with that the cheers broke out, a tumult! "Marelli! Marelli!" The name rang out. Achilles must bow. He must repeat his triumph. But he couldn't. He stood, his hands outstretched at his sides, asking his audience for its forbearance, its pardon.

At the end of the Act, Elliot scribbled a note upon his tablet and seeking out an usher, sent it to the Signor Marelli. He had written in English a message that he would be taking supper with Charles Williams at the Caffè Grimani and that he would be delighted to see Signor Marelli there or tomorrow morning at his apartment on the Grand Canal.

"Shall we walk during the entr'acte?" said Williams and the two men sauntered down on to the floor of the pit. "Did you notice a box on the side of the house opposite to ours and the third to the right from the stage?"

"No," answered Sir James. "I noticed nothing, of course, except—" and he stopped. "I mean that the auditorium was too dark."

Mr Williams agreed.

As they returned to their own box the usher brought a civil reply from Marelli. It was written in the Italian tongue and in a sloping foreign hand and in the third person. Signor Marelli understood that Sir James Elliot was kind enough to ask him to sup with him at the Caffè Grimani, but he had already been bidden to the house of the Conte Onocuto Vigano who, as Sir James would probably know, takes a great interest in the theatre of San Benedetto. Sir James knew nothing whatever of the Count Onocuto Vigano, but he understood that Julian Linchcombe refused to be recognised. That was as clear to him as that Marelli was Julian Linchcombe. If he had encouraged a tiny spark of doubt, it disappeared in the next act when the lad, dressed in the golden greaves and breastplate of the young Achilles with the golden helmet on his head, stood on the prow of Ulysses' ship as the curtain fell.

Sir James was hurt by the letter, but condemned himself for being hurt. Between Julian and himself there had been as close a friendship as is possible between a boy and a man, but he had no claim upon the boy's confidence. Sir James acknowledged it. He acknowledged too, that Julian, sunk forever in the grim reality of his unreal life, was ashamed and would always be ashamed, although no atom of the blame for it rested upon him. He would wish to hide away every association with his boyhood, his own familiar people, with the lost, beloved Grest; and above all, perhaps, with the older friend to whom he had talked of his ambitions. The recollection of those talks and of the scenes in which they took place must be, even now, poignant – intolerable. And indeed something of that anguish seemed to Elliot's attentive ears to have made the passion of Achilles wring the hearts of his audience.

"He has to forget what he can forget," Elliot agreed as he took his seat again in his box and the orchestra clattered back to its seats. "He has to build up his new shadow of a life into what solidity he can and find it in the idolisation of the public." Thus Elliot reasoned. But his love for the boy and his deep sympathy had sharpened his insight; and as the third act went forward, he felt a growing uneasiness. It was not caused by the struggles of Achilles between his ambitions and his love, however vividly acted or exquisitely sung – these were things of the theatre. Sir James Elliot was obsessed by the last scene in the previous act. He had before his eyes, not the distracted lovers, nor the gay marriage scene upon which the curtain fell – but the youth in the golden armour on the ship's prow with the naked sword held high and his great blue eyes, fierce as only blue eyes can be and full of doom. Surely he was crying, "Woe, Woe!" to much more than fabled Troy.

Chapter Twelve

THE IMPORTANCE OF THE THIRD BOX OPPOSITE

The falling curtain released such a fervid enthusiasm that it took Elliot's breath away; and he had seen the Opera House in Rome on the first night of Carnival. There were women sobbing, gondoliers in the Gallery calling down blessings on Marelli and his parents, and the young elegants leaned from their boxes and showered upon the stage sonnets scribbled during the performance to the new idol and his exquisite voice. Marelli led forward his Deidamia with a low bow and a word of thanks to her, but the audience had no eyes to see nor hands to applaud her with. It was "Bravo Marelli! Evviva Marelli!" until once more the curtains swept down upon the marriage scene. But still they must be raised again, so loud and violent were the cries, so resolutely did each one in the theatre hold his place. Or was there one box empty now? For a moment it seemed to Elliot that there was – that box, the third to the right across the auditorium at which Williams had bade him look. He did look now curiously; and he saw a dark figure at the back of it, quite still and silent and remote. Man or woman he could not tell. But Sir James was in his "romantic" mood that night. He discovered a menace in that dark figure and a menace of which his companion Williams had from the beginning been aware. Once more he was uneasy. His eyes sought to pierce the gloom of that box, but quite in vain, and his attention was suddenly caught back to the stage.

Twice Marelli had led forward Maria Baretti. She was a beautiful, tall, dark woman – if she had passed her youth, the loss of it was not visible on the stage – with a resonant but undistinguished voice and she was a favourite in Venice. But this was not her night. Every turn and twist of her voice was known, her movements and gestures were familiar. To watch and hear Maria Baretti was to walk through a garden for the thousandth time where all the flowers were charming and none surprised you. The newcomer, with his beauty, his freshness and the rare compass of his voice, had quite eclipsed her. The cries were all for him.

"Viva pure Marelli! Bravo pure Marelli!"

That "pure", however, was gall to Maria Baretti. Her smile became a grin of fury. When Marelli offered her his hand for the third time she refused it. She turned her back upon the audience, she raised her handkerchief to her eyes. Tears? Yes, but tears of rage. The curtains fell for the last time that night and Elliot looked again towards the third box. It was empty now and the door open. Whoever had occupied it had slipped away.

The Opera House emptied slowly. So many had so much to say that they must stop at every other step to say it; and those who were silent departed as reluctantly as pilgrims from a shrine. The two Englishmen were amongst the last to go, but gondolas still clustered about the portico of the theatre like a fleet, and they had much ado to find their own even with its orange liveries and still more to force a passage to the Grand Canal.

"To the Piazzetta," Elliot ordered, and he sank back upon his cushions with a sigh of relief.

The cool of the night and its sudden quiet and the pleasant drip of the water from the blades of the oars drove his forebodings away but left him with a troublesome little problem to resolve.

"Of all the gifts of life," – thus the argument ran – "music is the most divine. And of all the instruments of music the human voice is the most divine. I have heard it tonight, tender, glorious, moving as I have seldom heard it – Marelli's. Well, then?"

The wrong – Elliot was frank enough not to blink his problem – done to Marelli was the sacrifice of one for the highest delight of the many, lifting them for a few precious hours out of the morass of their daily cares. And weren't there compensations for the sacrificed? Elliot's meanest side was ranging up his arguments. They were accepted, almost as gods. They lived at the houses and in the company of the greatest – in England at all events – they made great fortunes; so long as they sang, they walked in a sunshine of flattery. Elliot was of his age, accustomed to its cruelties as to its elegances and fine manners, and contemplated this or that abomination as comfortably as his fellows. Indeed, as the gondola slid between the dark palaces and he still heard Galuppi's music soaring and falling in delicious cadences, he came for just a little time very nearly to condoning the horrible crime.

But when they had disembarked and were ascending the steps of the Piazzetta, Sir James was halted by a quite different argument. When all the lights were out, that boy – Achilles, Marelli – no, let him be honest! – Julian Linchcombe – must go to his home! And to what sort of home? There rose before his eyes a picture of Grest, of old Timbertoes stumping it in the Italian garden amongst the shrill, laughing children who were never to be.

"I'm not a romantic," Sir James cried aloud, much to his companion's astonishment. "I'm a blackguard. That's what I am, Sir," and he turned with so stern a face upon Williams that that unfortunate man almost toppled backwards into the water. "A cowardly, selfish blackguard! And if you can't stand on your feet, Sir, you'll get a bath in the Grand Canal."

He stalked on indignantly between the pillars on to the Piazza and then caught Mr Williams by the arm.

"I beg your pardon. I treated you with a lamentable want of ceremony.

"No one stands on it with me," said Williams.

"I was angry with myself—"

"And so fell foul of the nearest person. It was natural," said Williams, "and here we are at the Caffè Grimani."

Although it was one o'clock of the morning, the Piazza was lively with the lights of Cafés and Casinos and groups of gaily dressed people with masks covering their faces. They found a table and Elliot left the ordering of the supper to his companion.

"An omelette, some quails and a bottle of your Orvieto," said Williams and turning back to James Elliot, "It is the best wine they keep here and we should drink it, if only to grace an evening out of a thousand."

Elliot looked quickly at Williams.

"You enjoyed it?"

Mr Williams talked with his hands for a few enthusiastic moments and added: "When shall I enjoy such another? The surprise, the delight!" Only his fingers could express it.

The reply was a little too apposite to the problem which had been troubling Elliot, for him to refrain from probing a little deeper.

"And how many of those who were listening and seeing with us are at this moment saying what you say with the same pleasure?"

"All," cried Charles Williams, and then caught himself stiffly up. "All, that is, except one."

"Ah, yes."

Sir James Elliot smiled.

"I remember! The man – if it was a man, in the third box opposite."

Charles Williams drew back. He lowered his voice to a whisper.

"Yes, it was a man." He raised his voice again with a glance at his neighbours. "I was thinking of Maria Baretti."

But Elliot was not so easily to be diverted from the solitary secret man in the third box opposite. He had no wish to return to the callous problem which he had solved – hadn't he? – with shame that he had ever set it up. Moreover he was curious – not more than curious. The sharpened insight had ceased to worry him. He was just lazily, comfortably curious.

"You shall tell me as we sup the story of this man in the third box opposite," he said, and he saw Mr Williams' face grow blank and ignorance shroud him like a domino.

Sir James was to grow familiar during the next few weeks with that sudden change from animation to vacancy and hebetude when public affairs and Government men were mentioned in Venice, but he was surprised now.

"I have no story to tell you," said Williams simply, and he started up out of his chair with a wave of his hand and a greeting on his lips.

To Sir James Elliot the movement and the cry were a ruse to avoid an unwelcome subject. Certainly a small group of gaily-dressed, masked people had gathered just outside the open door of the café and were chattering noisily; and certainly Mr Williams went out and greeted a lady of that company. In a moment or two he brought her up to his table which was just within the door.

"Sir James, may I present you to the Signora Columba Tadino? The Signora is the chief mezzosoprano of the Opera Company."

Sir James rose and bowed over, the hand she held out to him.

"There was no part for her unfortunately in *Achilles in Scyros*," he said.

"No," she answered lightly, "so I went on in the Chorus."

Sir James' eyebrows went up to the curls of his peruke. Chief mezzosopranos were not usually so complaisant.

"It was an occasion not to be missed," she continued, "and I enjoyed myself immensely." She laughed mischievously. "It is not so often that we see our dear Maria Baretti weeping."

Sir James was not so engrossed in music as not to be well aware of the jealousies which it provoked amongst its exponents.

"Deidamia," he said, a trifle sternly, "is an emotional part."

"To be sure it is," said Columba Tadino merrily, "and especially so when the Achilles carries all the audience away with him to Troy."

"You will, I hope, have supper with us," said Sir James, who had a thought that he might hear from her lips something more of the history of the boy from the sea than he knew himself.

She dropped him a curtsey, laughing.

"I may not. A patron who has a casino next door has bidden some of us to celebrate the opening of the season."

"Ah!" The word slipped out of Elliot's unguarded mouth. "The Count Onocuto Vigano."

Mr Williams made a movement of surprise, but he said nothing. Columba Tadino shook her head.

"The Count is presenting his new wonder to the nobility of Venice. When you have a bright candle, your Excellency, you do not surround it with farthing dips – even if—" and again the mischievous smile played about her lips—"even if one is Columba Tadino, at your service, and the other Maria Baretti."

Mr Williams uttered a little exclamation of warning.

But Elliot had still a question to ask.

"In the theatre, he is happy? – you like him?"

Columba Tadino's face, or what they could see of it, changed. It seemed to the two men to become pitiful.

"Happy? He has not enough vanity. You must understand that whatever triumphs those singers carry off, without an insufferable vanity they cannot be happy. As for our liking him in the theatre, he is charming, modest, kind, and we love him. But—" she stopped and took a step nearer to Elliot. "You know Marelli, your Excellency?"

But Sir James had won his little battle with himself. The boy with whom he had ridden and indeed conspired against his tutor at Grest did not want to know him any more, and Sir James could understand his refusal.

"No. I have never seen Marelli before."

"It is a pity."

"Why?"

"Because," and she lowered her voice to a note so soft that it could hardly have been heard a yard away, "for a throat as delicate as his, the climate of Venice is not too healthy."

Columba Tadino resumed her vivacity with a laugh. "But I keep my friends waiting. I shall be in disgrace," she cried, and with a whisk of her skirts she was gone.

Sir James Elliot returned to his table, once more uneasy and bewildered. Charles Williams chattered away through the omelette and the quails and ordered coffee and a ratafia. Sir James meanwhile pursued his own thoughts.

"But if he has Onocuto Vigano and the nobility of Venice on his side, what has he to fear?" he asked suddenly.

"Nothing, of course, my friend, nothing," Williams answered hurriedly. "I must take you whilst you are here to the glass-blowing on the island of Murano. It is a sight which no stranger to Venice should omit."

Elliot could take a hint as quickly as another man and here was not so much a hint as a notice on a signboard. He was quite willing to visit Murano and make up his mind whether the fragility of blown glass was to be preferred to the more durable run glass. It was two o'clock in the morning before the last almond kernels at the bottom of the jug of ratafia were reached, and Sir James called for the bill.

"The gondola shall drop me at my steps and take you on to your house," he said.

83

The Piazza was growing quiet now. A few gondolas with their crews asleep waited at the steps of the Piazzetta. Sir James' drew quietly in and the two men stepped on board.

"To the Palazzo San Polo first," said Elliot, and with smooth strokes the gondola glided, over the black water. Sir James took off his hat and pushed back his peruke and after the agitations of the evening refreshed his soul with the cool silence. But he had covered no more than half the distance to his lodging when ahead, beyond the elbow of the canal, there rose the sound of voices singing to an accompaniment of violins.

"An accademia," said Elliot, but Mr Williams shook his head. The voices were louder with each stroke of the paddles. It was a concert, it was a concert on the water, and in a few moments a great cluster of boats with lanterns swinging on the bows swept round the bend. It was led by a single gondola with its canopy thrown back, and on the black cushions a youth dressed all in white reclined alone. The fitful light now gleamed on the embroidery and jewelled buttons of his white satin coat, now revealed the black mask which he wore upon his face. He did not join in the singing, he lay rather than sat, with his head thrown back, his face upwards to the stars. A few yards behind the escort followed. Now from one gondola the music rose and when that ceased from one further back; another set of voices with another set of instruments, horns and mandolins, took up the serenade.

"Let us stop!" said Williams, and he gave an order.

The two gondoliers stopped and the gondola remained hidden in the shadow of a great palace whilst this cavalcade of the lagoons swept by. Elliot and his friend waited until the voices and the music had dwindled into such silver melodies as the naiads might have sung and then gave the order to proceed.

"You saw who led the procession?" Williams asked.

"Marelli," answered Elliot.

"Yes. Onocuto Vigano lives just this side of the Rialto. It was to his palace no doubt that Marelli went after the Opera?"

It was a question which Williams put, but Elliot did not answer it directly.

"It might well be since Vigano directs the Opera," he said.

"And he was being escorted homewards with a serenade," said Williams. "Deidamia will shed some more tears when she hears of it."

His voice, however, had none of the lightness of his words. Elliot could not but put it side by side in his thoughts with Columba Tadino's warning. But he refused to accept it. Jealousies were as much part of a theatre as the painted scenery. The actors or singers put them on and off with their dresses. Maria Baretti might weep a few tears, she might even make a scene. Cuzzoni over in London at the Queen's Theatre in the Haymarket had made a hundred. And who cared except the gossip-writers?

The gondola stopped at the landing stage by the steps to Elliot's apartment.

"They'll take you on to your house," said Elliot as he stepped out. "I am very grateful to you for all the trouble you have taken to make my visit pleasant."

Mr Williams waved the gratitude aside.

"I have something to tell you," he said, speaking very carefully, "and I should choose another moment if I were not quite sure that these gondoliers do not understand one word of English. You are wrong if you think that the Venetian nobles have any power in this city either to protect or hurt. They do not meddle with affairs. You will not find one inside the doors of the English or any other Embassy. They dare not be seen there lest they should be thought to meddle. They have their toys to play with – the Opera, the casinos, women, cards. Onocuto Vigano – a charming fellow, a dilettante with a nice taste in the arts, but a wisp of straw if you leaned upon him."

"You have more to tell me than that," said Elliot standing very still and grave upon the steps.

"Very well," returned Charles Williams. "I do not want to interfere with what does not concern me. But it seemed to me that you were monstrously interested in the Opera tonight. You were surprised by this boy from the sea. You were a little troubled. You sent a note round to him and received an answer denying you. You were hurt by it—"

"You seem to have watched me closely," Elliot growled discontentedly.

"I hope not," said Williams, "and," he repeated, "I don't want to interfere. But if you were by any chance interested in his future, I think that I should listen to Columba Tadino. She is a good creature. And I don't like Deidamia's tears of rage. And I don't like this serenade. In

Milan, Turin, Florence, Naples – yes, all very gracious. But here?" and once more he talked with his hands.

Sir James stooped swiftly down.

"Who was the man in the third box opposite?"

"Names, my dear fellow, at this time of the night?" said Williams reproachfully. "Besides, names like throats can perhaps be too delicate for common use in Venice. Good night." And the gondola bore him away.

Sir James climbed the long flight of stone steps to his high balcony. He was not seriously distressed by Williams' or Columba Tadino's warnings. Columba Tadino was of the theatre – the most exclusive and enveloping of all the callings. For her a quarrel behind the scenes blackened all the sky. Williams, too, had lived so long in this small state that every tiny disturbance of its serenity would seem of earth-quaking importance. Sir James prided himself on his citizenship of the world. What did it matter whether Deidamia wept tears of rage and Achilles was paddled home with madrigals? That Deidamia had a lover of importance was clear – for all he knew, one of the famous Council of Ten. But the Council of Ten had other work than drying the angry tears of one of its member's mistresses.

Sir James might perhaps have given more value to these hints and reticences, but he had a picture never to be quite erased from his mind which at once distressed and angered him. It was the picture of the boy going home, masked and in his fine, gay clothes to an eternity of loneliness and disappointments and nullity. The very music which recorded his triumph must have been bitter to him as dust and ashes in the mouth. And he himself could do nothing except respect that solitude. Sir James Elliot made up his mind not to intrude himself upon Marelli, since that was his friend Julian Linchcombe's wish, not even to visit the Opera House of San Benedetto when Marelli was singing; and it so happened that by this real act of sacrifice, he did Julian Linchcombe the greatest service within his power.

Chapter Thirteen

A VISITOR FROM LONDON

Marelli – to give him his real name, Julian Linchcombe – occupied an apartment on the second floor of a house next to the Palazzo Fini. His windows looked across a narrow side canal to a small open square and were near to the Opera House of San Benedetto. His gondoliers wore a black and inconspicuous livery.

"I must be at the fencing school at eleven tomorrow," said Julian as he disembarked. "It is behind the Mocenigo Palace."

"At half-past ten then, Excellency," said the chief of the pair. "We would like to say that we are deeply honoured to serve you during your stay in Venice – may it be long! We were both in the gallery of the theatre tonight and wept one moment and called down God's blessings upon you the next. We are at your orders night and day."

Julian thanked them with a pleasant gravity for their courtesy. His door was opened, as he spoke, by a servant whom he had brought with him from Florence. Sandro Ricci had been in the pit and as he helped Julian to take off his embroidered coat and his sword and put on a dressing-gown, he too bubbled over with enthusiasm. He had seen Farinelli with his giant strides and his ugly movements as Achilles when he was a boy. If only the Signor would think less of the sense and make a few more flourishes and shakes. It was not a fault that he suggested – but people expected tricks and surprises.

Julian nodded good-humouredly.

"So my old music-master, the Cavalier Durante told me. Yet Sandro, the audience liked it without them."

"Oh! for that," cried Sandro, lifting his hands. "A riot! A delirium!"

"Well, one night just to please you, Sandro, I'll shake and flourish till the theatre falls and from the debris of the auditorium you shall send a message to the Cavalier, 'He has done it.'"

"I shall bring some hot coffee and cakes to the parlour," said Sandro.

"Thank you. I shall want nothing more tonight. You can go to bed."

But Sandro did not go to bed. He brought the pot of coffee and the cup and the sugar and the spoon and arranged them with care on an occasional mahogany table at Julian's elbow. Then he said: "There is an English gentleman waiting to see you."

"What?"

"It is as I say. An English gentleman is waiting to see you."

"So?"

Julian Linchcombe's face darkened.

"He comes too late. I will not see him."

"He came at once from the theatre. I told him, Signor, that he could not hope to see you tonight. He protested that it was of the utmost importance. He had come straight from England."

So James Elliot had written. He had come straight from England.

"But I denied him," Julian cried. "He wished to see me, but I denied him."

"He explained to me that he got your address from the manager of the theatre," said Sandro. "I told him to come back tomorrow, but, Signor, he was so urgent that it was for your good – he persuaded me to let him stay."

Julian had no difficulty in understanding the sort of persuasion which this Englishman had employed. On the other hand he was puzzled and distressed by Sir James Elliot's use of that persuasion. He had shown clearly that he did not wish a renewal of his friendship; and Sir James, as he remembered, was a considerate, reticent man who responded but did not intrude. Yet he was here, apparently determined to wait until the morning broke in order that he might talk with him. Why? For curiosity's sake? To see the monster? To learn how on the night of San Januarius the boy had been rapt away and the monster made? No!

Julian, looking back on a ride in the woods and on the uplands of Grest and on a moment of conspiracy when he had put a finger to his lips and Mr – as he was then – Mr Elliot had winked his encouragement, shook his head and repeated, "No!"

Why then? To offer his sympathy and commiseration? Julian's face hardened and his eyes grew sombre. He would rather curiosity than commiseration. One did not cry over irreparable wrongs. One avenged them in one's own good time when all the plans were laid – and Sandro saw so dark and bitter a look transform the delicate flower of a face which had been his master's into something so grim and satanic that he drew back a step or two, afraid.

"He had news of importance, Signor," he babbled.

What news and of how much importance to him—

Marelli? The new toy of the Opera-going public? Julian laughed sharply. He remained silent. Since Elliot persisted, perhaps Julian had better see him and get it over. He was Marelli, a stranger, he would put on the graces and insolence of a Caffarelli or a Senesino, he would soon rout the kindly Sir James Elliot – although – although – he longed for the grasp of his friendly hand.

"Very well, Sandro … I'll see him, late though it be … Wait! A few moments and then let him in!"

Left alone, Julian covered his face with his hands. Memories of Grest rushed back on him, old pleasures of the English countryside, old dreams of what he would do with his life, the lovely house – his. The gates which he had set up and barred with bolts stronger than steel against the time when he would unlock them himself were burst open as though they were lathes and in trooped, laughing, dancing, heartbreaking, a procession of days, sparkling with morning dew, ripe with the sunlight on the corn and grey in the cool of twilight.

When he took his hands from his face and raised his eyes, it was a stranger who stood before him, a burly, roundabout sort of man, dressed in a respectable new suit of brown cloth and a bob-wig. He had a broad face with a small snub nose like a thumb in the middle of it and a pair of lively grey eyes which seemed to have been stolen from someone of a sharper intelligence.

"Signor Marelli," said the man in a pleasant voice, as round as himself, and he bowed with a jerk like a toy on a spring.

The relief – he thought of it as a reprieve – so startled Julian that he could only stare at the visitor with his wits all afield.

"I make all the excuses on my knees for the unseemly hour of my intrusion," said the visitor in excellent Italian.

"It might be thought a trifle unceremonious," Julian answered dryly.

"Yet when you have heard what I have to say …"

"Shall we take the prologue for granted?" Julian suggested.

The stranger bowed again.

"My name is Sawl with a *w*. Paul Sawl. I fancy my parents had a distressing sense of humour."

"It certainly looks like that."

"I am by profession a merchant. I deal much with Italy."

Julian with difficulty suppressed a yawn.

"My dear Sir, why waste your time with me? I have no money wherewith to buy, and I have only a few crotchets and quavers to sell."

"I have come from London to buy them."

The fatigue vanished from Linchcombe's face. He was no longer a very tired boy wanting his bed. He leaned forward eagerly.

"On the part of whom?"

"Count Heidegger."

So it had come! The summons to London! Hoped for, worked for through the years at the St. Onofrio Institute, the months at the Opera House, but never expected so soon. Heidegger! Which was his Theatre? The King's or the Queen's? On the left hand or the right hand of the Haymarket? What did it matter? Heidegger was at the top of his fame as an impresario – the ugliest man in Europe, abused and praised. Factions quarrelled over him, but if he opened his stage-door to a singer in Italy – well, the singer could travel to London, could live handsomely for a season in London, could make his plans at his ease.

"You have Count Heidegger's authority?"

"I am the chief of his partners. I will arrange everything with you tomorrow. Then we will find a lawyer. In two days all will be settled."

Julian nodded his head.

"And when?" he asked.

"Towards the end of the year."

Mr Sawl tried to conceal an anxiety. It was clear to his auditor that Heidegger wanted new blood. A bad season perhaps had sent his partner scouring the towns of the Continent. He relieved Mr Sawl's anxiety with a smile.

"I can manage it. I am in Venice until the spring. Later on I must return to Naples." A curious smile sent a sudden chill down the worthy merchant's back. It was so secret, so full of a cruel enjoyment.

"Italians!" said Mr Paul Sawl to himself in alarm. He had a vivid picture in his mind of a beautiful fair-haired Borgia youth anticipating murder as his guests arrived to supper.

"I have business in Naples. In the early autumn I return for a few weeks to sing in Florence. Thereafter I shall be at your service."

Once more Mr Sawl jerked his body backwards and forwards as Julian rose from his chair.

"I shall then have the honour to call upon you at eleven tomorrow."

"Eleven?" and again the secret smile glimmered on the youth's face. "Eleven, I am afraid, is a sacred hour for me."

"Mass," thought Mr Sawl. Or even worse, High Mass – whatever that might be.

"Shall we say half-past twelve? I have no rehearsal tomorrow. It would be more convenient."

Mr Sawl was agreeable that they should meet at half-past twelve. He brought his heels together. He had a little speech to make.

"I arrived weary and disordered at Venice yesterday evening. I had just the time to repair my dress and rush to the Opera House. Signor, in a minute, my fatigue was forgotten. We English are supposed to be a dull, phlegmatic people, but I venture to assure you that your debut at the King's Theatre" – "Ah, it's the King's Theatre," said Julian to himself – "will be acclaimed with no less spirit and delight than it was last night at the San Benedetto."

"That is a very charming sentiment," said Julian with a laugh that was just a boy's frank laugh, without any hint of dark things behind it.

Mr Sawl took his leave. Julian went back into his room and threw the casements wide; and in the still night air his nostrils were once more filled with the scent of musk and amber; as they had been long ago on the hillside above Naples Bay. But the scent was more fragrant and stronger now.

Chapter Fourteen

JEALOUSY AND YET ANOTHER DEVIL

Maria Baretti was Venetian by birth and had learned her music at the Conservatory of the Mendicanti. Against these advantages she had to set the fickleness of her countrymen. The Count Onocuto Vigano put the case frankly to the young Marelli one day after a tempestuous rehearsal of *Dido Abandoned*, when Maria had stormed, wept and cursed the theatre, the management, the orchestra and Marelli and had rushed from the stage to fling herself into the lagoon. "She will come back tomorrow, damp," said the Maestro philosophically, "but only with her tears." Vigano carried off Columba Tadino and Marelli to dine with him at his casino in St Mark's Square.

"Venetians," he said, "are allowed no voice in their state affairs. They must show no concern or interest in them. Even I, a patrician, dare not say to you the little that I have said, if the waiter were in the room. There was never such a despot as our Republic and we walk, surrounded by spies, in search of some new glittering charm to keep our eyes away from serious things. You, my young friend," he continued, turning to Julian, "are the gem of this season. Maria Baretti has, of course, her friends. There will be quips and satires and, no doubt, a few scurrilities for you to put up with. But if you continue as wisely as now and hold aloof from all these squabbles, they will die down."

And so indeed it proved. Whenever the boy sang, the Opera House was crowded and no accademia was complete unless he had been persuaded to contribute an aria. Then men liked his modesty and his reticence; the women sighed with regret and listened with rapture; and Maria Baretti learned to hide the bitterness of her jealousy behind a smiling face, whilst she planned a shattering revenge.

She planned it secretly. For it was not until the last week of the season began that a breath of it reached Julian's ears. He had played that night in Jommelli's opera, *Demophoon*, for the first time and received during the course of it a message that his gondola would be waiting for him not at its usual station on the Rio dell'Albero, but on a small canal at the back of the Opera House. Julian was a little puzzled for his two gondoliers had enjoyed pushing their way in their smart black liveries through a crowd of boats, with a good many jests and almost as much abuse, to take up the idol of the moment at the principal steps and carry him away with a procession of idolaters following behind. But his thoughts were on his part of Timanthes and he forgot his puzzle until he was changing his dress at the end of the performance. He had no engagement upon that night and, wrapping his cloak about him, he went out at the back of the theatre. He had fallen into the Venetian habit of wearing a mask for the privacy which it gave to him, and so quite unrecognised he walked the few steps to the canal. As a rule a lantern burned on the long prow, but tonight it was unlit. As a rule there were two gondoliers, tonight there was only one behind the little cabin, the second of the two men, and he wore a brown suit of velveteen with a red sash about his waist, like nine out of ten of the gondoliers plying for hire.

"There are some steps, Signor," he said in a low voice, and Julian as he reached the quay looked down and stopped. His first gondolier was lying crouched upon the floor of the gondola, as though he was waiting for his patron to step on board before he rose – and struck.

"Is this the plot of a new opera, Paolo?" Julian asked.

"No, Signor. Giuseppe has something to tell you. I will paddle out into the Grand Canal where no one will recognise your gondola or overhear what is said."

The man spoke in the low voice he had used before and with the same urgency. Julian under the fold of his cloak made sure that his hanger was loose in its scabbard and stepped down warily into the gondola. Giuseppe did not move and from the stern Paolo drove the boat out into the middle of the Grand Canal.

It was a warm, clear night of spring, the sky patterned with stars. Gondolas clustered about the doorways of the palaces and from the windows above light poured out in tapering golden beams which shook in the ripple of the water like the bright blades of eastern krisses. And along those beams, music rode forth, weaving on each side of the canal a screen of melody. But here in the middle the gondola was lost in the darkness and the quiet. Paolo eased the thrust of his paddle and Giuseppe spoke, drawing himself close to Julian Linchcombe's knees.

"Yesterday, when your Excellency was rehearsing at the theatre – it was about one of the afternoon – a man with a parcel under his arm came in a gondola to your house. Paolo and I were drinking a glass in a little inn in the square opposite and we know that man. Trafelli. He is a paid informer of the Tribunal. He looked about and then he knocked and it was your servant Sandro who opened."

"Sandro?"

"Yes, Signor. Sandro takes the parcel from Trafelli and they chat a little and they laugh. We cannot hear except one sentence. 'And that exquisite voice! What a pity!' and both laugh again."

"Which of them used the words, Giuseppe?"

"Sandro, Signor."

"Sandro!" said Julian, leaning forward; and suddenly his hand struck like a snake and gripped Giuseppe's wrist. Giuseppe uttered a small cry of pain, but it was extorted by nothing more than that sharp grip. He looked down in wonder. He could not believe that the slim, white hand with the long, tapering fingers, could hold so much pain. Surely the Signor held within his palm a supple steel ring.

"You are speaking the truth to me, Giuseppe?"

"I swear it."

The boy's eyes stared into his for a few seconds.

"Whom shall I trust?" he said sombrely, and his grip relaxed and the fingers opened. In the darkness the difference between the sunburnt wrist and Julian's hand was the difference between black and white, between a bar of iron and a supple glove. Yet even now Giuseppe's arm was numb with the savage clasp, and it was plain that no band of steel was hidden within it.

"*Per Bacco!*" Giuseppe said ruefully as he rubbed his wrist, "you should keep that grip for your servant Sandro and give your trust to us.

We run a risk, Paolo and I, in telling you that something is planned against you, even though we tell it in whispers out here in the darkness of the canal. But we have found you always generous and fair, and you have given us great moments of pleasure. Believe us, Signor Marelli! The gondoliers, they know all that is said and all that happens. Maria Baretti does not love you."

Julian laughed harshly.

"Why indeed should she?"

"And she has in her hand," he looked with a grin at Julian's hand drooping from the lace ruffles of his sleeve, "a greater strength even than yours."

"You mean …"

"What you mean, Signor," interrupted Giuseppe.

"I have offended no law."

"But to this or that man, Signor, a woman is a law. We speak to you with all good will, Paolo and I. For the moment you are safe. Nothing will be done to make a scandal. No! These gentlemen," – and he waved his hand vaguely, leaving Julian to fill in the application – "like silence. A great singer finishes his season. The next morning he has gone. Where, Signor? To Russia, perhaps, like Luini Bonetto. He stayed there twelve years."

There was so much meaning behind his last two words, he so drawled them out to suggest an eternity of weariness and solitude that Julian fell back on his cushions with a shudder.

"Twelve years!" he whispered.

"So Maria Baretti said to her friend. Her gondolier Lelio told me."

"That you might warn me?"

Giuseppe shrugged his shoulders.

"We gossip about our patrons. We have so many hours to lie idle and wait. We cannot sleep all the time. So every little unimportant story goes the round."

Clearly the gondolier had more to say. He lay resting on an elbow on the floor of the gondola, his dark eyes shining upwards.

"For instance?" asked Julian.

"Maria wondered whether Bonetto would ever sing again. She thought, and from her laughter – Maria has a very pretty, tinkling laugh, though the Signor may not have heard it as often as luckier ones – the thought amused her like Punch at a Fair," says Lelio.

Julian seemed to hear the tinkling laughter travelling gaily over the water from some gondola in which she floated with her lover at her side.

"And what was this thought?" he asked.

"That twelve years of Russia with the horrors of its winter frosts and burning summers must destroy the sweetest voice as completely as twelve years under the leads of the Ducal Palace."

Julian stifled a cry. He covered his face with his hands, trembling from his head to his feet. He made himself small in a panic of fear. He had heard of those terrible prisons under the roof of the Doge's Palace – tombs into which live people vanished, never to be brought to trial, never to receive a message or a friend, to be kept there in darkness and loneliness as long as the State Inquisitors so willed. And he was nineteen! To a youth of nineteen, twelve years and life was over! Besides, there was something he had to do. He had set himself a task. For six years he had dreamt of it. He looked back over those six years of study and endeavour. They seemed in the retrospect to have been interminable and they were just half the time Maria Baretti had allotted to him in the dungeons under the leads.

"We are at your service, Signor, Paolo and I," – Giuseppe was still talking and in the trouble of his spirit Julian heard him from far away. "Night and day."

There would have to be a charge. Julian was clinging to the code of his own country. Maria Baretti! What folly to gild her with so much authority! Her – or her lover! Whatever the tyranny of the dreaded Council of Ten, there would have to be a case, the show and semblance of a case at all events; and looking back over his months in Venice he could find none.

"Whilst I have been talking, Paolo has changed again into his livery. I shall take my place. We shall paddle you back to your house openly as though we come from some accademia, some supper party, and we shall be at your door early tomorrow. But, Signor, there is work for you tonight – secret work. What was that parcel Trafelli the informer gave to Sandro? Search, Signor! Search and find!"

Yes, not for nothing had it been conveyed into his lodging. Julian leaned forward and laid his hand on his gondolier's shoulder.

"I thank you and Paolo, Giuseppe," he whispered in a voice which shook, and very humbly. The cry of disbelief which rises to most men's lips at the approach of calamity, "It can't happen to me," could never rise to his. Such horrors had happened to him as passed belief.

"Yes, take me home! Whatever comes, I have found two friends in Venice."

Sandro was waiting at the open door, all suppleness and smiles. Julian felt inclined to say: "No, I have not run away. There was no need to watch," but he held his tongue. In his parlour on the upper floor he took off his coat and slipped into his dressing-gown. A decanter of Lachryma Christi and a plate of cakes stood upon a small table with his coffee.

"I shall not want you, Sandro, until the morning. I have some letters to write and I may be late to bed."

Sandro carried the coat away, and for a little while Julian heard him moving about, preparing his room. Sandro slept some distance away at the end of the corridor and Julian gave him time to fall asleep. Then quietly he began his search. The big high-roofed sitting-room was furnished barely. A few cabinets stood against the walls. There was an old chest or two, a writing-table, a few chairs, a couple of divans. Julian examined everything. He opened each chest. Not one held more than a few draperies. He felt the darkest corners of the cabinets. He looked behind every curtain. He made sure that there was nothing new or strange anywhere. He turned out the light and lit the candles in his bedroom; and in the end, in a drawer at the bottom of his wardrobe, under a pile of his shirts, he found three books. They were not his; he had never seen them before. But they were old, in worn bindings and the pages were marked with thick pencil lines in the margins like books which had been deeply studied.

If must be that Trafelli's parcel contained these books, but the names of them baffled him. The *Grand Grimoire* for instance, and *The Key to the Temple of Solomon the King*. Julian retired to his bed with them, and as the night grew on to morning, he began to see with a rising terror the chasm widening before his feet. The *Grand Grimoire* set out the rules and invocations by which the Lord of all evil could be summoned out of his darkness. By the Key you learned how to bewitch and hurt your enemies. But the third book troubled him to the marrow. It was called *Adonis*, a work by some old German delver into mysteries, who had lost his wits in the delving and translated these mysteries many years back into Italian. *Adonis*, Julian read, was one of the names of Satan. By certain rites and ceremonial prayers, of which the formula was given, he could be evoked in the shape of the slender white shepherd boy with the blue eyes and the tossing curls to preside over the Black Mass and its abominations.

Julian had kept his modesty, but he was not a fool. He could not but know that he could pose as some jewelled and silken *Adonis* of his century – the young Satan summoned to grace a festival of blasphemy.

Did anyone now believe that these supplications were efficacious, that Satan could be made to appear, like a Genius out of a bottle in an Eastern fable? A few pale students overcharged with midnight oil perhaps. But the grave Venetian Council of Ten? Julian asked himself the question scornfully, but he gave to himself a reply which melted his heart like wax in a flame.

Yet the books had been hidden in his lodging by a paid informer. For a purpose then. Marelli might pretend – or might be held to pretend – to be that very *Adonis* of the volume at some private assembly held by the devotees – why, even in this apartment.

From time to time he had given an entertainment to acquaintances, musical people for the most part, singers, dilettantes. It would not be difficult, perhaps, to secure one of them to tell a fine, convincing story – if it was properly composed for him or her to learn by heart – of Marelli raising an elegant modish Devil in the shape of an eighteenth-century Adonis. And no more than one witness would be needed. And there would be no confrontation; no definite charge which the prisoner would be called upon to answer. Or would there be?

Julian had spoken boldly enough to his gondoliers, but he must assure himself. And he must get rid of those accursed books. He hid them away again under his shirts and put out his candles. He had no rehearsal in the morning; Demophoon was to be repeated in the evening. He had the day free. But he could not sleep. So bitter a sense of loneliness assailed him, so wide a sea rolled between him and Grest and all that he loved. The daylight was glimmering at the edges of his curtains before all these miseries drifted away.

He waked with a sudden fear that the day was gone, but it was merely Sandro setting his coffee on the table by his bed. Certain plans had been shaping themselves in the background of Julian's mind whilst he slept; and now as he stretched his arms above his head, he said with a yawn, "Sandro, I shall want you to take a letter from me to the Count Vigano. Giuseppe will put you across to the little square and you can walk. His house is this side of the Rialto and not so far."

Sandro was ready. He had but to bring the hot water and set out his master's clothes.

"I shall take the letter now?" he asked, crossing to a writing table which stood beside the window.

"It is not written," said Julian.

He wrote it whilst he dressed and sealed it with a seal of his own devising. It represented a mermaid, half fish, half woman, with a mirror in her hand, rising from the sea. He had drawn it in an hour of sharp raillery at his condition. In his letter he asked that he might be allowed to wait upon the Count at a convenient hour that morning.

"You will wait for an answer, Sandro," he said as he handed to him the letter; and he wondered whether that letter would go straight to Vigano's palace or pass thither by way of Trafelli's lodging. Trafelli, no doubt, was an expert at detaching and replacing seals. Well, the longer Sandro took over his mission the better. From the window Julian watched Sandro cross the canal in the gondola and disappear into a lane on the far side of the little square. Then he took the three books from their hiding place under his shirts and tied them up in a parcel. He looked for something which would act as a weight and yet could disappear from the house without provoking attention. He could find nothing.

"Well, there's another way," he said. He put on his hat, took the parcel under his left arm, adjusted his cloak over it so that it was completely hidden under its folds and sauntered down the stairs.

The gondola had returned to the steps of the house and with a nod to Giuseppe he stepped on board.

"Across the Grand Canal to the Giudecca," he said.

He had a fear that at any moment Messer-Grande of the Police might draw alongside, in his big boat, but there was no sign even that he was being followed.

"You have a little anchor," he said to Giuseppe, and when they had rounded the Customs House into the open water of the Giudecca, Giuseppe housed his long paddle and cut the anchor free of its rope. He handed it in to the little cabin and uttered a crow of pleasure.

"You found it, Signor?"

"Yes, I found it – hidden."

"What was it?"

"Books, Giuseppe! Dangerous books."

Giuseppe cursed Sandro fluently.

"He will burn in hell – that smiling scoundrel. Tie the anchor firmly, Signor. I will row far out between the two shores where the water is deep."

There were few gondolas in this stretch of water and those close to the shore.

"Now Signor. No one will notice."

Julian lifted the parcel with the anchor attached to it over the side of the gondola and let it sink without a splash. It would have needed a strong spy-glass in the hands of a sharp-sighted watchman to have discovered the reason of his movements from either shore. Julian drew a breath of relief as the bubbles winked and broke upon the surface of the water. There was no evidence now which could be twisted against him.

"I'll go back," he said. "I expect a letter."

They returned by the Rio delle Fornaci into the Grand Canal and, as they emerged from the narrow opening, they just cleared the bows of another gondola which was being driven at great speed down towards the Arsenal by two big gondoliers in orange liveries. The hood was removed and two men, one of them of a stately dress and presence, were lounging back side by side upon the cushions. Julian drew back and looked straight ahead with his face set.

Giuseppe quite mistook the reason for his patron's start.

"There is nothing there to disquiet you, Signor Marelli. It is the gondola of a multi-millionaire Englishman who lives at the corner of the Rio San Polo. It is natural that you should not know him, for though he has a box at the Benedetto, it is to lend to his friends. It seems that he himself has not the ear for music. He is the Right Honourable, my Lord, Sir James Elliot, Bart"

Giuseppe announced the medley of titles with the proper accent of awe and Julian smiled and began to wonder why this dilettante with the passion for music had avoided the Opera House ever since the opening performance four months ago. That he recognised Julian was beyond question. Did he accept placidly the rebuff of Julian's letter of denial? Was his pride hurt? Or – the poignant sting of humiliation was a familiar circumstance to Julian – or did he just simply despise him? The last explanation, no doubt, was the answer, Julian thought bitterly and unfairly.

Sandro was waiting with a reply from Vigano that he would see Julian at noon. Julian had the time to powder his hair and put on a more ceremonious laced coat of flame-coloured satin. Sandro helped him to adjust his cravat and arrange his hair in a bag at the back of his neck with all his usual servility and pleasure. "He has not found out yet," Julian reflected. "I am still the hoodwinked fool dancing in silk stockings towards the dungeons under the leads. Well, we shall see."

He took his cane and his three-cornered hat with its edging of white lace and descended to his gondola.

"The Palazzo Vigano," he said, and on the stroke of twelve he stood before the Count Onocuto's door.

Chapter Fifteen

JULIAN FINDS A FRIEND AND
A WAY OF ESCAPE

He was led by a footman up to a library on the second floor with large windows opening on to a balcony. Onocuto Vigano, a large man with a shrewd and kindly face, rose from a writing-table as Julian bowed to him.

"For a famous singer, Signor Marelli, you have a gift of punctuality which is the extreme of politeness and good breeding," he said agreeably. "But we will not stand upon ceremonies. I have some notion of the reason for your wish to see me, my dear Giovanni. I may take the liberty to call you Giovanni? I thank you," and the Count slipped his arm through Julian Linchcombe's and drew him towards the window. "It is, of course, to discuss your engagement for the next season at the Benedetto?"

Now no hint of such a project had been made to Julian, but before he could stammer out a word of surprise, a tight pressure upon his arm warned him to be silent.

"Of course I am not alone in the direction of the Benedetto, but we might talk it over," and across his shoulder he called to the footman who was still standing within the door. "Tomaso, bring a jug of ratafia and some biscuits on to the balcony."

"At once, your Excellency," said Tomaso, and he went out of the room. The balcony overhung a quay busy with stalls of fruit and the passage of people to and from the Rialto. Behind it the long room stretched away to the door.

"We shall talk here unheard," said Vigano with a smile.

Even now, Julian, with his experience of Sandro, thought it a fantastic thing that men of high place like the Count, should sit surrounded by spies in their own houses and take it easily as an ordinary practice of the day. Tomaso brought to a little table on the balcony the biscuits, the glasses and the jug of ratafia.

"You will shut the door after you, Tomaso. I don't like draughts and Signor Marelli, as you know, has a throat to be nursed."

"Certainly, your Excellency."

But Onocuto Vigano made sure. He crossed the room and tried the handle of the door. When he came back to the balcony all the liveliness had gone from his face. It was still friendly but there was a gravity in the friendliness, as though he sat by a death bed.

"You have something new to tell me? Let me tell you at once that although you have never breathed a word of it to me, or I to you, I know of the peril in which you stand."

The boy's spirits, which had been rising ever since he had dumped the accursed books in the water of the Giudecca, sank as deep and as fast as the books themselves had sunk.

"Yes, I have something new to tell you."

Vigano poured out two glasses of the ratafia; and that heady mixture of brandy, apricot stones, cinnamon and white sugar brought the colour back into the lad's white face. He told Vigano the story of the parcel smuggled into his apartment and its final disposal; and he saw his host's distress grow heavier and heavier as he spoke. Even when he described the silent dive of the anchor into the depths of the wide water of the Giudecca, Vigano's expression just lightened for a second with the sympathy one might feel for a child who goes out in the fairy stories to battle with the giants. Panic seized again upon Julian. He must get to England – he lived for that! – and soon.

"You see," he cried, "what false evidence there was to ruin me, I have destroyed. Once I am brought face to face with my accusers ..." but he might have been appealing to an image of stone.

"Why should you be brought face to face with your accusers?" asked Vigano.

"The natural justice in the hearts of men would demand it," cried Julian, but even to his ears the argument sounded weak. What justice had he met with in his short life? Wasn't he planning – hadn't he been for years planning – to do the work of justice, since justice stood aloof veiled and silent?

"The natural justice in the hearts of men," the Count repeated with a gentle mockery. "A phrase, my friend. A phrase for Achilles or Timanthes or Megacles, and worth many many *scudi* sung by you. But take another glass of this excellent ratafia and listen to the truth."

He took a pinch of snuff, refilled his glass and adjusted the order of his thoughts.

"The grand tribunal of the State of Venice consists of the Council of Ten with the seven secretaries to the Seigneurie, that is to say, the Senate and the whole College of government. But these seventeen men were thought too many to occupy themselves with breaches of the law. So every year they elect from their number three State Inquisitors, of whom one is specially concerned with matters of heresy. Understand that he is not appointed by the Church of Rome. He has nothing to do with the Roman Inquisition. The Pope fought for representation, the State of Venice forbade it. He is one of the three State Inquisitors and he can act only on charges of heresy. And those charges, before a sentence can be passed, must be confirmed by his two colleagues."

"Ah!" said Julian, but the Count Onocuto Vigano shook his head.

"It would never do to count upon a division. Heresy might be held to be subversive of the State, and on political grounds the two might – nay, would – agree with the one. And there is no confrontation of accusers and accused. The prisoner is not even told on what charge he was arrested, or on what evidence condemned. He has no appeal, no knowledge of the length of his sentence. He is *sous les Plombs*."

"And Marie Baretti's lover?" Julian asked in a whisper of despair.

"Is Ascanio Cavaletti, a patrician, a lawyer as so many of our patricians become, but of greater qualities than most of them, and this year – I beg you to mark this – the State Inquisitor who is concerned with heresy. The grimoires, the ceremonial of the Black Mass – tricks? Yes, but who practised them? The books were in your room, hidden under your shirts. Yes, but who hid them? You sank them in the Giudecca? Yes, but why? You were afraid they would be discovered."

104

Julian imagined these questions put by the lawyer Cavaletti, not to him but to his fellow Inquisitors. Julian knew Cavaletti, a bilious, dark man with thin lips and a pointed face and a grave dusty look as of one who lives amongst old tomes in unswept offices. He had spoken, from time to time, to the young soprano a word of praise with a disconsidering contemptuous manner which Julian had borne with what patience he could. It was the unluckiest thing in the world that such a man should have become enamoured of Maria Baretti. There had been no other woman in his arid existence and beyond her there would be none. She had lit a fire in his heart which utterly consumed him. She was romance, poetry, the complete amenity of life; and anyone who caused her an inquietude or a tear must receive so long a lesson for his temerity that he would remember it to his dying day. All this Julian had only begun to understand during this last week, but now as he watched the sorrowful face of his friend, he once more sat shivering in a panic.

"There's little that I can do," Vigano considered. "But something I have done. I have arranged, and tonight it will be announced, that on Sunday, the last night of the season, you shall appear again in *Achilles in Scyros*. It was the first opera in which you sang. It established your fame. And the fact that you will make it your farewell will create an excitement and draw a crowded house. I think the Police will persuade the Government not to interfere with it. They want no riots, no popular indignation."

"But after that performance is over?" Julian asked.

"Yes," Vigano agreed. "Yes, the next morning whilst you are still in your bed, Messer-Grande, with his sbirri, is likely enough to call upon you."

Julian rose from his chair and leaned over the balcony, his eyes on the garden of a house across the canal. The greenery and the colour of flowers caught suddenly at his heart. This silent city of water and palaces and small streets, where few trees grew and no birds sang, became a horror to him. He must escape from it.

"Then I must not be asleep in bed the next morning," he said; turning again, to Vigano.

"No."

"There is a canal at the back of the Opera House. I will have my gondola waiting there."

"You can trust your gondoliers?"

"Yes. I am sure of them," said Julian, and his plan of escape became clear in his mind. "I shall leave my apartment just as it is with nothing packed. I shall tell Sandro that I shall remain in Venice for a week or two. Fortunately, I have already been measured and fitted for some travelling clothes. Giuseppe shall collect them and buy for me in the Merceria what else I want. These he will pack into a portmanteau and have ready in the gondola."

"Yes. That would be wise," the Count agreed.

"I'll have a cloak ready in the wings. I'll slip it over my dress and whilst the stage is still crowded and the theatre full, I'll slip out to my gondola and go as fast as it will carry me by the Canal di Canaregio to Mestre."

"Good!" cried Vigano.

"It will take me two hours to reach Mestre."

"And there I can help you."

"You?"

"Yes."

"But you will run a risk, Count."

"Oh no, no."

"Yes, you will be helping a criminal to escape."

"No! I am clever enough to guard against that."

Vigano waved the objection aside. His anxiety had gone. He was alight. He began to pace the room, smiling and chuckling and helping himself to great pinches of snuff.

"At Mestre I'll have a chaise waiting for you – hired not in my name nor in yours. I have a friend at Mestre who'll see to it."

"But then he'll run the risk," objected Julian.

"Risk! Risk!" cried the Count, stopping in front of his friend. "I never saw such a pernickety, argumentative fellow in my life. There'll be no risk. My friend's the discreetest little man you'll ever come across. You can change your clothes in the gondola and the gondoliers can bring the Achilles dress back. That's right. There will be two spanking horses in the chaise, and before the alarm's given, you'll be over the frontier."

The Count Onocuto Vigano slapped his thigh. His chuckle became a laugh. He was not only helping his young artist to escape from a great

106

danger, he was upsetting the Inquisitors' apple-cart, he was making fools of Messer-Grande and all his damned interfering sbirri.

"They'll never look for you that night," he cried. "Marelli – the last night of the season – there will be a supper party in a casino … Oh! by the way …"

Vigano suddenly ceased to laugh and sat down again on the balcony opposite to Julian.

"You don't sing on Saturday night at the Benedetto?"

"No."

"But you do at the Rezzonico Palace."

"Yes."

"There is a concert there. You are the attraction. Yes. I have a card for it somewhere."

He sat and looked at Julian with his underlip thrust forward and a frown gathering on his face.

"Count Rocca …" he continued.

"He is giving the party," said Julian.

"Yes, Rocca. An excellent fellow. A great nobleman. Rich as the Chinese Emperor. A friend of mine."

But the Count Rocca with all these excellent qualities did not satisfy the Count Onocuto Vigano. Vigano sat playing scales with his fingers on the arms of his chair and staring gloomily until the boy felt that if the suspense lasted a moment longer, he must scream.

"A beautiful Palace, the Rezzonico," Vigano continued. "Ceilings by Tiepolo. I wish mine had been," and he cast a wistful eye up to his plain white plaster.

"But even my voice won't shake the paint off the ceiling," Julian said helplessly.

"No, Giovanni, no," Vigano replied quite seriously. "I am not afraid of that. There's no danger there. No! You can loose freely your highest notes, there won't be a crack across the …" he suddenly became aware of the nonsense he was talking. "I beg your pardon. I forget my manners. I was thinking – I don't want to exaggerate – that it was perhaps a little unfortunate that you should be singing for Count Rocca."

"Why?" Julian asked anxiously.

"He's an Austrian."

"An Austrian is not an enemy."

"No. We are very good friends. But the house of a Venetian patrician is safe from the police. Messer-Grande may not enter it. But an Austrian, unless he were an Ambassador or on the Ambassador's staff, has no such privileges. Messer-Grande can enter at will."

Julian sat back in his chair. If he had only learned the intricate laws of Venice! There were half a dozen houses belonging, to the patricians who would have welcomed his assistance.

"I can't change my engagements now," he said.

Vigano nodded his head vigorously.

"It would be fatal if you did. It would be suspected at once that you had laid some cunning plan. You must know nothing of any design against you."

Vigano rose again from his chair.

"But come!" he cried. "I am making too much of this accident. The last performance of *Achilles in Scyros* will take place. I am having it billed everywhere. It is afterwards that you must hurry;" and as Julian stepped down from the balcony into the room, Vigano laid a friendly hand on his shoulder.

"Courage! The chaise shall be waiting for you at Mestre and in the autumn I shall give myself the pleasure of hearing you in some new opera, perhaps at Florence."

Julian had quite other views for the autumn and he was speaking of them to no one. But as he took his leave, he said with a warmth which made his voice shake.

"Whatever happens to me, Signor Count Onocuto Vigano, I shall remember, what I have a great need to remember when I meet them, your hospitality and your friendship."

Vigano was moved as much by the quiet and candid manner of his young guest as by his words. He held out his hand to him as equal to equal and the two shook hands cordially.

"I have always had a fancy, Giovanni, which the morning has made a conviction, that we both belong to the same world, perhaps to the same rank. I know nothing and I ask no questions. I only say to you words which it may be that you understand," – and with a pleasant but rather complacent smile, as though he was shaking hands with himself as well as with Marelli, he spoke in English, English with an accent which made havoc of it, but still English – "God send you a good deliverance."

A wave of red swept over Julian's face and receded, leaving him white as his shirt. He dared not reply in English; yet it seemed to him that it would be discourteous to a man who wished him well, if he pretended not to understand that courtesy of the English law towards men upon their trial. He was standing at his wits' end to know how fitly to answer this farewell, but Vigano had made his departure easy. Vigano had turned back to his writing-table, as though Julian had already gone from the room.

Chapter Sixteen

THE CONCERT AT THE REZZONICO
PALACE:THE ESCAPE FORESTALLED

"The Signor's coiffeur has arrived."

"The rogue's late, Sandro. Bring him up instantly."

It was the evening of Saturday. There were still thirty hours to run before he could hope to feel his chaise bouncing on the road between Mestre and the Frontier. And all was ready. A portmanteau packed with new clothes was hidden on the gondola. The Count Vigano held money to settle all his bills and charges after he had gone. Julian had been careful not to alter by an accent or a look the friendly good-humour with which he had used his servant Sandro; and Sandro, still all smiles and willingness, had obviously not discovered that the damning heretical books were no longer beneath the pile of shirts in the wardrobe.

Julian had nothing to do but to play out his part during the next thirty hours, and a calmness of spirit and with it a sense of amusement were helping him to play it with ease. Thus tonight.

"Vanity and affectation are the badge of our tribe. From Caffarelli, Senesino and the rest of us – graces, impertinences, a superfluity of fine clothes and ornaments are expected. So tonight I'll be the perfect coxcomb, as difficult and exigent as a woman, with an eye for every mirror in the room."

And it is to be granted that there was underlying the pretence a real vanity in the boy. He kept watch and ward over it as a rule, being warned thereto by a little book which Durante, the Maestro di Capella, had given him when he took his leave of the Conservatory of Saint Onofrio. But tonight he gave that fault its way. He was young and stirred to a trifle of bravado. This was to be his last appearance in his own person in Venice. Very well. He meant to leave behind him the memory of a gracious and charming picture as well as of an exquisite voice. The vanity of his kind! He railed at it and was aware of it – and seated before a mirror gave his orders to his coiffeur.

For greater convenience in the parts which he took, he wore his own hair which was thick and lustrous. He had it curled now with two rolls above each ear, heavily powdered, drawn back with a black satin ribbon and the ends fixed in the usual velvet bag. His shirt and cravat were delicate with lace, and ruffles of fine Mechlin lace covered his hands to the fingertips. The two long ends of the black satin ribbon which gathered his hair at the back were brought loosely round to the front and fixed with a jewelled brooch in a big bow in front of his cravat. With these he put on a coat of the palest blue velvet, lined with white satin and embroidered with gold. The coat was flared so as to stand out round the hips and was decorated at the edges and the cuffs with large buttons of filigree gold. His breeches were of the same colour and material as his coat. But his waistcoat was of white satin worked with gold thread and was embroidered absurdly enough at the hem with a procession of little pale blue monkeys carrying little gold umbrellas. With this dress he wore white silk stockings and lacquered shoes with red heels and big buckles of brilliants. He stuck a little black patch, cut like his seal in the shape of a mermaid with a mirror, high up on the bone of his cheek, buckled about his waist a sword with a jewelled hilt, put a watch with a gold chain hung with tinkling ornaments in each fob, and with a pirouette set himself in front of a long mirror.

"Giovanni Marelli," he said as he contemplated the slender modish youth before him, and suddenly in the blue eyes which met his, he saw opening such depths of sadness that he turned away with a shiver. A pretty enough fellow, no doubt. But what woman would go home that night with a pang at her heart because he was not beside her in her gondola? And what man would look at him with a fancy that here was a youth who, once free from a youth's vanities, might take a worthy place in great affairs? Not one! Neither woman nor man.

111

"So, Giovanni," and he made to his image a little bow of bitter mockery, "all that remains for you is to sing with a bird's clear passion and a bird's breaking heart. Well, I can depend upon you for the last of it."

The coiffeur, who was standing with his hands joined in an ecstasy, cried: "Oh! If only your Excellency sings the half as well as he looks—"

"The Count Rocca will have a right to think himself cheated," said Julian. He slung a cloak of a silvery grey damask over his shoulders, took a chapeau-bras under his arm and ran down the stairs to his gondola.

Across the Grand Canal the windows of the Rezzonico Palace blazed, the sounds of a harpsichord and violins and a woman's voice poured out in melody. It was a warm, clear night of spring and it seemed as though all the gondolas in Venice were gathered about the landing stage of that massive and beautiful house. Julian could hear his name uttered with a gleeful anticipation as his gondoliers pushed their way to the lighted torches on each side of the great porch.

"It is Marelli! We shall hear him."

"Out here! In the dark! It will break my heart with pleasure," cried a woman.

As he got out, Julian said: "I shall be late, Giuseppe. For I shall sing three times."

"And an encore for each time," Giuseppe said. "We shall be here when the Signor is ready to go."

It seemed to Julian that Giuseppe had it in his mind to say something more, but other gondolas with guests were pressing up each moment, and Rocca's lackeys ordered him away. A servant took his cloak and hat at the foot of the great staircase on which so many hoops of satin and silk swirled and rustled, so many coats of velvet gleamed that it had the look of a field of flowers in a gale. Julian added his periwinkle to the field and heard the cries from the gondolas repeated in subdued and charming whispers. "It is Marelli. See, in front of you! See, behind you!" At the head of the stairs Count Rocca was greeting his guests just within the doorway of the great ballroom.

"I can leave my post now," he said politely as he received Julian.

At the end of the room, opposite to the balcony and the great windows, a dais had been built for the musicians and singers, and behind it a smaller apartment had been reserved for their use.

"There is a buffet supper with little tables beyond the ball-room and there and here you will find many friends."

So loud a clatter of shrill voices and clinking ornaments filled the air that Julian wondered whether any more than a stray bar or two would ever be heard at all. But when he stepped forward to the front of the platform, a gasp of astonishment at the splendour and beauty of his appearance died away to a flattering silence.

He sang first "Sento nel Cor", a delicious aria by Alessandro Scarlatti, and followed it with the song made famous by Farinelli, who had sung it every night for twenty years at Aranjuez to conjure the melancholy of the King of Spain. "Son qual nave", from Porpora's opera of *Eumene*, was to Julian, as it had been to Farinelli, for it called for a sweetness, a high clear note and a prolonged power which the young soprano had especially at his command. The height of the ceiling with the Tiepolo painting made the acoustics admirable, so that his voice now held his audience in a delighted suspense, now moved them like the sight of tears, now soared and dropped upon their senses like the soothing fragrance of a magnolia bloom. So complete was the boy's triumph that when he had finished the great room was still possessed by silence. It had been transformed by the magic wand of a voice into the very home and citadel of melody. And no one moved or spoke, lest a harsh whisper or the beat of a foot should drive that fugitive spirit away. Julian, indeed, had bowed and was descending the steps of the platform when the applause broke out; and it did not stop until Count Rocca, mounting the steps, announced that Signor Marelli would sing again later in the evening.

Julian was surrounded with dilettanti and fine ladies, complimented and flattered. Orpheus was a faded nightjar in comparison. Eurydice would never have looked back, had Marelli led her through the corridors of Hell. All were convinced of that and fluttered their fans or took pinches of snuff according to their sex; but no one asked him to sit down. Nor did he dream of doing it. Here was all patrician Venice assembled with such high personages as the visitors' list included. They sat or stood as they willed, but in their presence, singers, actors, artists of all kinds only stood. So Julian stood. He saw across the room his old friend" The Right Honourable, my Lord, Sir James Elliot, Bart," holding quite a Court all to himself and enjoying the experience. Julian was amused and pleased. He knew quite well that his denial of all knowledge of their old friendship had hurt the Baronet. But he hoped that Elliot had understood his need to keep the lovely life at Grest quite apart from this irremediable transmutation which he had undergone. He was grateful to the older man for his reticence and now enjoyed his admirable performance of a grand seigneur as much as Sir James was obviously enjoying it himself. For a second or two Julian had recalled the great processions of his father through Italy with a pang of grief. But there was no jealousy in the grief, and with a smile he looked away, lest unavoidably their eyes should meet. But if there was nothing but pleasure for him in the airs and condescensions of Sir James, there was surprise and discomfort in the behaviour of another of that company. Of all the men from whom Julian expected a word of greeting, the Count Onocuto Vigano was the first, so warm and friendly had their meeting been in the palace by the Rialto.

"Yet he's avoiding me," Julian realised. "If I pass near him, he is at once deep in conversation with his neighbour. If my eyes turn towards him, he shows me the bag of his wig. Why?"

And the question was disturbing. Fear of the authorities, of the Council of Ten and the three Inquisitors? Julian could find no other answer. One of the Inquisitors, by the way, was present, Ascanio Cavaletti. From time to time Julian saw that tall and arid figure stalking, generally alone, about the rooms.

Someone touched Julian upon the arm. He turned and Columba Tadino, with a laugh between mockery and tenderness, said to him: "It is our turn next, *molto amato, squisito, gagliardo elegante*."

"You are already in the mood for our comedy. Let us go," answered Julian, and they moved together towards the door.

A genuine affection had sprung up between these two during the season. She had found him thoughtful for his fellow-singers, gentle to her and with more than a touch of deprecation for his triumphs. She liked and was disturbed by the loneliness which hung about him like a cloak. Moreover, he had often gone out of his way to insist that she should share his success at an important accademia, like this one of Count Rocca. He, on the other hand, met with a friend of much insight and no jealousy, of a lively spirit and a deep tenderness.

They sang tonight a sequence of duets from *La Serva Padrona*, the comic opera by Pergolesi. The music was light, the melodies had a lilting gaiety and infected these two, so accustomed to the sighs and passions of tragedy, with their own zest and sparkle. The audience was swept off its feet. There was an amusement in seeing these artists of the high emotions disporting themselves, with the enjoyment of children on a holiday, on the easier ground of farce, and so warm and delighted was the applause, it seemed that Rocca's guests would never let them go; and whilst they slipped at last from the platform, Rocca was surrounded and submerged in congratulations.

They were undeserved. Rocca had protested. Arias which called for a couple of octaves, songs which were ornamented with shakes and flourishes and crescendos and diminuendos, these were what an accademia of importance required. Julian, however, had insisted and Count Rocca had shrugged his shoulders. These sopranos were kittle-cattle who must be indulged, if you needed them to fill your reception rooms for you. And now that the experiment had been acclaimed, he was taking the credit of it to himself.

"Yes, I had that idea. The native comedy of Italy and the great voices to subdue themselves to it. The result, I think, delicious. You agree?"

Wise people might perhaps have foreseen in this revolt against the turgid declamations and dead themes of the conventional operas the lovely compromise which was soon to be struck by the exquisite music of Mozart. But Count Rocca was no forerunner.

"Marelli will sing again. Meanwhile there is a concerto for violins, hautbois, flutes and harpsichords; and there is supper. Pickled sturgeon and lark pâtés, and a turkey, I think, with chopped mushrooms and a few green onions. You will see the buffet in the next room."

Meanwhile in the artists' retiring room behind the dais, since in the next item no voices were required, Columba Tadino and Julian stood alone.

"I am your servant, my sweet friend," he said, giving her his hand. "One day perhaps we shall sing together again."

"*Molto amato*, with all my heart," she began in jest, and something deeper took her, an intense pity, a conviction that there were secret fires burning and torturing that young heart of which she knew nothing. She sank in a low curtsey in front of him and taking his hand in hers kissed it. When she stood up again, Julian saw that her eyes were drowned in tears.

"But not in Venice," she added, and even in this room her eyes sought the corners lest they should hide someone to overhear them.

"Where you will, Columba."

"You depart tomorrow night? Yes? At once, when the curtain falls?" she asked eagerly. "Write to me from Borgo. It's the first little town beyond the Frontier."

"I will."

"Promise!"

"See! I cross my finger."

"But you are laughing."

"With a heart very full of gratitude."

"*Molto amato!*" she repeated softly. "I shall not come to the theatre tomorrow. I do not sing in *Achilles in Scyros* and … I dare not." She drew him towards her and kissed him. "But I shall not sleep until a letter – oh! only one line in your hand – comes from Borgo. However, I shall hear you again tonight. I shall be in the corner far away by the window on the left hand. Sing to me, boy that came out of the sea."

"As I have never sung before," said Julian.

But he was wrong. He was to sing a fourth time that night and under such a stress of contained emotion as he had never had occasion to know.

He returned to the great reception room. In the doorway stood Rocca and his enemy, Ascanio Cavaletti.

"Ah!" cried the Count, and he pulled at Cavaletti's sleeve. "You see, Signor, you see!" He turned to Julian with a joyous relief. "The Signor Cavaletti would have it that you had gone. But I assured him that you were to sing again."

"That was agreed and I keep my agreements," said Julian politely.

But he had a little trouble to keep his voice quite steady. Why, he was thinking uneasily, should Cavaletti fear that he would seize this favourable moment between two performances to disappear? He was in no danger tonight. But he had been living for so many days now on the edge of panic that the least shadow of a new threat made his heart turn over within him. Rocca, however, was in too exuberant a mood to observe the expressions upon faces.

"Aha!" he exclaimed, nodding his head. "*La Serva Padrona!* What did I say, my young friend?" He had forgotten altogether his fight against so homely an item in the programme. "A triumph! I had no doubts. A novelty, human and charming. My compliments, my dear Marelli. You must sing in Vienna. I shall see to it," and he fluttered away.

Julian found himself face to face with his enemy in a curious isolation. Cavaletti was smiling, his thin lips parted, his white teeth shining between them.

"Yes, a great evening for Count Rocca and a consoling memory for Signor Marelli," he said slowly.

Julian went forward to meet the attack.

"I think men look for their consolations to the future," he said, with a curious smile upon his face.

"Men? Yes, no doubt," Cavaletti returned dryly, and saw the blood mount into the boy's face and his eyes darken with pain. Cavaletti's tongue tip appeared between his lips, moistening them. He was smiling now. There was a gleam of enjoyment in his eyes. Julian had never seen cruelty so perfect, the slow approach, so that not one flavour of it should be lost. The words dropped one by one in the smoothest courtesy.

"Metastasio, Signor Marelli, is no doubt a great poet. The world tells me so. But though he writes without verse or rhyme, I have a preference for Plato."

"Indeed?" said Julian politely.

"You, with your days and nights filled with music and songs and the glamour of applause, will have had no leisure for the dialogues of Plato."

"No, Sir," and a recollection of his old tutor hunting him vainly through the corridors of Grest and up into the lumber room under the roof burnt for a second incongruously in his memory. "I was brought up to admire rather the sobriety of the Latins," he replied.

Cavaletti's face was suddenly black with anger. This boy was answering him and with spirit. An impertinence! But the black look passed. Twelve years under the lead roof of the Ducal Palace would write paid to a good many impertinences.

"You are nineteen years old, I think," he said, and laughed.

"I am in my twentieth year," Julian answered boyishly and haughtily.

Cavaletti laughed again and again, his tongue flickered across his lips. He looked Julian slowly over from his shoe-buckles to the delicate lace of his ruffles, the little blue monkeys with the gold umbrellas embroidered on his waistcoat, the big bow at his throat. And in spite of his efforts, Julian felt his feet trembling, his hands shaking, and knew that Cavaletti saw them too and was ravished with the sight.

"It is fortunate that Plato did not live in this state, at this time," Cavaletti continued, "or Venice would have lost a good many hours of pleasure."

"He is coming at last to the unpleasant message he has for me," thought Julian, "but I'll be hanged if I help him to deliver it." So he merely bowed and Cavaletti was disappointed; and in the pause he noticed a little confusion at one point in the room. From that confusion, one of farewells and compliments, Elliot with Rocca upon his heels emerged. They passed close by Julian and out of the room. In a moment Julian heard his host's voice bawling from the top of the stairs.

"Sir James Elliot's gondola! Look to it, rascals!" Julian was seized with a wild impulse to break away from his prosy tormentor, bolt down the stairs and leap into Sir James' gondola at the same time when the stately Baronet stepped magnificently into it. But Cavaletti held him, gloating over him as some dainty morsel reserved to complete the feast.

"No, Plato had no place in his community for pretty fellows like singers and actors and artists. As they approached they were to be received with roses and fair words, but they were to be escorted at once out of sight – quite out of sight into another land, as people disturbing the order of the State."

On just such a plea the State Inquisitors could act today in Venice. Was that what Cavaletti had taken all this time to say? Was that all? Julian wondered and doubted and shifted from one foot on to the other.

"But I must not keep you," said Cavaletti. "I am already suffering a great many black looks from the ladies for keeping so modish and famous a young gentleman from their company. Besides, you have still to sing your farewell to Venice."

Julian stood still, as still as though he had been frozen to the ground. "My farewell?" he repeated.

"Yes! It will be something we shall remember with infinite regret."

"I sing it tomorrow."

"And where?"

Cavaletti was eager to hear it tomorrow. He stepped forward, so eager he was, his eyes aflame with the pleasure of anticipation.

"At the Benedetto."

"But, my young friend …" Cavaletti was puzzled.

"In *Achilles in Scyros*. It is announced."

Cavaletti was in despair.

"But have you not heard?" He looked round the great room. "No! You were singing, your ears shut to everything but your work."

"What should I have heard had my ears been open?"

"That there has been a fire at the Benedetto."

"A fire?" Julian stammered.

His knees as well as his feet, as well as his voice, were shaking now. It was to this climax that Cavaletti had been working; Marelli was not to know of the disaster until his knowledge was too late to save him. It was for this reason that Cavaletti had held him so long with his talk of Plato.

"It is not so disastrous apparently as was feared," Cavaletti continued. "There was water close at hand. But the orchestra and the dressing-rooms have been flooded. There will, alas! be no performance at the Benedetto tomorrow night. The news has already been cried in the streets."

Cavaletti once more looked Julian over from his shoe buckles to his ruffles, the monkeys with the gold parasols on his embroidered waistcoat, his cravat and his powdered hair. He made no effort to dissimulate his pleasure now.

"And so, I beg, the prettiest of adieux tonight," he said with a wave of a hand towards the platform, and he turned on his heel and went away.

So that was the story which had been put about. No wonder Vigano had refused to meet his eyes. Vigano had his orders. He must keep quiet and not interfere. The flight to Mestre and Borgo beyond the frontier had been foreseen.

There was a touch upon Julian Linchcombe's arm. "What? Already?" he asked. "Here? In this room?" He remembered some troubled words of Onocuto Vigano. Only the houses of the born patricians of Venice were safe from the irruptions of Messer-Grancle and his sbirri. Julian turned, but it was only Count Rocca who stood at his elbow.

"It is half-past two of the morning," said Rocca, "and they will not let you go too easily. Perhaps when this concerto which is coming to its end has finished … What do you say?"

"I am your servant," said Julian.

Were all his fine plans in the dust? The fragrance of musk and amber to fade in the prison under the leads? Heidegger in the Haymarket to wait in vain for his new recruit, and Marelli to sing his last aria in the Rezzonico Palace? Well, it should be worth hearing. Julian set back his shoulders and holding his head high, walked down the corridor towards the platform steps.

Chapter Seventeen

THE CONCERT AT THE REZZONICO PALACE: DISASTER AND RECOVERY

Julian had a hope that he would find Columba Tadino in the makeshift green-room. He could send through her a message to his waiting gondoliers. But she was not to be seen. Julian gathered up the copies of his songs. Columba Tadino was waiting, no doubt, but in the place she had appointed, the corner by the great window and the balcony. He walked up the steps to the rostrum to much clapping of hands and cries of "Marelli!" and flutterings of programmes and handkerchiefs. As he bowed, he looked with a smile towards Columba's corner, and the smile took an edge of bitterness. For Columba was not there.

"The sinking ship," he thought. "Well, let me go down with every flag flying." And with a bow to the conductor of the little orchestra, he sang Handel's exquisite song from the opera *Acis*, which begins "As when the Dove …" and sang it with a faultless tenderness. He followed it with yet another aria from the same hand, Semele's lament from *Semele*, "Oh, Sleep, why dost thou leave me?" But whilst he sang, that curious gift of great speakers and executive artists which enables them to criticise and hold a secret conference with themselves, whilst they are giving the very best which they have to give to their audience, was awake in him and at work. He had stood by the side of Handel and sung in his boy's treble long ago at Grest. Perhaps that incident, he conjectured, brought back his memories of Grest. Perhaps it was just

Columba's absence and the conventional image it had suggested. But whilst he sang he trod the quarter-deck of a great ship of the Line. It was lurching and shaking under him and every second sinking deeper into the trough of the sea. But above his head the great flags which decked in battle a ship of the Line were streaming out on the wind, the Cross of St. George, the Union Flag and, higher than them all at the mainmast head, the giant banner of England. The roll of a drum, as his voice soared and stopped, sounded in his ears like the last thunder of his great ship's guns. There was the death glorious – not here, under the leads of the Ducal roof, to appease the sordid hatred of a rival – and the rival a woman.

But here he was, a singer bowing his farewell to Venice – a little pale blue monkey under the gold parasol of an artificial voice. Would it avail him now, that gold parasol? He turned and stepped down from the rostrum. He had no valedictions to make; he was not a guest but a performer for a fee. He walked straight to the head of the stairs. In his mind there was just a hope.

"It will take these polite people half an hour to pay their compliments to their host. There will be confusion, delays. If Giuseppe is on the watch waiting for me – and he will be, for the gondolier is the first to hear the news – I might be away to the Giudecca and Mestre before my disappearance is noticed."

Someone brushed by him, a woman going up – Columba Tadino. She had not a word, not a gesture for Marelli. "The sinking ship," he repeated. But he did not hurry although he longed to. The staircase was empty, but in the porch, at the landing stage, there were torches flaming, footmen bawling and a throng of guests who had made their farewells betimes. Julian walked sedately down. He saw two of the footmen detach themselves from the crowd and run back to a little door at the side of the staircase. They came out again, leaving the door open. One of them held his cloak, the other his hat. Julian laughed quietly. After all Marelli had his privileges. To footmen, to gondoliers, to the people who slept on the stones of the squares and the quays, he had a special meaning. He meant music and in return they were ready with his cloak and his hat when he was in a hurry.

At the foot of the stairs Julian turned back round the newel post to where the two lackeys waited. The one with the cloak held it spread wide, and Julian turned his back to him so that he might adjust it on his shoulders and held out his hand to the second footman for his hat. He was taken completely off his guard. The lackey with the cloak made a screen of it between Julian and the staircase. The man with the hat plucked Julian into the room so violently that he stumbled. He heard the door slammed behind him, he felt a pair of arms pinion his elbows to his sides in an embrace of iron. Before he could recover from his stumble, a pair of handcuffs gripped his wrists together. The two men stood away from him. His cloak was now lying on the floor behind him.

"Messer-Grande, at your service," said the man with the hat. "You will stay in this room until his Excellency's guests have gone and the house is quiet. Then we will come for you. If you utter one cry, we will come back and gag your mouth."

Messer-Grande stooped and unbuckled the sword from Julian's waist. "You will not want this again," he said.

He laid it with the hat on a square oak table. The two men went out of the room. Julian heard the key turn in the lock. He stood without moving where they left him, his hands, manacled and helpless, dangling in front of him. Outside there was still the bawling in the porch and the silence on the staircase. Hardly five minutes could have elapsed since he had passed Columba Tadino at the head of the stairs.

"So it's over," he said.

He had jumped with both feet into the neat trap prepared for him. Vanity again was the cause and explanation. Marelli – the boy from the sea with the golden voice – to be sure, lackeys would rush to set his cloak about his shoulders and present his hat to him with an obsequious bow. No doubt of it! But here he was, on his way to the Leads, with handcuffs on his wrists and the threat of a gag if he raised a cry. And all those fine plans – the season at Heidegger's theatre in the Haymarket, the great opportunity which he was going there to discover, the settlement of a terrible account! All vanity! For him the Leads. Twelve years of them! Did one live for twelve years under the Leads?

On the staircase suddenly there was a chatter of voices, a hiss of silken skirts like a smooth sea breaking on a beach. Count Rocca's guests were taking their departure from the Rezzonico Palace. Julian waked from his stupor. He was in a porter's side-room. There was an oak table on which his sword and hat were laid, a three-legged stool by the table and over the table an oil lamp burning dimly hung from a hook in the ceiling. This meagre furniture was on his left hand against the outer wall. In front of him, as he stood with his back to the door, a small unglazed window, high up in the wall, let through the stars. Did one ever see stars, he wondered, under the Leads of the Ducal Palace?

He was asking himself the question idly – for in an hour or two he would know – still possessed of only half his wits, when from that high small window, a few bars of music, sung by a woman's voice, floated down to his ears. Familiar music – yes, he had heard it, shared it that night – music from *La Serva Padrona* – and the singer was Columba Tadino. Julian raised his head, but he dared not answer. He had a friend out there then, and his heart rose in gratitude and remorse. Whilst he had been reproaching her, she had been seeking a way to help. Could it succeed?

Julian measured with a glance the wall between the window and the floor. He examined the unglazed window. It was long enough, but between the lintel and the sill it was narrow – perhaps too narrow. It might depend upon – and he looked closely now at the manacles on his wrists. The locks were too strong to break, even if he had risked the noise of smashing them against the stone wall; and slender though his hands were, he could not slip them through the rings. But his hands were not crossed, and there were a couple of links between them. He could just place his hands with the palms side by side instead of face to face. For the first time he drew a breath of hope.

The chatter on the stairs was louder, but he dared not drag the table along the floor and he could not stretch out his arms and carry it. He removed his sword and hat and laid them carefully on the floor. He stooped under the table, rounded his back, raised it so, balancing it carefully and sidled along the wall until he was directly below the window. Then he kneeled again and let the legs of the table come silently to the ground. He drew himself from under it. He had judged the distance accurately. The table was exactly below the window.

But he could not reach from its surface to the windowsill. He was sure of it. There was still, however, the stool. He could lift that and he set it up on the table. For a moment he listened and made a little bow of apology towards the door. He had cursed the whole tribe of women often enough for their habit of blocking doorways and staircases whilst they chattered with complete indifference to the wishes of any who were in a hurry to go. The bow of recantation was certainly their due now.

"Stay, fair ladies, as long as you please. Flirt, sneer, laugh! Recall the pickled sturgeon, the lark pâtés, the purple figs and the still champagne at the buffet! How good they were and how villainously the little Marelli sang! Take your time, ladies. There is so much to say."

He was standing on the table. He balanced himself on the stool, a rickety wobbling thing. He reached up his arms, standing on his toes. He could lay the palms of his hands flat upon the sill, with the tips of his fingers he could get a grasp on the outer ledge. He laid them so at the left hand corner of the window. Julian had good reason now to bless the hours spent in the fencing room, the dancing-school and the water of the lagunes. He was light of weight, slim as a girl, supple as an acrobat. Without a spring, which would certainly have sent the stool clattering to the floor, he drew himself up the wall, got his right leg over the sill and with a jerk was astride. He could not sit up, the lintel was too low, but he could lie hunched up along the sill, half within the window, half without. He put his head out and looked down the outer wall.

A small canal ran along this side of the Rezzonico Palace. Beyond the mouth of it, in the Grand Canal, there was a great cluster of gondolas, bright as day with Chinese lanterns and flaming torches and noisy as the fruit market by the Rialto. But underneath him it was all silent and all dark. Columba's voice had stopped. From below, his head projected from the window had been seen against the skyline; and in a moment, his eyes becoming accustomed to the darkness made out a thicker blot of darkness, and a white patch or two, the shirts of Columba's gondoliers.

But they seemed a mile beneath him. He had not thought of the steps down from the porch to the landing stage or the height of the landing stage. If he dropped from the window, he would make such a clatter in the gondola, upset its occupants with himself into the water with so much noise and splashing that certainly his attempt at flight would be discovered. He would probably break his legs into the bargain and be fished out by Messer-Grande, if fished out at all, in a condition which would make escape quite impossible for the future.

But he could make out now a narrow ledge or coping halfway down between himself and the water. He compared its level with the level of the stool inside the room. "About the same," he thought. He turned his hands so that now his fingers grasped the inside of the sill and drew his left leg out of the window, so that from his head to his waist he was in the porter's lodge, whilst from his waist to his feet he was stretched out in the air.

He lowered himself gently and his toes touched the ledge. He could stand on it, so long as he pressed against the wall. Now all that he had to do was to lower himself on to his knees, get his hands on the ledge and swing down until he could drop into the gondola. But those simple movements with all his suppleness he could not make. The ledge on which, he stood was too narrow and his wrists were handcuffed in front of him. Had they been free, he could have spread-eagled his arms against the stone and thus balanced, with his body pressed against it, slip down first on to one knee, then on to the other. But if he brought his hands down in front of him, he pushed himself backwards off the ledge, and instead of his legs, he would break his neck. He had to keep his hands at arm's length above his head. But he did manage to keep his balance and scrape down the wall. There were, alas! casualties among the pale blue monkeys with the gold parasols, but he was at last precariously on his knees and sure that, what with the strain upon his body and the narrowness of the ledge, he could not stay there for more than the fraction of a minute. If he could have dropped his hands to the ledge on which he knelt the rest of the descent would have been easy.

"Hist! Hist!"

The gondolier might hiss up to him as much as he liked, but since Julian could not turn his head or twist his shoulders and keep his balance, whatever advice he had to give was going to be wasted. Julian had his own problem to consider. He must drop plumb down and catch the ledge under the palms of his hands as he dropped. That they would do more than break the length of his fall, he could not believe. They would strike on a flat surface. There was not a chink nor an edge on which they could grip.

"Hist! Hist!" the gondolier whispered; and Julian whispered back, oh, most unwisely, in his own tongue.

"Buz, buz! The actors are come hither, my Lord," and he gathered himself for the drop.

But there was more sense after all in the gondolier's hisses than in Julian's quotation from Hamlet. For before he could push himself off, there was a slight rattle of wood by the side of his knees. It was the butt of the gondolier's long sweep. He had jammed the blade between the strong rowlock and the wall and was holding it there. Julian felt it with the side of his knee, pushed himself off the ledge and caught it as he fell. The second gondolier took his legs as he dangled.

"Let go!" and the next moment he was seated by the side of Columba. She drew him back under the canopy and threw a cloak across his knees.

"Quick!" she whispered, pushing her head forward towards her gondoliers, "Mario! Renzo!"

They drove their great sweeps into the water. Columba looked back to the high window of the porter's room.

"How slow you were, Giovanni! I thought that you would never come."

Julian tossed back his ruffles and showed her his wrists.

"Awkward ornaments," he said, and Columba uttered a little cry.

"They did that to you! My poor boy! I promised to hear your last song. I heard of the fire. I ran down to get my gondola to the steps, ready. As I ran up the stairs again, I passed you. I thought it would be madness to show I was your friend. From the landing above, I saw you pushed into the empty room. I brought my gondola under the window, and with – those," she touched the manacles on his wrists, "you still escaped. Faster, Mario!" And her eyes still searched for that dark window in the side of the Rezzonico Palace.

But no light showed in it. The gondola was still in the black shadow of the great house. The only light in this dark cleft came from the white of the water as the oars churned it.

"Look at those lights," she cried. They were driving forwards to the Grand Canal where the shouts rose and the lights flared and the gondolas clashed and jostled in a swaying mass. Beyond them all, alone by the left bank of the Grand Canal, one big gondola rode, silent, unlit, shrouded in black.

"The police-boat waiting for me," said Julian, and at the change in his voice Columba turned quickly towards him. The bravado, the

127

raillery had all gone out of him with the coming of this moment of relief. He was sitting back, making himself small, his feet drawn back under his knees, his voice shaking, and his body shaking with his voice. His eyes were fixed in a dreadful look of terror upon the black prison barge, and to Columba he had actually grown small. He was a boy in a gala dress, breaking with fear.

"Courage! A moment more! Once we are lost in that swirl of boats!" She snatched the wrap from her shoulders and arranged it over his knees and drew it down to the floor. "We are so near to safety."

But they were not near enough. A head was thrust out of that high window from which Julian had climbed. A cry rang out over the water above the bawling voices.

"Take care!" and the water flashed from the sweeps of the police gondola as it turned towards the Palace.

Columba rose to the dire need. She had a flashing inspiration. Since secrecy had failed, advertisement must serve. She tore the wrap away from the boy's knees. She pushed the awning back from above their heads so that all could see.

"Sing Giovanni! Sing as you have never sung! And, Mario, faster, faster!"

Julian stared at her.

"What, you too, Columba?"

"Sing, Giovanni! For the love of God!"

And still not understanding what she would be at, Julian threw back his head and sang – the first song which came into his head – that air of bravura from *Artaxerxes*, which he had sung at the Villa Angelica under Vesuvius. And as the well-known voice with its liquid notes leapt and swooned from the dark, narrow mouth of the lateral canal, cries of delight and surprise rang out and the crowded gondolas surged forward as though they had ears and a motion of their own.

"Marelli! Marelli! Viva Marelli!" and the gondolas were about them.

"Sing Giovanni! The police won't interfere now. See, their gondola has stopped! They don't want a riot, a scandal, Maria Baretti and her lover, the Inquisitor. The game's up. Mario, keep to the side!"

Columba's brains were working shrewdly. A water-party! On the loveliest of spring nights, Marelli to sing, and not a copper to pay!

"Keep into the bank, Mario."

It was not only that she wanted the throng of gondolas between her and the police boat. She had vividly in her mind a map of the Grand Canal.

"We'll sing the duet from the *Olympiade*," she whispered. "And make the most of it, my dear. Come!"

She pushed her hand through his arm, but Julian now understood. Her tender courage had revived his spirit. He had sung Pergolesi's opera with Columba at the Benedetto Theatre only a week ago. He raised his hand for silence and then in a clear, low voice breathed out the first notes of the most moving, the most simple of all Pergolesi's melodies.

"*Ne giorni tuoi felici.*"

And as he sang, the whole fleet of gondolas, Rocca's guests and the lookers on, swept in a cavalcade down the Grand Canal. Every homeward-bound reveller turned aside to swell it; and here a violin, there a guitar volunteered an accompaniment. Columba took up the strain as Aristea, and in a little while the voices blended. Down the canal the great procession floated, torches and lanterns burning, Columba's gondola always on the inner rim; and on the other, side, unobtrusively, like a boat cruising to be hired, the black police barge kept it company. They passed the Contarini Palace. Columba's voice dropped away and Julian took up alone his resolve to go and his prayer not to be forgotten.

"At the next rio, Giovanni," Columba whispered. "Your own men are coming up by the side of us. I'll hold the procession until it's seen that you have gone – as long as I can. In this confusion of lights it won't be seen at once. Giuseppe must free your wrists. And then to Mestre."

Julian sang the great farewell as he had never sung. Durante, his old tutor at the Onofrio, would never that night have warned him against the simplicity of his style. He trilled and he shook; he ornamented and improved and decorated; his voice mounted like a bird and diminished on the same pure note in the blue of the heaven and swelled out again in organ-strength as it hovered down to earth. Little muted cries of delight broke from the people. They knew the music so well; they adored the embroideries which a lovely voice could weave on it; and Julian was playing every lesson which he had learned, every natural gift he possessed against the black police boat and twelve years under the Leads.

A swish of oars and his own gondola was beside him. Columba whispered to her gondoliers to back water. The water-party was halted as the dark cavern of the small rio opened between two great mansions to the right.

"Ready!" whispered Columba; and Megacles of the *Olympiade* poured out his last despairing loud appeal. As the applause broke out and the flambeaux drew across the night a quivering screen of flame, Columba whispered again.

"Now! God be with you, my dear!"

Julian dropped his forehead on her lap and kissed her hands. He lifted himself from his seat or began to lift himself. For Giuseppe swooped down and picked him up in his arms as though he had been a child. The cheers were still rising as the gondola swept between the two towering houses. Julian looked back. The flotilla still covered the mouth of the narrow rio, the torches were still blazing. Columba began to sing. In that confusion only the nearest of her audience could have seen that now she was alone.

Giuseppe and Paolo were stripped to their waists. They drove their gondola along this high cleft like slaves on a galley. The music died away; the sky widened to a vast canopy of stars; the houses dwindled; a white causeway of stone glimmered on one bank of the canal. No one walked on it. There was no sound but water dripping back to water from the blades of the sweeps.

"To Mestre, Signor?" said Giuseppe quietly.

"No!"

There was no carriage waiting at Mestre tonight and there was a police boat at this moment perhaps on his heels. There was but one refuge safe for him – if he could reach it.

"The Englishman at San Polo! By the little canals! The police boat will make for the Giudecca and Mestre."

Giuseppe turned off to the right. The gondola twisted and turned through a labyrinth of tiny waterways. Here and there a group of drunken men, tumbling from a drinking shop, shouted at them. Here and there a man walking stopped in his walk and peered at them over a balustrade. Julian's heart was in his mouth. Panic was again clutching his heart. But they had passed back beyond the Rezzonico Palace, and suddenly, at a bend, the width of the Grand Canal opened out in front.

"Here are the steps, Signor," said Giuseppe, bringing the gondola gently against them.

Julian was standing on them the next moment.

"Giuseppe, the Count Onocuto Vigano has money for you. You shall hear from him. Now slip on your coats and go quietly back to the Rezzonico Palace, as if you were still waiting to take me home. You know nothing."

He heard a word of good wishes and hurried up the stairs. Turn after turn! Would they never end? A heavy door faced him at the top. Julian beat upon it with his chained fists. Not a sound answered him. Had Elliot gone from the Rezzonico Palace to some other party? In despair Julian beat again and again upon the door, bruising hands and wrists and unconscious of the pain. And every other second he was looking over his shoulder, expecting Messer-Grande and his servants to turn the last corner of the stairs. At last, after an eternity, feet approached from within the apartment, a key turned in the lock, the door opened, and as Julian tumbled through the doorway, he saw James Elliot, in a dressing-gown, with a great pistol in his hand.

"You?" cried Elliot.

"Lock the door!" and Julian spoke in English.

Without a word Elliot locked the door and shot the bolts.

When he had done, he turned and saw Julian drawn up at the side, his head thrown back against the panelling of the wall, his face sickly as a dying man's.

"Yes," said Julian, "I am Linchcombe. Julian Linchcombe of Grest;" and suddenly, he covered his face with his hands and the tears ran out between his fingers.

Sir James Elliot saw with a shock of horror the handcuffs shining on Julian's wrists. But he was a man with great self-possession and great consideration for his friends. He said gently "I was hoping that you would come to me;" and placing his arm round the boy's shoulders, he led him into his sitting-room and set him on a couch.

Thus they met for the first time since an afternoon nearly eight years back at the inn of "The Golden Ox" in Naples.

Chapter Eighteen

THE REFUGE

Both wisdom and friendship bade Sir James Elliot to continue to be the imperturbable Englishman. Julian Linchcombe, having reached at last this haven, had reached the end of his valour. He was broken in spirit. He sat on the couch, white and shaking like a man with a palsy.

"You want a posset, Julian. So do I," said Sir James. "I have taken to my heart the liquors of this country."

"Lemonade?" Julian asked faintly with the shadow of a smile.

"Come! That's better," Sir James reflected; aloud, he cried: "Lemonade! Faugh! A child's drink and cold on the stomach. No, Sir. A ratafia. And I have some which has been standing for four months. Meanwhile, the sooner those irons are off, the more conveniently you'll drink it."

He spoke as if the visit at half-past two in the morning of an unusually exquisite young gentleman, dishevelled and in handcuffs, was the sort of humdrum incident anyone might expect.

"I'll wake up my servant."

"Your servant?"

"Thomas Biggin. I'm a fumbler with my fingers. Thomas was a sailor before he took to valeting and is handy with any kind of tool. He has been with me for twenty years."

"He was with you at Grest then?"

"You were a boy."

For a moment or two Julian was silent. Then, with a touch of eagerness: "Yes. It will be as well to make sure whether he knows me again," he said slowly.

"You can trust him to keep your secret if he does."

Again the wan smile glimmered in the boy's face. "Thomas Biggin. The name's comforting, Sir. It sounds like farm hands in smocks sitting outside an ale house with mugs of beer and saying 'Eh?' when they didn't hear you, and 'Ah!' when they did." He broke off suddenly with a cry. "My God, I wish I was one of them!"

He put his elbows on his knees and buried his face in his hands. Sir James patted him on the shoulder.

"I'll bring Thomas to you." He went to the door on the inner side of the room which opened upon the service quarters. "You are safe here, Julian."

Julian nodded his head and looked up with a full smile.

"Yes. You are The Right Honourable, my Lord, Sir James Elliot, Bart Besides, you went but the once to the Benedetto Theatre and liked the opera so little that you never returned."

"You guessed why, I hope," said Elliot gently. "I remembered you. I thought it out. Oh, Messer-Grande will not come here to search for me."

But when he ended, as if there and then to prove his confidence mere folly, someone knocked upon the outer door.

"At this hour … !" said Elliot, under his breath.

For a little while the two stared at one another in a dreadful silence. Elliot saw panic smoulder and glare red like madness in Linchcombe's eyes. He rose awkwardly, unsteadily to his feet. Searching the room for an issue? No! Elliot was never to forget that moment. By some miracle the lad lifted high his head and brought his red heels together with a click.

"If they have come for me," he said quietly, "you must hand me over to them."

Sir James thrust out his underlip. A boy with this spirit?

"Not even to the Duke of Venice himself," he said stubbornly. "Stay here!"

He went out of the room into the lobby. On his left was the strong door locked and bolted. On his right was the inner door opening on to the terrace above the Grand Canal. A lamp swung from the roof above his head. He stood without a movement, his great pistol in his hand.

The knocking was repeated. But it pleaded, it asked, it prayed.

"By Gad," he said, "no police in any country ever knocked on a door with so much modesty."

He stepped forward, withdrew the bolts, turned the key in the lock and pulled the door open.

Who is it?

"Giuseppe, the Signor's gondolier."

He was carrying a portmanteau on his shoulder and he swung it down into the lobby.

"It must not be found on the Signor's gondola," and Giuseppe turned and ran down the stairs. Sir James leaned against the wall with his hand to his heart.

"By Gad, I might be the boy himself," he said angrily. "What nonsense! I won't have it!"

He thumped his heart. It must behave itself in a more orderly manner if they were to remain friends. He locked and bolted the door again. Then he went back into the parlour where Julian was still standing as he had left him. He said roughly, being still angry with himself: "It was your damned gondolier with your baggage. If I may say so, a deuced inconvenient time …" but he never finished the acrimonious sentence. For now Julian's day was full and this reprieve surcharged it. He dropped on to the couch as though he had been felled and slid off it on to the ground.

Elliot was stricken with remorse. He started forward.

"Julian! It was a false alarm. Don't you hear me?"

Julian didn't. His eyes were closed. He heard nothing whatever. Elliot lifted him back on to the couch. With a sudden, sharp fear he unbuttoned his waistcoat and thrust his hand in over his shirt. But Julian's heart was beating.

"He has got the vapours now!" cried Sir James.

It was really a most agitating night. What did one do? One burned a feather under the nose of people who swooned. But there was not a feather in the room. Nonsense! Whenever people swooned there was always a plethora of feathers. He had read it, he had seen it. Amelia faints and you light a feather and there she is languidly smiling her gratitude. But this boy oughtn't to want a feather. "As if I would have handed him over!" exclaimed Sir James.

A bright idea flashed upon him. He would get the handcuffs off before the lad recovered consciousness. He hurried off by the door to the service quarters, thanking Heaven that the women slept in their own homes. Thomas Biggin, aroused by the noise, was already drawing on his breeches in the light of his candle.

"Thomas, there's a young gentleman in the parlour in an unusual predicament."

"Now, what might that be, Sir James?" asked Thomas, scratching his head.

Sir James explained in words of one syllable, and, pulling on a linen jacket, Thomas, with no more surprise than if he had been asked to prepare a cup of chocolate, laid his hands on a file, a length of wire and a spike, and followed Sir James into the parlour.

"Now, not a word, Thomas, to a living soul! And keep your head!"

Julian was still deep in his swoon. Elliot turned back his ruffles. Under the handcuffs the wrists were black with bruises and the skin torn.

"Get those pesky things off, Thomas! Gently now! Keep your head!"

Thomas Biggin knelt down by the couch, and Sir James, hovering over him like a mother-rook over her nest, was amazed at the delicacy with which his servant's great hands did their work. He felt the spring of the lock with the wire, then bent the wire and inserted it again, and got a pressure on the end of the spring with his spike.

"Don't let that slip! Keep your head, Thomas!" implored Sir James, and it was only when he realised that each time he urged Thomas to keep his head, Thomas stopped his work to turn a wondering wooden face upon his master, that he desisted from his advice.

"She's a-coming now," said Thomas.

Elliot heard a tiny click and the iron ring opened.

"Excellent, Thomas!"

"T'other'll be easier to handle," said Thomas, and Sir James saw Julian's eyelids flutter on his cheeks.

"He oughtn't to have those long eyelashes with the curve up at the end of them," said Sir James. "They give him a melting look and he doesn't melt, Thomas. Don't you think that, Thomas, or we shall quarrel!" he added fiercely.

Thomas was thinking of nothing but freeing the second wrist from its manacle, but Elliot had got it into his head that Thomas was despising the boy as a weakling.

"Just because he's handsomer and better-dressed than most of us, you mustn't run away with the notion that he's breakable. He's neither glass nor china. He's steel, Thomas, though you mightn't understand it from the look of him. But I am forgetting the ratafia."

When he came back with the jug and glasses, he saw Julian sitting up pale and worn, and his wrists free.

"I behaved like a baby, Sir," he said.

"You wanted your bottle," Sir James agreed. "It's ready now. Try it!"

He filled a glass to the brim and handed it to Julian.

"Whilst you are drinking that, Thomas and I will get a room ready."

Julian began to protest, but Elliot would not listen.

He took the handcuffs out on to the terrace and, swinging back his arm, flung them far into the air.

"Listen, Thomas!"

And standing in the darkness they heard the plop as those implements of Messer-Grande struck the water. Julian, within the room, heard it too.

Thomas Biggin carried the portmanteau into the guest room at the end of the terrace.

"We'll keep the lobby door on to the terrace and the inner door of the bedroom locked," said Elliot. "Then the only approach to my friend will be by the glass doors of the parlour. We'll see that the women don't use that for a day or two. You must warn them, Thomas, very discreetly. There mustn't be a whisper that there's a guest in the house."

Thomas scratched his head doubtfully.

"Women!" he said.

"I know. But it's only for a day or two."

"Clack-clack! If it isn't their tongues it's their clogs," said Thomas.

"Their clogs will be a warning."

Thomas ruminated and at last a smile spread slowly over his face.

"I can manage it, Sir James."

136

Elliot went back into the parlour and saw Julian with the glass empty at his elbow, colour in his cheeks and a light in his eyes.

"That's better! Off you go to bed, my lad. We'll talk tomorrow – no, by Gad, today. I am next door to you if you want any help."

Julian murmured a few words.

"I shall thank you better in the morning. I don't suppose anyone living has such a friend as I have in you."

He was hardly aware that he undressed, brushed the powder from his hair and washed the blood from his wrists. For a few seconds he was conscious of the cool, clean luxury of lavender-scented sheets and waked to see the afternoon sun chasing the shadows on the terrace.

Chapter Nineteen

OLD CONSPIRATORS CONSPIRE AGAIN

Julian Linchcombe and Sir James Elliot supped together in the parlour that evening. The two women had gone to their homes and Thomas Biggin dished and served the meal. They drank soup, ate a magnificent turbot with lobster sauce and big peppers, a leg of veal garnished with rice, an apricot cream and macaroons, and for dessert, figs and grapes and pistachio nuts. They drank Lachryma Christi of a beautiful orange colour, Elliot gorgeous in maroon velvet and gold, Julian spruce in a plain suit of fine green cloth with a modest lacing of silver. There was an air of profusion habitual nowadays in the dress of Sir James, which he was never quite able to control, and he looked across the table with a touch of envy at the trim elegance of his guest.

"I wish you could teach me to tie a cravat like yours," he said, gazing with despair at the big bow of snow-white muslin at the youth's throat and at the unruffled fall of lace which hung below it. "But you never could. Whatever I put on, I manage to look a sloven at the end of it." He sighed deeply. "It's a tragedy."

Julian laughed.

"A trifle of carelessness, Sir, which would be unbecoming in me, is quite appropriate to the Right Honourable, my Lord, Sir ..."

Elliot interrupted with a grin.

"That'll be enough. I regret to notice that you are just as impudent as you were when you expected me to join you in deceiving that unfortunate old shortwinded tutor of yours on the stairs at Grest."

"Which, by the way, Sir, I think you did."

Elliot laughed.

"Well, it's good to play truant if only by deputy." He had to come soon to Julian's tragic state and history, but he was keeping it as far away from his consciousness as he could, for as long as he could; and Julian's boyish impudence and humour helped him. Moreover, though he had recovered much of his old spirit, Julian's face was pale and his eyes were tired. Elliot made the conversation light, whilst he insisted that the lad should eat his fair share of supper and drink glass for glass of the Lachryrna Christi. But the supper had to come to an end.

"We'll take our coffee on the terrace, Thomas. Set out two chairs and bring out my tobacco pipe."

Sir James Elliot rose reluctantly and they went through the glass doors. It was quite dark, and Elliot welcomed the darkness for the youth's sake. "He will talk more easily if his face can't be seen." It was only when standing up that the lit windows of Venice and the bright loom over the Piazza could be seen. Seated behind the parapet one had only the vast embroidered hood of the sky overhead, the caress of the warm air, a scent now and again of the sea, and a distant murmur from far below to make a floor of sound. Here Sir James Elliot filled the bowl of his long pipe and lit it. He puffed for a little while under the pretence that the pipe did not draw well. Then he reached out a hand and laid it on Julian's sleeve.

"Now, boy, if we are to find your way out of this bad trouble, I have got to have your story. What brought you to my door last night?"

Julian at once began with the opening of his season at the Benedetto Theatre; and Elliot listened to the first sentences with a relief which he recognised as cowardly. The episode of Venice stood apart then. It was not linked with that story of irremediable wrong which Elliot shrank from hearing the more he loved its victim. He wanted Julian as he remembered him, as from time to time in some flashing moment he met him again, a boy of a quiet gaiety, full of spirit, full of ambition and yet ready with a laugh at his own extravagance. He wanted him unusual only by reason of his charm and the freshness of his mind, not because he was crippled for life by the most dastardly of crimes.

But as he listened, this episode of Venice, with a jealousy of the theatre deepening into hatred and a thirst for an abominable revenge, took hold of him. The license of an Inquisitor to use for his own ends his silent and unquestioned power horrified him.

"I have to get you away and at once," he cried when Julian had finished. "Maria Baretti! Who would imagine a woman so cruel?" and a short, bitter laugh from the youth at his side suggested that more than one example could be cited. "The man in the third box. Cavaletti, of course. I was warned, too, on your behalf—" Suddenly Sir James Elliot broke off.

What was the use of blaming himself for his indifference to that warning? The danger was too immediate. Messer-Grande might not come knocking at his door, but he might set a watch upon it; and here perhaps was a hope of finding a safe way out. He turned quickly towards Julian.

"There's a man here at the British Embassy – Charles Williams. He has spent his life in Venice. He was in my box that night when you played Achilles. It was he who warned me of your peril."

Elliot felt rather than saw Julian draw away.

"You want to call him in?"

"Yes. He is my very good friend. He will help."

"You told him—who I was?"

"Not a word. Not even that I knew you."

Elliot heard a sigh of relief, imagined a smile and once more saw the young Achilles with the hard, blue eyes threatening doom to more than Troy. Well, since Achilles wanted his secret kept, he would help him to keep it.

"Let us see, Julian, what we can tell Charles Williams."

The reply came at once, rather sullen, very obstinate.

"I am Giovanni Ferrer, known as Marelli."

Sir James accepted the premise.

"We build our story up on that. Agreed. But I knew you before you came to Venice."

"You did?"

Julian was startled.

"To be sure." Sir James recalled the details of the opening night at the Benedetto Theatre. "I sent a note to you during the interval. Charles Williams was at my elbow when your answer was brought to me. I fancy – no, I am certain, that he thought that I was hurt by it – as indeed I was."

A hand timidly rested on his arm.

"You'll forgive me?"

"Since it was to me that you turned for help," said Sir James. "So then I already knew you. How? When? Where?"

Julian found the answers to those questions quickly.

"You came to visit the school of St Onofrio at Naples. The Cavalier Durante, the Maestro di Capella brought you."

"That might be," Elliot agreed. "And I was struck by your singing."

"You were kind enough to think well of it. You used your acquaintanceship with the British Minister to secure for me an audition at the Villa Angelica."

"Did I have enough influence?"

"You, Sir? The Right Honourable, my Lord …"

"I thought that I had hinted that not all jokes bore repetition," Sir James interrupted with a grin. This story was working out very well – plausible in every detail. Sir James began to feel more comfortable.

"But I left Naples before you made your debut at the San Carlo Opera House. Is that right?"

"Quite."

"And I didn't know that you had taken the stage name of Marelli?"

"So my appearance at the Benedetto was a complete surprise to you."

"But I was not sufficiently interested in you to do more than send round to your dressing-room a cold word of congratulation," said Elliot. "Really, this is an excellent story."

"To which," replied Julian, "I seem to have returned an insolent rejoinder; and how, if you please, Sir, do we go on from there?"

"Quite easily."

Sir James was once more imperturbable.

"In your predicament you sought a refuge in the house of a patron of importance."

"And he being the most generous of men …"

"He being that lowest of all God's creatures, a dilettante – did you speak, Julian?"

"Sir, my good manners forbade me either to contradict or interrupt."

"For such good manners boys were horsed in my young days," said Sir James, and both of them broke into a laugh. Then Sir James jumped up from his chair.

"So the plot's laid. Once more we are in a conspiracy. I shall, send for Charles Williams tomorrow morning, and meanwhile we ought to prepare ourselves for a sound long sleep ..."

"By a jug of ratafia," cried Julian.

Sir James went back into the dining-room to find it, but whilst he stirred it up in its big glass demijohn, so that the cinnamon and the apricots and the kernels and the sugar and the brandy might all blend in one delectable drink, he discovered a flaw in the conspiracy. He had taken Charles Williams and his help for granted. But had he the right to do so? It was clear from Julian's story that the Count Onocuto Vigano had abandoned his friend, the singer, from fear. It was true that Vigano was a Venetian and Charles Williams an Englishman on the Embassy staff. He could not be secretly imprisoned, but his recall might be demanded, and Charles Williams dismissed from Venice would hardly be alive. He might refuse, therefore, to move a finger to save Marelli from the claws of Maria Baretti.

"But I am not going to allow it," said Sir James as he shook and stirred the ratafia. He was John Bull in an instant. If there had been a bottle of beer handy for them, he might have poured the ratafia down the sink with a curse upon all foreigners. "No, I won't. But I must warn Julian."

He carried his tray into the parlour. Julian was still upon the terrace. Sir James put the tray down upon a table and found Julian leaning over the parapet and staring down towards the water.

"What is it, Julian?"

Julian turned round, and the light of the window fell upon a very troubled and anxious face.

"I have been wondering what has happened to Columba Tadino?" he explained. "She saved me last night. I can't let her suffer for me."

"By Gad! I never knew a boy invent so many miseries and hug them to his breast," cried Elliot in exasperation. "I saw Columba Tadino in the Piazza at five o'clock this afternoon with Charles Williams, and she was in the highest spirits."

Julian's face was changed in an instant. "Good news, Sir James. Thank you!"

He followed Elliot into the parlour and stood smiling eagerly whilst Elliot filled the two glasses. But as he raised his to his lips, Elliot planted himself squarely in front of him.

"I want to tell you something."

And at once there were two antagonists in the room instead of two friends, Sir James, bluff portly, with an out-thrust jaw and a red face; Julian, wary, erect, with his blue eyes as hard as pebbles.

"Yes, Sir?" said Julian. "I am listening."

"I ask no questions," Elliot continued. "I probe no secrets. But I know you, my Lord of Linchcombe," and he made a stiff correct bow, "and I am not going to leave you, however things go, to sweat and freeze under the Leads of the Ducal Palace. I shall go back to England and scream from every house top the real name and title of Giovanni Ferrer, known as Marelli."

"You will have no proofs," said Julian.

"Admitted," replied Elliot. "But – and I dare you to laugh – the Right Honourable, my Lord, Sir James Elliot, Bart, can make a stink. And, believe me, I'll make so foul a stink that they'll smell it in Venice, and open the Ducal doors wide enough for you to saunter out between them with your congé in your pocket. That is what is going to happen unless Charles Williams helps us," and he uttered every word as if he were a man with a hammer driving a great nail into a stubborn beam. "Then, my Lord," and again the formal bow followed on the words, "I take my cue from you. For your sake, and for your father's sake, I am at your elbow when you call."

For a few moments, the blue pebbles, hard, unrevealing, imperious, met his. Then they softened until they were – what were the words in the song which Julian sang at Grest and again at Naples? – "deeper and kinder than sapphires."

"I think I am the most graceless beast alive," Julian said, with a tremor in his voice. "I come to you for help, and for the sake of old memories you give it with both your hands. And I show my gratitude by silence. For one reason. I, the most pitiable of men, cannot bear pity."

143

Sir James had no words wherewith to answer him. This youth with his looks, his birth, his wealth, his talents, should have had the world at his feet. Yet he stood there, the most pitiable of men, refusing pity. Silently, solemnly, they raised their glasses and drank to one another.

"I know," Julian continued, "but I have no proofs. I had, no money to go in search of them. I have money now and I shall find them. Then my friend, I shall tell you everything."

He did not ask Elliot to stand at his elbow when he had his proofs. He just raised his head as though some strange perfume reached his nostrils, of which he could not have enough.

"The musk and amber of revenge," he said with a grim smile. "I once found that phrase in an old book."

He drank his glass of ratafia slowly, his eyes smiling upon Elliot.

Chapter Twenty

THE PLAN OF ESCAPE

Charles Williams, who throughout the day was at the service of his friends, did not allow the day to begin at the hour suitable for a farmer. He was a townsman. To be asleep after nine he thought slothful; to be abroad before ten ungentlemanly. Sir James Elliot was mindful of these principles and sent his gondola at half-past nine to Mr Williams' door with a letter asking for his help. Mr Williams chuckled over the letter and the discretion of its wording. He changed from his old brown cloth coat to his new plum-coloured velvet one, set his hat jauntily on the curls of his wig and was conveyed to the Palazzo San Polo.

Thomas Biggin received him at the top of the stairs, and, showing him into the parlour, closed the door behind him. Sir James was waiting for him alone.

"It was good of you to come so quickly," said Elliot and was astonished by a sudden contraction of the muscles on the left side of Mr Williams' face.

"Of course I came quickly," replied Williams, and repeated the gymnastic movement of his face. It occurred to the Baronet that his friend was winking. He sniffed the air with a curious archness. He advanced roguishly across the carpet. He poked a finger roguishly into Elliot's ribs.

"You're a fox, aren't you? Cunning's the word. Oh, you quiet ones!"

"God bless my soul!" said Sir James Elliot.

"Just a peep, eh?" pleaded Mr Williams. "I'll be as close as an oyster," and he tip-toed towards the glass doors to the balcony.

Elliot planted himself firmly in the way.

"What do you expect to see?"

Charles Williams grinned and the grin became a laugh.

"Oh! aren't you the innocent? What a rascal!" he cried.

Now there was never a man who looked less of a rascal than Sir James Elliot. Rascality and he were at opposite poles. He disliked the epithet even though its application was obviously meant to be humorous. There was a familiarity in the use of it which he found distasteful. He had dropped in the estimate of Charles Williams somehow and his face flushed with indignation. "But I mustn't lose my temper," he warned himself. "That would spoil all."

He took Charles Williams by the arm and led him back to a chair.

"Come! What is all this?" he asked, pleasantly.

"My dear fellow!" Charles Williams expostulated. "Don't you know that my old servant, Bettina, is the aunt of your two girls?"

"Oh?"

And Sir James, in his turn, sat down. But he sat down rather heavily. Could Thomas, the invaluable Thomas Biggin, have become a gossip?

"And you couldn't expect two girls who had been locked out of the guest-room and the terrace and told to prepare supper for two not to carry the tale to their own aunt, now could you?"

"Oh!"

Sir James was now alarmed. What tale had the two girls told?

"But you needn't be disquieted, my dear man!" Yes, it was my dear man now. "Bettina won't talk and your two girls daren't. Bettina is a terrifying woman, I can tell you, and she has given her orders. You mustn't really blame your maids."

"No?"

"No, indeed. Your man let it out first."

"What!"

Sir James jumped out of his chair.

"Thomas?"

"If that's his name."

"By Gad, I'd never have believed it!"

"He did," and again Charles Williams laughed roguishly, and again he winked portentously. "Let me have a peep at her!" he whispered.

Sir James stood and gaped like a fish. So that was the story which Thomas Biggin had invented to appease the curiosity of his servants; and in it was the reason for Mr Williams' hilarity. Sir James was vastly relieved.

"Carried her off did you?" continued Mr Williams with a chuckle. "It'll be someone we all know. You wouldn't take all this trouble to hide a girl from the Erboria, would you now? Took her away from Rocca's party, eh? Carried the fortifications by storm. Well, well, well, what a hero!"

These lush flatteries fell more pleasantly upon the ears of Sir James, now that he knew what error had provoked them. Even the most sedate of Baronets will walk with a sprightlier step if he is thought capable of a place in the storm-troops at a rape of the Sabines. He would certainly have to disabuse Charles Williams of a – well, of a not improbable mistake. And meanwhile a path out of all this trouble began dimly to glimmer in his mind.

"But, my dear man," – yes, Charles Williams was now my dear man – "I asked you for your help. I hope that, should the case in your mind occur, I should be equal to my own emergencies."

Sir James was, no doubt, a trifle fatuous, but the worthiest of men have their moments of fatuity. And his hardly lasted for a second. He ceased to simper.

"But this is a very different affair."

"Oh?"

It was now for Charles Williams to look blank.

"Yes."

Sir James went out on to the terrace. He returned immediately with Julian.

"Signor Giovanni Ferrer," he said, and Williams stared with his mouth open and his eyes starting out of his head.

"Marelli!" he cried.

"Not so loud!" said Elliot.

Mr Charles Williams whistled.

"So you ran to earth here!" said Williams to Julian. "That was a clever trick." He swung round to Elliot. "Then you did know him," he exclaimed accusingly.

Elliot was quite at his ease now.

"These young singers!" he said with a shrug of his shoulders. "They forget their patrons in success and remember them in defeat. But they sing."

"Yes, no doubt," said Charles Williams with a cynical glance at Julian. "That excuses all. They sing."

"But Columba Tadino sings too," Julian exclaimed eagerly. He cared little for Elliot's reproaches – they were part of the conspiracy. But Columba had helped him in his need and he was still in doubt whether she had suffered because she had helped.

Charles Williams looked at him with a greater friendliness.

"Columba Tadino? You need not be anxious for her, Signor. Columba Tadino is a clever girl. All yesterday she was telling to me, to her friends, at the top of her voice, her amusing story. She was going home by the small canal which runs by the Rezzonico Palace to the Giudecca, when you suddenly dropped into her gondola from the window of the porter's lodge. You told her that since the fire at the Benedetto theatre had cancelled your last appearance, and since your baggage had already been sent forward to the mainland, you had determined to go there at once. But there was such a crowd in the porch and on the staircase that you wouldn't get away for an hour. Columba, accordingly, turned her gondola about and took you back to, the Grand Canal to find your own. But you were recognised, surrounded, and there was nothing left for you to do except to sing your way down the Grand Canal. An empty gondola was alongside and at the first opportunity you slipped on board of it and got away to the Giudecca and Mestre. What could anyone do to Columba? It wasn't known that the police wanted you. It isn't known now."

No doubt Columba had failed to mention the handcuffs and he would be thought to have slipped them. Such things had happened.

"But," continued Williams, "they are searching Mestre for you and no doubt Venice too – very quietly, very thoroughly."

"Do you know that?" asked Elliot.

Williams nodded his head.

148

"A whisper reached, me. Cavaletti doesn't mean to let you go, Signor Marelli."

Sir James Elliot crossed his legs and took a pinch of snuff.

"That's a plaguy nuisance," said he comfortably. "For I propose to set off on a visit to Ferrara tomorrow."

Julian looked at his host in consternation.

"Yes, I wish to spend a few days in that famous town. In fact, my dear Williams, I sent for you to ask you to come with me as my guest and cicerone."

"That is most kind of you," exclaimed Charles Williams. The time of the year was suitable. "I could certainly get leave from my duties." Ferrara in the spring! What could be more charming? "But Marelli? You can't leave him here to be waited on by your two maids. Even Bettina couldn't keep them from talking."

"Oh, Marelli?" said Elliot, sitting back easily in his chair. "He will think of another hiding-place and get away to it during the night;" and he dismissed Marelli with a wave of his hand.

Julian, for his part, was wondering what Charles Williams could have said to set Elliot suddenly against him. He was to find another refuge! With a sinking heart he began to search his memory for names. The Count Onocuto Vigano? There was no hope in that quarter – and Elliot was speaking again.

"We shall not go by Mestre, Williams, a long, dusty, uneven road. No, but up the River Brenta by water."

Charles Williams was delighted with the prospect.

"And we shall travel in comfort – as indeed the English milords are expected to travel," Elliot announced with a deprecatory smirk. "For instance, there will be a separate gondola for our baggage of which Thomas will be in charge."

"Thomas?" Julian interrupted aghast.

"Yes."

"Thomas Biggin?"

"Who else?" Sir James Elliot asked smoothly. "Oh, I would do anything for your safety within reason, Giovanni. But I could not leave Thomas Biggin behind. He is an attribute, a personal adjective. I should not be half myself without him."

Julian looked down upon the floor, his wits all dazed. Had Sir James been nursing some subtle idea of punishing him for his reply to the letter sent round to him at the Benedetto theatre? Was he too drawing into his nostrils the pungent savour of musk and amber? His chin dropped forward on his breast in despair.

"Thomas will be in one boat with the baggage. A second will carry musicians. Yes, it will be pleasant to have water-music as we ascend the Brenta. We shall have, of course, to travel in my present gondola – you, my dear Williams, myself, and, since I may as well profit by the reputation which you and Bettina and my maids have given me, I shall bring a lady with me to cheer our way."

"A lady?" cried Charles Williams.

"You will not be inconvenienced, I hope," replied Elliot politely. "She will not come from the fruit market, I promise you."

"My dear fellow!" Williams expostulated. Then he fell again into his roguish mood. Marelli was quite forgotten. He must make what he could of his hapless destiny. Julian sat with his eyes upon the floor. He felt the handcuffs once more cold upon his wrists.

"Do I know her?" Williams asked.

"You do."

"Ah, foxy, foxy," and Mr Williams laid a forefinger against the side of his nose. "Her name, or I die here on your floor?"

"You'll keep it secret?"

"As the grave."

"Pyrrha," said Sir James Elliot.

Mr Williams frowned. His face was lined and furrowed by perplexity. "Pyrrha!" he repeated. He ran over the names of such ladies – and they were not few – as might fall victims to the charms and the pocket-book of my Lord, the Baronet – Lucrezia, Giannina, Camilla, Caterina – but there wasn't a Pyrrha amongst them. And then he lifted his head to see Marelli upon his feet, blushing, laughing and blushing again.

Mr Williams was more puzzled than before.

"I don't understand," he stammered.

"My dear fellow!" cried Sir James with the very accent of Mr Williams, "Pyrrha is the name which in the very excellent libretto of Signor Metastasio, the young Achilles bore amongst the maidens of Scyros."

A moment of stupefaction for Charles Williams, and the same moment of uneasiness for Julian. Then Williams broke into a loud guffaw, and never had humiliation so poignant, in all these eight years of humiliation, so wounded Julian Linchcombe.

"To be sure," cried Williams, thumping with the palms of his hands upon the arms of his chair. "Signor Marelli, I make you my compliments," and he swept a bow towards the floor.

To his impish humour the plan was most amusing. The great English Baronet in a stately procession up the Brenta with a lady at his side, and Mr Williams of the English Embassy on the seat in front of him. Music to waft him on his lordly way. His baggage on a third gondola behind him. Who would venture to ask the name of the lady he took with him on this adventure? No one. And Giovanni Ferrer, known as Marelli, would slip between the claws of Cavaletti and Maria Baretti and Messer-Grande and his satellites as easily as – nay, more easily than – he had slipped from the window of the porter's lodge in the Palace Rezzonico.

"Maria Baretti – that gentle one – will take to her bed in a rage and Cavaletti will bruise his knuckles as he knocks upon her bedroom door. He hasn't caged the shining singing-bird for her, the unforgivable fellow!" and checking his laughter, Charles Williams went into a conference on ways and means with Elliot. Julian was not consulted. He was left to stand much as he had stood years before in the music-room of Sir Edward Place at Naples whilst the ladies decided how he must be dressed and furbelowed for his debut. All that Julian had to do was to hold his tongue now and do as he was told afterwards. People with a knowledge of the world and the habit of affairs would arrange what was best for him.

Barges, not gondolas, would be wanted, said Mr Williams. Sir James had his friends amongst the musicians. It would be wise that he should collect the little orchestra. It would be thought just the seemly proper way of travel for a rich English milord.

"We will have Handel's water-music to waft us up the Brenta," cried Sir James. It was that work which had reconciled George I and Handel on the Thames years ago. The villas and orangeries on the banks of the Brenta should hear it now.

"We will give out that we are going to Padua," said Mr Williams. "We must leave that charming town until we return."

Julian was not so submissive as he had been in the presence of the ladies at Naples.

"But I would like to stop for an hour or so at Padua," he interrupted.

Both Sir James and Mr Williams looked at him with an air of surprise as if whilst they were deep in their provisions for his safety, they had forgotten his presence in the room.

"That's quite out of the question," said Charles Williams brusquely.

"I have a special reason," Julian returned sullenly, changing from one foot to the other.

After all, during the last eighteen months he had managed his life with some success. Why should he not have a place in the discussion?

Sir James smiled at him in amusement.

"But, child, Padua is in the State of Venice. Stop at Padua, and Messer-Grande will have his handcuffs on your wrists again."

He turned back to Williams.

"Perhaps Columba Tadino could provide a woman's dress?"

Mr Williams shook his head.

"Columba Tadino may be watched. I have little doubt that she is. No! But I have friends. I can borrow what is wanted and no questions asked. He'll wear a mask, of course, as any woman would on such a journey." He measured Julian with his eye. "And with his hair piled high on a comb he'll pass very well."

They would want beds for the cabin, since they would certainly pass one night and perhaps two in the barge. Mr Williams charged himself with that duty. Sir James was to order provisions and wine and dainties for his lady, and he made out a list whilst they talked. Both he and Mr Williams were getting a vast deal of enjoyment out of their conspiracy against the State of Venice.

"I shall not be home again before supper-time," said Sir James. "But this will be your last day of imprisonment, Giovanni," and Sir James went upon his various errands with Charles Williams, leaving Julian thoroughly ashamed of his fractiousness. Here were very good friends putting themselves to a great inconvenience for his safety, and he must needs reply to it with the behaviour of a fractious child.

Chapter Twenty-One

A WATER-PARTY ON THE BRENTA

At half-past eight on the following morning the luggage of Sir James Elliot, Bart, who was setting out on a discreet tour through the waterways of the Terra Firma of Venice, was piled into the smallest of the barges. At nine, the second barge, with its little company of musicians, took its place opposite to the steps of the Palazzo San Polo. Some five minutes later a third barge arrived; it was decorated with flowers, the boards of the deck were hidden under rich carpets; baskets of fruit were sheltered from the sun; chairs were placed under a canopy in front of the cabin. The barge was bright with ornaments of silver and polished brass. The third barge slipped in between the barge of the musicians and the steps. It had hardly stopped when Mr Charles Williams ran down and stepped on board. He was or seemed to be busy satisfying himself that all the appurtenances of the barge were worthy of the high dignity reserved for it. He also satisfied himself that no inquisitive black gondola manned by sbirri was lurking near at hand in the Grand Canal. Having taken these precautions, he clapped his hands and after just that interval of time which it took to descend the stairs, Sir James led out his lady with a sedate and protective grace. Elliot's chief gondolier stepped forward in his orange livery and held his arm so that she could rest her hand upon it as she stepped on to the barge.

"Pyrrha, my charmer, you can trust all your weight to that ruffian's muscles."

Gaiety never sat easy upon Sir James Elliot. He was better as the stalwart oak than as the lively sapling, and Pyrrha knew too well the quick and curious eyes of the race of gondoliers to stay chattering on the steps.

"Nay, I want no help, Sir James."

Pyrrha was on board and in her chair at the back of the awning.

"Let us go, my friend. I am in a fever for green trees and the scent of flowers in the gardens of the Brenta," and with a little imperious touch upon his sleeve, she drew Elliot down beside her. Williams at once gave the order to proceed and the barge with the musicians behind and the baggage behind the musicians, set off upon its journey.

There was no fear that the sharpest of the gondoliers could find anything strange in the aspect of Pyrrha. Julian's brown hair was not dressed high over a comb, but lay flat upon his head and streamed down his back in curls after the Venetian style. On the top of it he wore a three-cornered hat trimmed with white lace and his face was hidden by a mask. A full black silk skirt, flounced with black gauze, touched the deck, and the upper part of the dress was covered by a black silk cloak which showed no more of him than the whiteness of his throat.

The barges were poled along the small canal and into the open water of the Giudecca. There a light wind was blowing out of the east and sails were hoisted. There, too, the musicians broke into Handel's water-music. Charles Williams sat in the front, turning this way and that with a wave of the hand for any other party on the Giudecca that morning, the great Lord, sedate, almost disdainful, certainly aloof in the cabin porch, his lady lost in his shadow.

They were just emerging into the lagoon, when a gondola patrolling the shore darted out at them. It seemed to Williams that he could hear the hearts of his companions beating. But he kept his head and as the gondola turned at their side to keep pace with them, such a stream of jests and gossip passed between the gondoliers that he, too, sank back in his chair with a gasp of relief.

"He is hoping that more seigneurs like you will visit Venice," Mr Williams explained, translating the gondolier's dialect to Elliot.

Shortly after noon, the barges reached the Brenta, and with the gentle wind still filling the red sails and the oars assisting, they slowly ascended the narrow stream. On each side country houses, set amongst the fresh green of gardens and trees and gay with flowers, comforted their eyes. Greetings and cheers waved them on. The violins and the hautbols sweetened the air with melody. No one challenged them. To the house-owners and the wayfarers on the banks of the river, the expedition was all lunacy and extravagance and princeliness – in a word it was English. Let it go forward then, in God's name, whither it would.

Thomas Biggin cooked them a dinner which they ate in the cabin and when they had eaten it they were at the village of Doglio and the bridge across the river. But they did not pass beneath the bridge. Beyond it lay Padua. They entered the canal which ran southwards for twenty-two miles to the Po. Here horses were awaiting them upon the towing-path, and a very short time after they had started on this new stage of their journey, twilight came and the swift night. They were moored against the bank, but they covered the windows of the cabin with black cloth so that no lights should show.

These hours of darkness were the most onerous that the fugitives had to endure. Throughout the day there had been movement and a tingle of excitement. Now there was merely the slow passage of the minutes and a rush of fears and a sense of helplessness. They were still within the State of Venice. If a branch cracked by the canal side, one of them would whisper "Listen!" and they would sit holding their breath until they choked. If a flaw of wind set the water tinkling against the planks, they imagined Messer-Grande's black prison boat sliding noiselessly to their side. Elliot smoked his tobacco pipe and let it go out and lit it again. Even Charles Williams, who at the very worst had nothing to dread but a short banishment from the chosen city, slept only by fitful snatches; whilst Julian sat with his hands idle on a table in front of him and still as a dead man.

Williams flung on his clothes and went out from the cabin. After ages had passed, he returned and flung back the heavy curtains and put wide the doors. The colourless light of the morning was welling out under the lid of the sky. Above a mist the mulberry trees stood out upon the plain. In a little while a jingle of harness was heard and the cries of men upon the towing-path. The barge moved forward, and as though a word of command had been given, all three dropped upon their beds and slept. When they waked the sun was high and they were breaking the shining current of the Po. The State of Venice was behind them; they were within the borders of the Pope's domains.

Elliot and Williams shaved, dressed and set their wigs upon their heads.

"We will take our coffee on the porch as soon as you are ready, Giovanni," said Elliot, and Julian, who was sitting up in his bed with his eyes shining, flung out his arms and cried: "Surely no one had ever two such good friends as you."

"Nonsense!" said Sir James gruffly, and "Fiddlesticks!" Mr Williams exclaimed.

He was annoyed. He stumped out of the cabin and sat himself down with a thump in one of the chairs; and when Elliot joined him, he turned on him in an odd exasperation.

"Why should I care whether a little, impudent, Italian musico is shut up under the Leads for a few years?" he asked. "Explain that to me! But when he thanked me so prettily, damn it, I was moved! Elliot, I was moved! I am getting old, you know. An Italian musico! Why should I care? Only—only—" and Mr Williams looked perplexed—"an insolent, vanity-ridden tribe! Why should I care? Only he didn't seem to belong to the tribe!"

Sir James was anxious to divert his companion from these speculations. What Williams was stumbling over was the fact that this boy had the manners of his race and his breeding and his education; and it was just as well that Williams should get no nearer at the present moment to the truth.

"I am told," said Elliot, "that Farinelli has the modesty of a great gentleman."

"May be," grunted Williams. "No doubt! You know more about these singing people than I do."

But he was not satisfied and he looked at Julian with a keen curiosity when he joined them in the porch of the cabin. He was not the only one, however, to be curious. The orange-livened gondoliers saw, instead of the lady Pyrrha, a trim youth with his brown hair tied back with a ribbon and a muslin cravat knotted with a careless grace about his throat. He was dressed in a green suit laced with silver, white silk stockings and silver-buckled shoes. All that remained of Pyrrha was her three-cornered hat.

"The Marelli," whispered one of the gondoliers to the other. Here was gossip, to be sure, to satisfy every gondolier from Santa Maria della Salute to the Burchi Canal. But there was perhaps danger in it. A closed mouth would be wise, even with so marvellous a tale clamouring to be told.

The barges arrived towards nightfall at Ferrara, that once-ducal town with the great empty palaces and the grass growing in the streets.

Chapter Twenty-Two

THE INCORRIGIBLE PAST

"You have made your arrangements?" Sir James asked.

"Yes, Sir," Julian answered. "The roads between here and Bologna according to the landlord are deep and heavy. So I am travelling with six horses to my chaise, just as if I were an English milord;" and a smile without a trace of bitterness in it danced in the lad's eyes.

They were taking their supper in the public room at the inn by the light of candles. It was a big room of a decayed magnificence, with painted walls and gilded pediments and, but for the three travellers, it was quite empty. Both Sir James and Julian used the Italian tongue since Charles Williams was at the table. Williams lifted his hands.

"Six horses! And you are not yet twenty! What it is to be a singer!"

Julian laughed.

"An extravagant, foolish person," he agreed. "But perhaps I am to be forgiven. I am anxious to put as wide a distance as possible between myself and the State of Venice."

"And yet," replied Mr Williams, looking over the rim of his glass of red Chianti, "... and yet – if I am impertinent, put it down to the inquisitiveness of an old gossip, Signor Giovanni – it seemed to me that in spite of the danger you ran in the State of Venice, you were still anxious to waste some valuable hours at Padua."

Julian laughed again and again with nothing but gaiety in his voice.

"That is true," he said. "I appeared no doubt to be merely fractious and troublesome after the manner of singers, Signor Williams. But I was putting great trust in your protection and I had a reason. I admit that I was fractious, but only for a part of me. I shall show you my reason."

He went up to his room and came back with a slim book bound in white vellum and ornamented with gold which he laid on his place at the table in front of him. He turned to Elliot, his eyes dancing: "You, Sir, who, if I remember aright, are pleased to call yourself that happiest of all God's creatures, a dilettante—" Julian was watching Elliot with a shy, impish look sideways under his eyelashes. He had the very air of the boy who had ridden with him one morning at Grest, and had talked of his ambitions and interspaced the talk now and then with some quite disarming piece of impudence. Elliot began to laugh, but was checked by the sudden wrench of the knowledge that the boy whom he seemed to see by the candlelight in this painted room at Ferrara, could never come to life again. But he was aware that Williams was looking at him curiously and he covered over his discomfort as best he could.

"I was speaking, you may perhaps remember, Giovanni, with reference to the treatment dilettantes might recommend for young singers."

"And what was that, Sir James?" asked Williams.

"Well," replied Sir James easily, "I told Giovanni that in England we birched little boys who were impudent, whether they sang or not."

Mr Williams jumped. Not even impresarios talked in Italy to their famous singers in that strain, though, "by Gad!" he thought, "it would teach 'em better manners if they did." But Giovanni was still laughing with amusement.

"My tutor, Sir, at the Conservatory, the Cavalier Durante, had no doubt the same views as you, but he had, perhaps, a subtler method of applying them. He gave me this book."

"Yes?"

"He tied it in paper and he sealed it."

"Yes."

"I was forbidden to break the seals until I had made my debut."

"And then?"

"As soon as I was back at my lodging, I was to read it. I did. Written with a delicate pen, steeped in vinegar, it took the skin off my back. It was written by the Abbate Benedetto Marcello."

159

"A patrician of Venice," cried Williams.

"And a great composer," Sir James exclaimed.

"And he lives at Padua," Julian added. "I was hoping, Sir, that you knew him. I was sure that you had a letter of introduction to him. I was going to ask you to take me with you, so that I might offer to him my most respectful thanks."

And Julian handed the little volume across the table to Elliot.

It was called *Opera à la Mode*, and it was written with all the simplicity of genuine conviction, as a manual of conduct for all concerned in the operatic theatre, from the tumblers up to the prima donnas and their mothers, if they wished to align themselves with the taste of the day. Sometimes a bear appeared on the scene, so there were rules for the bear. The three sacred unities of the drama were to be preserved and they were stated, but they were not quite the unities of the higher dramatic criticism. Place, time, action – certainly. But place meant the theatre at which the performance took place; time, the six hours after sundown; action, that was easy to define – the ruin of the manager. Proceeding with the same serious absurdity, the author instructed the singers. Never, never must they forget their private dignity, their great names. They represented, say, Artaxerxes or Dido. That really was of no importance. The audience must never be allowed to forget that this is really Signor Salimbeni or the Signora Cuzzoni. The effect can be properly gained if the singer carefully avoids listening whilst any other singer is singing and chooses that moment to smile at a friend in a box or crack a private joke with the leader of the orchestra. He must on principle make the librettist change his dialogue and the composer his harmonies. It would diminish him to be satisfied. In almost all operas, at some time or another, the hero appeared in chains. It was incumbent on the actor at such times to wear his best jewels and his prettiest sword and to see that his wig was well-powdered and his chains nice and bright. He was to shake them too and make them jingle in order to wake the compassion of the audience, especially if someone else was singing. All the follies and pretensions, all the conceit and impertinence of those strutting favourites were marked down and scarified in a phrase or two of droll recommendation. Sir James Elliot read extracts and if the light flickered, Julian, from his memory, could supply the word.

"I should have liked Signor Marcello to have written his name in the cover," he said with a smile of regret as he took back the book. "For I owe to him the abstention from many sins."

"Do you?"

Williams, more curious than ever, shot the question at Julian with a thrust of his chin.

"Do you now?"

Williams shook his head.

"For my part I think that primer was put into the hands of the one scholar in his class who didn't need to study it."

Julian pushed back his chair abruptly enough to startle his companions.

"You are wrong, I think, Mr Williams," he said, but quite gently, and he sat with the little book upon his knees. A look of concern clouded Elliot's face, and he moved his shoulders uneasily. Once or twice he had seen the breastplate of gaiety and patience and conformity which Julian wore, split and had been forced to watch with anger and horror, a boy whom he loved, eating his heart out in a distress which no one could ever allay. The Leads of the Doge's Palace! After all something could have been done. Ambassadors raised to enquiry and protest, a Foreign Office stirred to threats, and the doors opened. But here, nothing – nothing at all – ever. What other young life had budded to wither so soon in so much pain! Once or twice, since Julian had stumbled into the lobby at Venice, Elliot had been a helpless witness of that pain and he hated the sight of it. Even now in his middle age the tears were springing to his eyes.

"You are wrong, if you'll pardon the contradiction from one who knows," Julian repeated, not looking at either of his friends. But though his face was not visible, his fingers tightened on the book upon his knees.

"All the students of my special class need the lesson of this little book," he continued in a low and troubled voice. "Vanity – impertinence – coxcombry – affectations, even in dress – we all succumb to them. Did you ever see before such a Harlequin as me at Rocca's party? But you will again. Vanity! It's our defence against the world. It's our refusal to submit. A few inches of lace more than others wear, a few more jewels – to match, no, to defeat the women. They come naturally to the students of my class. You have made us different, you have put us outside the pale. What have we got for a consolation? Vanity, Sir, and I am sure we are all very grateful."

The bitter words were spoken as quietly as a lover's plea to his mistress in a crowded room, but they were as passionate; and they seared both the men who listened, as they might have done, had those men been guilty of the crime.

Julian raised his face. For a fraction of a second Elliot saw it ravaged with despair, then the mask shot over it again. Julian rose.

"But we are in danger of becoming serious and that would never do," he said lightly. "I leave at daybreak for Bologna, for even my six horses can hardly cope with the road there. So I take my leave of two unforgettable friends."

He shook hands with them both and went from the room. Mr Williams said "Ha!" and resumed his seat. Then he said "Hm," and after that it seemed that he had no more to say. Sir James had a little trouble with his throat which impeded his utterance. Finally he banged the table and cried with an exasperated bellow.

"I know what we want."

"And what's that?" asked Mr Williams.

"A ratafia," Sir James shouted defiantly.

"My dear fellow, I haven't the slightest objection," said Mr Williams.

Over the ratafia, however, Sir James became once more gloomy.

"I can't let that boy go just so," he said. "There was something I had it in mind to ask him. But I can't remem—by Gad, I've got it. Of course! I'll be with you again in a minute."

He went quickly out into the hall where a porter waited with the candles. Elliot took one and mounted the stairs. He knocked upon Julian's door.

"Come in!"

Julian was in his shirt and his breeches, stooping over his portmanteau. He stood up.

"I wanted to make sure that you had money for your journey."

Julian lifted from the mantelshelf a bag which jangled, tied with a string.

"Thank you, old friend," he said warmly. "I packed more than enough in my portmanteau, and I have a banker at Naples."

Then he moved with two quick steps over to Elliot and said: "Do you, Sir, remember an evening when you were brought to see me in bed, and I was supposed to be asleep, and at the last moment I opened my eyes and showed you that I was awake?"

"Yes," Elliot answered, looking over the lighted candle at Julian. "Yes, I remember it very well."

"I rode with you the next day. I was drawn to explain to you why I sent that appeal to you – for it was an appeal."

"Yes. It was an appeal. So much I understood, but only so much."

"But I wasn't sure," Julian continued. "I was the merest boy. I said nothing – although every look, every word of yours, invited my confidence."

"I couldn't pry," said Elliot.

"No, it was for me to speak," answered Julian. "I think I made the deadly mistake. I believe that if I had been open with you," he laughed like some desolate creature away in the moon, "old Timbertoes might have stumped the Italian Garden at Grest with his wife on his arm and his children shouting about the hedges. For you would have stood by me."

"I hope that I should," Elliot answered.

For a moment or two Julian looked into the candle flame with a smile, as though the Italian Garden, ringing with the laughter of his children, was there, visible, audible.

"She used to come every night to my room and bend over me when I was asleep," he continued. "She tried with all her will to poison my dreams – like a witch – just like a witch – only she was beautiful – a witch who hated a boy of twelve who stood in her way."

Elliot felt his flesh creep, so vividly he remembered Frances Scoble's intense concentration as she hovered over the child and the one fixed frightening stare she turned her head aside to give to him, the visitor. The horror of the recollection was made all the more real by the quiet certain tone which Julian used.

"And she was succeeding," he resumed. "I was tormented. Great swollen faces, horribly bright, swam and dipped over me in the darkness, but quite low, almost brushing my forehead and my cheeks, and whispering words I could never hear. I was so frightened that I thought that I was dying. I used to wake up screaming and then she would hold me close to her, consoling me, but so pleased – oh, so pleased. In myself I knew."

"So you kept awake?" said Elliot as quietly as Julian had spoken. But it seemed to him that he was looking right through the kind and friendly world into a wild carnival of Hell.

"I had to keep awake. I took things to bed with me, horse-chestnuts – prickly things. I showed you that I was awake. I asked you to keep my secret, for I was terrified what else she might do, if she guessed that I was awake. And you did, of course." He ended his story with a smile.

"I never heard of anything so wicked," said Elliot.

"It was hatred," said Julian, "stark, unvarnished hatred. But, oh, how I wish that I had told you when we rode together at Grest rather than tonight here in Ferrara."

He broke off, and the longing dying out of his voice, added: "Well, Sir, I shall see you again at the end of the year."

"Where?" Elliot exclaimed eagerly. "In Florence? In Naples? I shall come to your first night."

"You will not have to travel so far. I sing for Count Heidegger, or rather," and Julian smiled, "for Mr Paul Sawl, the greengrocer, at the King's Theatre, in the Haymarket."

For a moment Elliot's heart stood still. Julian stood so motionless, his voice was again so quiet, so sure. The plans of a man wronged behind that boy's face of pure beauty were working out to some deadly climax. Step by step Julian was moving forwards, unhurried, yet swift, like some avenger of old Greece upon an accursed family.

"What will you do, Julian?" he cried.

"In good time, Sir, you, to whom I owe so much, will know. I must have my knowledge proved. Till then, I beg you to keep my secret."

He laid his finger on his lips with that impish smile which had bound Elliot to secrecy long ago on the little staircase in the corridor of Grest.

"Good night!"

"No," said Elliot very gravely. He remained standing with the candle in his hand. "You shall tell me, as you say, in your good time. But you should know what there is to know – now."

"I am not to be dissuaded," Julian returned.

Elliot inclined his head.

"And I am not trespassing on your secrets or your plans."

Julian looked steadily into the flame of Elliot's candle, with a face set and mutinous,

"I am listening, Sir."

"They are married."

"Frances Scoble and Henry? No doubt. For decency they would let a year pass."

"Wrong! They married within three months of their return to England."

Julian lifted his eyes from the flame of the candle to Elliot's face.

"Yes," said Elliot. "There were reasons. A child was born in February of the next year."

"Yes?"

"A son," Elliot answered.

The dreadful, bitter smile which a few months before had frightened Mr Paul Sawl swept all the beauty out of Julian's face. For a few moments he stood in silence. Then he said: "Whilst I was at school in the Conservatory of St Onofrio;" and he stood without moving. He did not even answer Elliot's second farewell; for he had not heard it.

There was certainly to be no good night for Sir James. He tossed from side to side in his bed. He had been in the right when he told Julian of the marriage of Henry, the new Earl, to Frances Scoble and of the son born to them. Ought he to have told more – that the pair of them were happy, liked, respected and notable for their wise management and benefactions; that Henry was making a reputation as a speaker in the House of Lords and was marked for office? But Julian's last words, "Whilst I was at school at the Conservatory of St Onofrio," stopped him altogether. There would have been too sharp a cruelty. Moreover, the horror of the story which Julian had told him – the witch and the boy – burnt in his brain.

Then by one of those leaps of thought with which a sleepless night makes everyone familiar, he remembered a conversation on a balcony below his window which he had overheard at the Inn of "The Golden Ox" at Naples. He had made a note of it – yes – at once – after it had been exchanged. He searched in an old letter case which he carried about with him on his travels, and found it tucked away in a pocket. A conspiracy – yes – in which the woman Frances Scoble, now Countess of Linchcombe, had faltered, and the man Henry Scoble, now Earl of Linchcombe, had reassured her. But there were a question and an answer, yes, and a comment on the answer, which he had omitted and had remembered afterwards and inserted. Yes, here it was.

"Wouldn't it be better if we waited?"

"Not unless there is something you have planned of which you have never told me."

Frances Scoble had put the question. Henry Scoble had replied to it. Elliot seemed to hear her too eager answer. "Nothing, Henry, I swear," and Henry's doubtful comment. "I am not sure that I trust you once you're t'other side of the hedge."

There was a conspiracy – yes – in which Frances Scoble was concealing something from her lover. And suddenly Elliot remembered more, and was looking once more into the very pit of Hell. Frances Scoble had talked with him, played with him, played with him on the same balcony the next day. Did he think – oh, and how anxiously she had asked – that Julian could become a great singer? And he had answered "No," – no, with all the complacency of the dilettante comparing the amateur with the professional, but never understanding, poor fool, that the amateur with the professional's training added on, might excel them all. It was not Julian's reticence which had destroyed him. It was Elliot's own easy confidence in his judgement.

Chapter Twenty-Three

THE PROOFS ARE FOUND

The house was not an inn, nor was it a private house. It stood in a valley of the green island of Ischia under Monte Epomeo, above the track from Casamicciola. A small vineyard rose in earth terraces on the hillside behind it and it stood in the midst of an orchard of cherry trees and pomegranates, of limes and oranges, offering with two or three little tables under brightly-coloured awnings an irresistible attraction to the few travellers who passed that way. On some days there were none. But on others, visitors to the convent of San Nicola or curious tourists to the crater of the dead volcano rode by on asses or mules, and few of them but broke their journey there to gossip for half an hour over their host's white wine or his wife's ice-cold lemonade. For the little estate had a clean and prosperous look.

Three men at all events turned off from the track towards it on this afternoon of May and leaving their mules to the care of the muleteer, took their seats at one of the tables. One of them – from his dried-up face, his sober, shabby dress, his horn-rimmed spectacles and a certain musty air as though he had become himself an old yellow document from one of his shelves, he smelt the attorney a mile away – did all the talking.

"The world has gone well with the fellow, not a doubt of it. He has kept his pace with it too. Squalor for the squalid is a maxim, Sirs, which is not so often contradicted but that a man may be astonished and pleased when it is. Let us try whether he brews a white wine to match the daintiness of his upholstery."

He clapped his hands and a woman of about fifty years, stout and rosy and neatly dressed, came to them from the house.

"What can I offer you for your pleasure, gentlemen?" she asked.

"Your best white wine, my good hostess," said the lawyer, as he took a pinch of snuff from a big brass snuff-box.

"In a moment, Sirs," she said and as she turned, her eyes fell upon the youngest of her three visitors. "*Gesù!*" she cried, her mouth agape, "but it is an angel the good God has sent to us this blessed afternoon."

The youth to whom she spoke had, with his fair brown hair, his blue eyes, and the delicacy of his features, a beauty spiritual enough to justify her admiring cry. He blushed and looked as uncomfortable under her praise as a schoolboy. The third of the party, a man, oldish and spare, with a lined, tired face, in which a pair of lively dark eyes twinkled incongruously, slapped his hand on the table.

"If you had had the schooling of that angel, my good soul, you would not call the afternoon of his first visit to your house blessed," he cried with a laugh. "For it is his first visit, isn't it?"

"*Madre Maria*, yes!" she answered. "Would I forget, even if I passed him in the city street?" And she went back to the house to fetch the wine.

The three men waited. About them were ridges of bare rock, with here and there on a spur, a grey column, like a splinter, pointing upwards to the sky. But between the ridges, wherever, plants or trees could grow, they grew. Little forests of chestnut trees darkened the flanks of the hills, vines climbed them, or thickets of myrtle. Below, sheep and goats pastured on the lush grass; below the grass, orchards made a pattern of all the happy colours, red and green, orange and white; straight in front across the wide bay of Naples, the smoke of Vesuvius rose lazily into the sky.

"That was a point well taken," said the attorney, rapping on his brass box with his knuckles. "An excellent point! I make you my compliments, Signor il Cavaliere."

The Signor Cavalier lifted up a warning hand as the woman of the house brought glasses and a bottle of wine to the table.

"In a moment, my gentlemen, I shall bring you cakes and fruit. Cherries and figs and melons for your pleasure," but it was at the lad of the party that her smiles and glances were directed. "You are from Pozzuoli perhaps? You will have ridden from Ischia town. You must eat, my young one," and she bustled back to the house.

The lawyer laughed dryly, finding an ironical amusement in the woman's attentions.

"She is embarrassing, perhaps?" he said with a glance at the youth.

"She is surprising," the oldest of the three observed. "I am myself in the dark, for I am here only as a witness of my young friend, but I'll warrant that that good woman is more in the dark than I am."

The young friend moved restlessly.

"It would be better, perhaps, to ask for her husband," he said. He took his hat from his head and laid it on the ground beside his chair, but the lawyer would have none of such misplaced expedition. He filled his glass with wine and tasted it with relish and sat back in his chair.

"That would be an error. Let us proceed without haste! Or we shall meet with nothing but the shut mouth and the stubborn ignorance. And already I see someone coming down from the vineyard on the hill. It is very likely our man."

When the others looked, they too saw him. He came down through the orchard with a, swinging easy walk, a man on his own domain. He, too, was about the age of fifty, ruddy and cheerful, a big strong contented man. He came without hesitation straight up to the table and addressed himself to the Cavalier as the chief amongst his guests.

"The wine is to your liking, Sir, I hope?"

The Cavalier bowed with an uncomfortable word of thanks, but the lawyer straightened his shoulders. He looked round with a start and then a smile of recognition altered his face.

"But it is Crespino!" he cried. "You remember me, Crespino? The lawyer Zanotti – Lelio Zanotti of the Via di Toledo. Nay, never look so disturbed!"

For at the sight of Zanotti's face and the sound of his voice, Crespino's manner had changed. The ease and cheerfulness had gone and in their place were discomfort and uneasiness. Zanotti the lawyer, however, was as genial as any piece of parchment ever could be.

"There was a little trouble once, to be sure, when you were fishing over there in the village of Portici. Yes, I prosecuted, but *Dio Mio*, all that is past and forgotten. Come, you shall drink a glass of your own wine with us to show that no rancour remains. Bring up a chair – Crespino – let me see! Crespino Ferrer. Yes, that was the name."

Crespino Ferrer brought another chair to the table reluctantly.

"There is no rancour, Signor Zanotti," he answered simply. "You got me six weeks in the prison," and he laughed with a return of his good humour. "But you see I have a different life here, long good nights of sleep, long good days of not too hard work, and a full belly. One does not wish the old days to encroach upon it."

"That I understand very well, Crespino," the lawyer said heartily. "From there," he waved a hand towards the shore of Vesuvius across the bay, "to this little Paradise of Ischia – yes, keep the bay between them, my friend, whilst you can. Come, sit down, and your good wife with you—" For he saw Ferrer's wife carrying towards them a tray piled with cakes and fruit. As she set out her dainties upon the table with a smile of invitation to the youth to set to, Zanotti called out: "And we shall want another bottle and more glasses, one for Crespino here and one–"

"Crespino? Then you know him?"

Her interruption was sharp, and from her face in its turn, the smile and the pleasure fled. But it was no more than disappointment which replaced them. In this green corner of their contentment some old patron by chance had found them out. It was to be expected. She turned back to the house for the glasses. As she took them from the shelf her red cheeks dimpled and her mouth softened. She would ask the boy with the angel's beauty and the pale rose of an angel in his face, to swear his friends to silence. For what were angels sent down to earth, except to grant the prayers of their supplicants?

She carried out the glasses and hurried a little faster than was her habit. For her husband had apparently already made her prayer for her.

"I understand that, Crespino," the lawyer was saying. "*Gesù Cristo!* one does not want the riff-raff of Portici drinking you out of house and ease for the sake of old acquaintanceship. No, no, we have a secret here to keep. Madam, a glass," and he took it from her and filled it to the brim. "And for you, madam! So! Now you shall tell us, Crespino, how this good fortune came."

Crespino drank his glass. He sat and smiled.

"It was a gift of God," he said, and the woman who had not sat down nodded her head behind him, her eyes shining.

"Never was a truer word spoken," she said fervently.

"But there are in God's lucky bag many kinds of gifts," said Lelio Zanotti, laughing. "Which came to your fingers?"

"The most precious of all, Signor," the wife replied immediately. "A son."

Even Lelio Zanotti, the lawyer, was caught by surprise. He splashed his wine on the table. That poor little skeleton washed up on a beach in the fine clothes of a patrician. This kindly, pleasant woman had the effrontery to acknowledge that their fortune was owed to that piece of roguery?

"A son!" he exclaimed.

The woman's smile became triumphant.

"Giovanni."

"The singer?"

"Giovanni Ferrer. A great singer, my gentlemen, but a greater son. To him we owe everything. It isn't always so, no, parents must pray like beggars in the streets and be grudged perhaps just enough to keep a roof over their heads. But our Giovanni – oh! a son amongst a thousand."

"But—but—" Lelio Zanotti pushed back his wig and scratched his head, a man bewildered. "You had a son, Crespino. Certainly you had a son, and no doubt his name was Giovanni. I never heard. But he was sick – yes, I remember that – and he died—"

"No!"

Both Crespino and his wife interrupted with the same cry. But the odd circumstance was the spontaneity of the cry. In neither case was it a cry of defence, or defiance. There was almost a note of horror in the denial. It was intolerable that anyone should doubt the existence of this noble and generous son.

"He was near to death," said Crespino, "but we sent him away from our village up into the hills."

"To Traetta, I suppose," the youth at the table interposed quietly.

"Yes, Sir, exactly," Crespino returned. "To Traetta—" but he did not finish the name. His mouth fell open. He stared across the table. "How should you, Sir, know of Traetta?"

"I am Giovanni Ferrer, known as Marelli," said Julian.

The third of the travellers was Durante, the Maestro di Capella of the St Onofrio Conservatory, but his evidence was not needed. The woman uttered a cry, her glass slipped from her hand, she stared for a while at Julian, without any enmity, and burst into tears. Crespino was on his feet before anyone else could move. With a remarkable tenderness, he put his arm about her waist and placed her in his chair.

"There, there, mother!" he said in a helpless voice, seeking to comfort her. And between her sobs, she gasped: "And we almost believed it to be true."

"Yes, old lady," Crespino answered. "Another month or two, perhaps, with no neighbours to disturb us, in the quiet of our vines and our cherry trees, we should have quite believed it, fought for it, perhaps, as people fight for a belief. But what is, is, and dreams have their end."

He stood upright and faced the three men at the table. With him, too, there was no anger, but a great sadness and a surprising dignity.

"You must understand us, gentlemen. In our hovel over there at Portici, dirty, stinking of old fish, we fished a little, starved a good deal, quarrelled, and at times imagined a small farm such as others have – a farm like this, a long way off like this. When Giovanni died – yes, Signor Zanotti, he did die – and we had money given, we said nothing to our neighbours. We found this little plot, we made it as you see it, we missed nothing but Giovanni. Then a year and a half ago, some time like that, news reached us, when we were in the town of Ischia, of a boy with our dead boy's name, whose voice and beauty had brought to him fame and riches in a night. We began to say to each other, 'If only it had been our Giovanni. We made a little play with the fancy to pass the evenings. It was he who had given his old father and mother the farm and paid them so much, through the lawyer at Ischia, so much every quarter out of his great earnings. We said to people, 'Oh, yes, this is Giovanni's gift. You have heard him perhaps at Florence, or Naples – our son.' People asked what news we had of him. As mother here says, the poor woman, we almost believed it."

He patted his wife on the shoulder and braced himself.

"I don't know what has brought you gentlemen here. But if there is some trouble and we have to leave here and go back to Portici—"

"I am not going to say that that will be necessary," Julian said gently, and the woman looked up with a gleam of hope in her eyes.

"What was this money which you had after Giovanni died?" asked Zanotti.

"I will tell you all that I know," said Crespino.

"Wait," said Zanotti.

He took from one pocket an inkhorn and a pen, from another a scroll of paper which he unrolled and reversed until it lay flat upon the table.

"It was seven years ago," Crespino resumed. "Giovanni was dying of a consumption."

Late one night a man had crept down the alley of the fishing village and rapped gently on the door. He proposed an infamous bargain. When Giovanni died, his parents were to sell his body and his name. "My wife, the poor woman, wept – she said we were murdering our own child by bartering him away before he died. But that of course was nonsense. We were very poor, we could not buy anything to keep him alive – and the price offered was very high."

On the day that the boy died, Crespino had himself carried the news into Naples.

"To a house or an inn?" asked Zanotti, lifting his eyes from his parchment.

"To neither, Signor. It was a matter of a day or two, you understand. At noon on each day, there would be someone waiting for five minutes under the great Head of Naples near the Church of St Eligio."

"Ah!" exclaimed Julian. "By the Mercato."

Zanotti turned his head towards his employer in surprise.

"You know that rendezvous, Signor?"

"I know none so well, though I saw it but once, and in the dark," Julian replied with a sombre quietude. "Continue, Crespino?"

"That night the man came again to my house in the fishing village, but with a companion."

"Traetta," said Zanotti, making a statement rather than asking a question.

"Yes, Signor, the old Traetta."

Between them they had carried the boy's body down to the beach and laid it carefully in a boat as though he still lived, and the Traettas sailed it away. "I was to say what I did say, Signors, that I had sent Giovanni up the hill and that he was recovering his health."

Two days afterwards Crespino had called upon a lawyer at the top of a great house in the Via di Lepri.

"Fabricio Menico," said Zanotti, as he wrote, "a pettifogging scoundrel of the lowest class."

"He is not of your Excellency's eminence, no doubt," Crespino returned, "but he is well known amongst the fishermen."

"That is what I said," Zanotti observed dryly.

Menico had given Crespino Ferrer money. He was to find a new home and as long as he stayed quietly in it and kept to his story, he would draw another sum of money every quarter.

"I knew of course," Crespino declared, "that there was trickery – a substitution – perhaps crime. So much money would not else have been given. But we were very poor, we had lost the boy, there were still the little vineyard and the orchard for the price of a fable. We paid the price, Signors, and we began to believe the fable. That is all I have to tell you."

"No, no, Crespino."

The lawyer raised his hand.

"You have omitted the most important item in your story, the very heart and kernel of it."

Crespino Ferrer looked blank.

"The name of the man who called on you in the night and bought the dead body of your son. Ah!" and he pointed the butt of his quill menacingly at Ferrer's breast, "you are holding out against me, are you – Adam?"

"Adam," the man stammered. "There was no Adam."

"But there will be one, my good fellow, unless you recover your memory," said the lawyer with a ferocious spasm of laughter. "Adam lived in the Garden of Eden until an angel," and he indicated Julian to the wife with his finger, "said 'March!' And Adam marched."

Crespino wrung his hands.

"But Signor, I swore by—"

"No doubt by San Januarius. Yes, yes, it was in fact at the time of that Saint's festival that a great crime was committed. The name of the criminal, Crespino?"

Ferrer's wife touched him on the arm, and he gave in.

"It was Domenico, the courier."

"You knew him before?"

"I had taken parties for him to fish in the bay and to visit Herculaneum."

"He came twice? Once alone, once with Traetta, and a third time you met him under the Head of Naples," said Zanotti, writing vigorously. "There! It is done. You can sign your name?"

"I can't write."

"You shall make a cross then and the Cavalier Durante will attest it."

He made room for Crespino. The tears were rolling down Ferrer's cheeks now, but he took the pen from the lawyer's hand and made a big black cross beneath the writing. Then Durante in his turn wrote in his fine small hand the date of the month and year and that he witnessed the mark as Ferrer's signature. Zanotti rolled up his scroll and tied it round with a ribbon and tucked it away with his inkhorn and his pen in his pocket. He rose and bowed to Julian.

"I am at the Signor's service."

Julian sat at his place, his forehead resting on his hand, whilst the others waited upon his word. Then he too rose to his feet, and in a bitter voice he cried: "It is not here that I shall seek justice. I shall exact it in my own time, in my own way. Crespino Ferrer and his wife have nothing to fear from me."

Crespino's wife flung herself on her knees in front of him and tried to seize his hand. But he would not yield it to her.

"You don't go scot-free," he said to her with a gentle smile. "You have lost a dream, an illusion on which you had set your heart, and you will never recover it. The pleasant talks in the long evenings before a fire of cherry-tree logs – the generous son, his fame in the great cities – at an end, my poor woman! You must find another theme."

He put his hat upon his head and led his companions back to the gate where their muleteer was squatting with his mules.

With the confessions of the Ferrers, Julian's savings and his own ingenuity, Lelio Zanotti had an easy task. But, as so often throughout this strange affair, seeming accidents helped to discover the crime. On the third day of Julian's sojourn in Naples, he was stopped by a woman outside "The Golden Ox". For a moment he did not recognise her, so old and ravaged she looked, so coarsened in face and form.

"So, my little one!" she cried boldly, with her hands upon her hips, "what did I tell you? The Dukedom – it is in your pocket. You have not forgotten Costanza and what you owe to her?"

Through her the Traettas were found. Squalor for the squalid was a maxim which applied to them. They were living in Portici, rich for a week once a quarter and beggars for the rest of the year. As Zanotti pointed out to them in his office, they lay under a charge, if Julian cared to bring it, for which the penalty was death, and their only hope was a full confession. By the help of the Traettas, Zanotti reached Domenico.

Domenico blustered a little, but he was at Zanotti's mercy and the last bit of truth was got from him. Henry Scoble had planned murder; but a swift, unexpected, unfelt death did not content the hatred of Frances. Her subtle mind gloated over years of suffering, of destitution, of starvation, made doubly and trebly hideous by the recollection of other days of ease and luxury. She had gone "t'other side of the hedge", as Henry Scoble had suspected. She had bribed Domenico to vary Henry Scoble's plan, but had not foreseen that Giovanni Ferrer, instead of sinking into the gutter, was going to fill the continent with the sweetness of his voice.

"Ah, if we had only guessed that!" cried Domenico in a sudden exasperation; and Zanotti with a little cackle of laughter handed him his quill; and Domenico wrote.

There remained Fabricio Menico, the paymaster of these scoundrels. But a clerk betrayed him, and before the summer was out, Julian had all the evidence of which he stood in need.

Chapter Twenty-Four

A LETTER FROM LONDON

On the twentieth morning of May in the following year, Mrs Dermaine took up her pen in London to write a letter to her cousin, Mrs Coleby, in Yorkshire. The letter was a monthly ceremony. Mrs Dermaine denied her door during its compilation to her dearest friends. There must be absolute quiet throughout the house. To seclude herself the more completely with her thoughts and inspirations, she wrote in a room at the back of her house in Dorset Gardens which looked out only upon the noiseless growth of flowers. She was not a blue-stocking. She prided herself indeed, on moving upon other days in the very maelstrom of polite society. But she undoubtedly nursed a hope that at some future date a dainty volume with decorative uncials would correct the historians of her time by the observations of a shrewd and impartial witness. It is to be deplored that Mrs Coleby, less concerned with the gossip of London town than with her dogs and horses, dropped the letters into the fire as soon as she had read them. One or two sheets with burnt edges, however, were retrieved by one of the chambermaids and made pleasant reading in the servants' hall for the gentlemen's gentlemen who came with their masters to The Chase and for a wider circle afterwards.

"The latest news in the world of politics is of a speech made three days ago in the House of Lords by the Earl of Linchcombe, a fine oration, in which vigour was expressed with the highest elegance and adorned with the most gentlemanly quotations from the Latin poets. What it was all about, my dear Anastasia, no one seems willing to explain to me, but the London Daily Post, which of course is Whig to the last drop of its ink, hailed – yes, actually hailed – his Lordship as a great landlord who had harnessed science to the service of the fields and both by the zeal of his public and the discretion of his private life set an example to the youth of the country. It is said, too, that the King on reading his daily summary of Parliament cried out: 'Dat is one damn big speech.' In consequence, Lord Linchcombe is spoken of for the Ministry of the Board of Fisheries, which, for some reason beyond the comprehension of a poor little piece of frippery like me, is the Department of Agriculture.

"His good lady, the Countess of Linchcombe, kept his house for him in St. James' at the beginning and made it an oasis, my dear, a veritable oasis of decorous conversation amidst the frivolities of the season. Not that cards or music or an occasional ball were eschewed, but the tone was solid, the stately aphorism rather than the crackle of the bon mot, a meeting of lofty spirits rather than of notable wits. Dull, to be sure, but highly respectable and the ante-room to Office.

"Lady Linchcombe, however, to the astonishment of the polite world, sometime in April closed her doors and retired to her great house of Grest Park. 'We are both, in truth, country mice,' his Lordship explained with a sigh. 'Heigh-ho! But for my duties as a senator, I should follow in my humble way the example of Cincinnatus.' Charming? A little grandiose perhaps and condescending, but the very accent of a nobleman destined for the Cabinet. There is, to be sure, a curious little whisper running round the town which, far from explaining the disappearance of so serene and indeed masterful a woman as the Countess of Linchcombe, makes it something of a mystery. Gossip, Anastasia, but we lap up gossip with our tea and exchange it as uncharitably as we can, like counters at a game of lansquenet. However, for your amusement rather than your credence, here it is.

"The chief, I might almost say the only, sensation of the season is the new soprano from Italy – Marelli. He has quite restored the fortunes of Heidegger at the King's Theatre in the Haymarket and has driven poor Mr Handel back upon his oratorios and cantatas. Marelli is the most astonishing creature. There has been nothing like the furore he has caused since Farinelli was in London. He has the same wide compass, the same swell and shake, the same flutelike melting notes. But whereas Farinelli was a veritable Maypole, ungainly in his movements and with the face of a pug, this lad with his fair hair, his blue eyes, his supple form and a curious mixture of imp and seraph, has quite ravished the town. Moreover, he is, what we all love in our hearts, *farouche*. He will not sing at private houses, he is never seen at a fashionable rout, he has taken a villa at Twickenham, from which he drives in a chaise to the King's Theatre, and, though he stayed at Burlington House for a day or two on his arrival in England, he sees only a few musicians, and at times, I am told, dines *en famille* with a Mr Paul Sawl, a merchant of Italian goods, who is the chief of Heidegger's supporters. The consequence is, of course, that the indifferent creature is more sought than ever. He went in company with a well-known dilettante, Sir James Elliot, once, on an afternoon, wrapped in a blue cloak to Vauxhall Gardens, but was recognised and so mobbed and jostled by his admirers that he and his friend had to take refuge in a funeral coach which happened to be returning empty from a churchyard. To such a pitch of extravagance has the adoration soared that a painter was introduced into the pit surreptitiously to take his portrait, and now little medallions with his likeness framed in silver are sold by the score, and not to wear upon one's dress or coat – for even the men have gone music-mad – is to confess oneself quite outside the world of bon ton.

"Is the prelude over long? The prelude to a whisper! Is not that a title simply dying for an author? It means so little and sounds so much. Well, it is breathed that the Countess of Linchcombe, curious about one of these medallions, which a friend was wearing, asked for a nearer look at it; and when it was put into her hands, flushed scarlet in the most unbecoming way, and then turned of a deadly pallor.

"'It can't be,' she murmured, sinking down upon a couch. Again she stared at the medallion and then returned it with a smile. 'It can't be more than an artist's fancy. Pretty, to be sure, and a charming ornament.'

"But it was noticed, or it was supposed to be noticed, that she pleaded a headache and shortly afterwards left the house. 'A *coup de coeur*, my dear,' said the friend who told me the story, but I asked her with some asperity not to make herself ridiculous. *Coups de coeur* were not occasioned by pretty singing birds from Italy. But she told me that I ought to study the doctrine of the attraction of opposites.

"Instead of doing anything so foolish and wasteful in the height of the season, I made a party for the Opera. My dear, the house was crowded, and in a box opposite to me I saw Lady Linchcombe. Her husband was not with her. He, I am told, has no ear for music and if he goes anywhere, goes when the King goes to the oratorios, where at all events there is a vast amount of noise.

"The Opera which I saw was too confused in its plot for me to relate it; and the confusion was the greater because some of it was sung in English and some in Italian. I do not remember whether the name was Elmira or Almena. But there was a Dragon in it, an excellent Dragon who breathed fire and required for his meals a quota of the tenderest creatures, male and female, chosen from the choicest families. The scene opened with the landing on the island of a fresh batch of victims. They were charming, my dear. Although the scene was placed in legendary days, the young ladies wore the widest hoops and fluttered with ribands, whilst the young gentlemen were all with powdered heads, embroidered coats, high red heels and wore swords with jewelled hilts. They danced a minuet upon the sands, which was quite ravishing; and Marelli, who was condemned to be eaten because he was the true King, sang with the Signora Mancita a love duet which lifted us into the skies. Of course, I need hardly tell you, the sorceress who guarded the Dragon and fattened the young ladies and gentlemen to make them properly succulent, fell desperately in love with Marelli. There was a vast deal of intriguing between the two ladies. But, in the end, the passion of the sorceress led her to sacrifice herself. As a plot it was absurdity itself. But, my dear, the singing! There were some songs – the opera was composed by Mr Handel's rival, Bononcini – which I hope to hear upon my death-bed. They were so melodious and sung by Marelli with an exquisite and celestial simplicity. You will remember, Anastasia, how the second-rate torture the notes they sing. Frankly, my dear, amongst all the absurdities of the performance, the absurdity of a *coup de coeur* for Marelli seemed not so absurd after all.

"I was not so entranced but that I had an eye for my Lady Linchcombe. She sat well back in her box, so that with the wavering light of the wax candles it was difficult to read the expression on her face. Only once or twice she leaned forward and then held her fan before her face, so that only her eyes were visible. But she left before the curtain fell and two days later she was gone to Grest ...

At this point, Mrs Dermaine had worn down her quill and her vocabulary was exhausted.

Chapter Twenty-Five

KIDNAPPED AND GLAD OF IT

The season was over, the windows of the great houses were dark, the lamps burned on deserted alleys in Vauxhall Gardens, the Opera Houses and Theatres had barred their doors, Parliament had adjourned. Lord Linchcombe was Minister for Agriculture, partridge shooting was beginning, Marelli had departed from Twickenham in his chaise; and in his parlour of the Angel, the great Posting Inn in Winchester, halfway between London and Grest, Sir James Elliot sat before a writing-table in a quandary.

He, too, had to write a letter, but he could not begin it. He was gravelled by the opening salutation.

"My dear Lord Linchcombe," he wrote, and threw his pen down and sat back in his chair.

"But, damn it, the man's a murderer," he cried aloud and looked hastily round the room. Fortunately there was no one to overhear him.

All the statements and confessions which Zanotti's subtlety and Julian's savings had procured in Italy had been read by Elliot. There was never a clearer case to his thinking. Greed and ambition had led Henry Scoble to a plan of murder. Hatred – stark, unvarnished hatred, as Julian had called it – had urged Frances Scoble to plot a more savage and a more subtle form of the same crime. Julian had been saved – if it could be said that he had been saved – because his voice was so much finer than Frances Scoble knew, and the boy himself had subdued himself to its training.

But Elliot had pledged himself to silence; and that pledge had put him into his present quandary. Sir James was not at all a dilettante with a shotgun. He was by some accident of nature a very good shot, and each year, right away back to the days of the old Earl, he had been one of the first party to shoot the partridges at Grest. This year the invitation had come before Sir James had read Julian's full report, and he had accepted it. After he had read the report, he had prided himself upon his diplomacy.

"If I now write excuses and say that I won't come, I am in a way breaking my promise to Julian. I should be arousing suspicion that I know something which I am not prepared to disclose. No! I will start in my coach for Grest, making my usual stop at the Angel, and there I will be seized with a violent colic."

This was all very good and clever. But Sir James had not remembered that he must begin with a form of address – "My dear Linchcombe", or, since he inclined to a formality in his manners – "My dear Lord Linchcombe".

"Well, I'll be damned if I address the fellow so," he reflected stubbornly.

Yet, a letter of explanation must be sent. He was expected for dinner at Grest Park the very next day. Sir James was still staring at his letter paper when the porter thrust his head in at the door.

"There's a gentleman below asking for you, Sir James."

"Is there, now?"

"There is."

"And who may it be, Sam?"

Sir James had already turned his chair round in an eagerness to shut from his sight that offending sheet of paper.

"Mr Brute Bellingham."

A smile spread over Elliot's face. A messenger from Heaven, a Mercury! Brute Bellingham was on his way to Grest, a thousand pounds to sixpence. Brute Bellingham should carry the sad news of his colic. Brute Bellingham should have seen him in his contortions.

"Show him up, Sam, and bring a bottle of the old Madeira," and a moment later, "Brute, you're a welcome sight to me."

Brute, a broad, ruddy country Squire, who farmed a small estate seven miles from Grest, responded with a grin which split his face as a fruit knife splits a melon. A queer, unlikely friendship between Brute and Sir James had begun amongst the turnips and the furrows of Grest when Brute shot over them for the first time at the age of twenty. He had watched with the supercilious amusement of his years Elliot take his place in the row of walkers.

"Musical people can't shoot," he whispered to a friend. "The Lord be praised I'm not next to him!"

But his amusement changed to surprise, and his surprise to awe, as the morning advanced. For on the line which Elliot followed, birds fell, and more than fell in front of Brute Bellingham. Brute sidled up to Elliot after the ladies had left the table and with an awkward prettiness made his apologies. Elliot was delighted. What man of the town doesn't feel an inch or so taller when he is congratulated upon his prowess in field sports? Brute Bellingham found his companion amenable to country talk, with never a word about a cantata. He began to pride himself on his association with the Arts. "My friend, Mr Elliot – you know, the man Handel listens to when he's in a rage," – dropped in and out of his conversation.

"I'll do anything you wish, Sir James," said Brute as he smacked his lips over his Madeira.

"I want you to tell them at Grest" – Elliot could not bring his lips to shape the name – "a lie – a big, fat partridge of a lie. You saw me at the Angel, writhing, with a steaming hot poultice on my stomach, and my knees up to my chin. I couldn't write a word, I was in such pain. What in the world is the matter?"

For Brute Bellingham was sitting with his mouth open and such a look of consternation upon his face as the Maréchal de Saxe might have worn after Fontenoy.

"My dear Sir! I counted on you – my word I did! You would show the fellow the ropes, choose the songs …"

"Songs?" cried Sir James. "I haven't an idea what you're talking about."

"No, I don't suppose you have," Bellingham returned with a chuckle. "No, nor anybody else. I thought of it, Sir James. Yes, I was the one. It wasn't Bob Joyce of Crofton, nor Charlie Bassett of Dingle Hall. They were both – what's the word? – Bill Joyce knew it. I've got it – confederates. But I thought of it all alone "

Mr Brute Bellingham grinned with the pride of a schoolboy who suddenly discovers that he has a brain.

"What mad scrape have you got into now?" asked Sir James.

And out the incredible fact popped.

"We've kidnapped the Marelli."

"What?"

Sir James sprang to his feet. He gasped, he set his hand on the table to make sure that the world was not turning upside down. Mr Bellingham took the Baronet's amazement for a compliment.

"Devilish dull those little dinner parties at Grest before the shooting. Just the family, one or two relations, one or two honoured guests like you and me and Charlie Bassett. No sittin' over your port lest you should be squint-eyed in the mornin'. Have to join the ladies over their tea and play Pope Joan for spillikins afterwards. Devilish dull. Besides, Henry is a Minister, got his hand in the till, eh? His politics are damnable – of course, as a Tory, I know that – but if he wasn't a Whig we'd be proud of him, with all those Latin tags catching each other up out of his mouth."

"But what in the world has that to do with kidnapping Marelli?" cried the exasperated Sir James.

"I thought I'd make this party memorable. D'you see, Sir? Suddenly, when everybody's yawning enough to split their faces, up I jump with my hand on my heart and say, 'Ladies and Gentlemen, the famous Italian will now sing a couple of serenatas, and my friend Sir James Elliot will do the notes on the harpsichord.' Enter Marelli, ladies in ecstasies, gentlemen 'anything for a change', Frances Linchcombe flattered, Henry, 'Ha! Ha! a kind thought, my dear Brute', and off we go."

Sir James left aside the remarkable effort which would be required even from a Marelli, if he were to sing a serenata by himself and cried: "Marelli! He'll never consent!"

"But he has consented."

And Sir James sat down in his chair again. He was very quiet now and his voice thoughtful.

"I should like to hear a little more."

Brute Bellingham obliged, beaming with pride. He had discovered when Marelli was to leave Twickenham. It was the height of good fortune that Marelli should be travelling on that western road.

"He might have been making for Grest," said Bellingham.

Sir James thought grimly, "He was," but took care not to say it aloud. Bellingham and his friends had lain in wait in a thicket close by the road ten miles from Winchester. They mounted their horses as Marelli's chaise approached.

"He thought us High Toby men," Brute Bellingham continued, "and he was out of his chair before Bob Joyce had stopped it, with a big horse pistol in his left hand and a drawn sword in his right. I was diplomatic – cracked a joke, you know. I said, 'Come, come, Signor Macaroni, we're not Captains of the Road,' and what d'you think he answered? 'You look-a so like-a it, I'll blow the brains you 'aven't got-a out of your calf's head if you come-a one leetle step nearer.' The sort of reply which makes conversation difficult."

Sir James chuckled.

"I think your Italian accent is wonderful," he said. "I can hear Marelli talking. Continue please."

Brute Bellingham continued. He had no wish to be shot or to shoot. He explained what he wanted, where he stood, and Marelli listened, first with surprise, then with a secret laugh. The honest Brute Bellingham described that laugh with a grimace, as though he had bitten upon an unsavoury morsel in his food.

"Italianish – all venom and stilettos – and not a sound with it – eyes like flints – shoulders shaking and not a sound from his lips. I shivered. I thought of one of those sparks who asked you to supper and pricked your finger with his ring as he shook hands and you went home and died five hours later as big as an elephant. When he had laughed enough, he put up his sword and pistol and agreed to come on his own terms – the secret to be kept to the last moment, and he would drive to the house and away from it in his own chaise. I said I'd pay him his fee."

"And what did he say to that?" asked Elliot with a grin.

Brute Bellingham, with a sour expression, filled himself another glass of the Madeira.

"He was damned impolite. He told me I was a comical fellow to fancy I could afford it. He'd pay himself, thank you. Now what did he mean by that?"

Sir James shook his head. Julian certainly did not propose to sing for nothing at Grest, but his price was buried in his own fierce heart. Sir James, however, had not to answer. For Brute Bellingham suddenly drew up a chair to the side of the writing-table and sat down on it.

"He said that he would wait in the Library with the big bookcase until I came for him. Now, how the devil did he know that the Library opened into the drawing-room? Or of the big book-case?"

"The big book-case is famous," Elliot replied instantly.

"Oh, is it?"

Mr Bellingham pushed his chair a trifle closer to the table. There was a heavy perplexity in his face, even a trace of suspicion.

"Did you ever see an Italiano with blue eyes as sharp as swords?"

"Many," said Sir James.

"All those Connoisseurs and Spectators jeer at 'em as melting."

"It's the ladies who melt," said Sir James.

"And a lot of use that'd be," cried Brute Bellingham with a roar of laughter.

Elliot thrust his chair back with a movement of disgust, but Bellingham was, at all events, diverted from a dangerous line of speculation and Elliot hurried on to ask: "Where is Marelli now?"

"He's on his way to my house with Bob Joyce and Charlie Bassett in his chaise with him. He changed horses here and should be there before midnight."

"He changed horses here! When?"

"Half an hour ago. Just before I sent up my name to you."

"Did he know I was in the Inn?"

"Not unless he was to meet you here. I didn't know until he had gone, and he didn't leave his chaise."

Sir James nodded his head. An old notion had returned to him that there was a design and pattern in all these accidental happenings against which it was useless to struggle. The stage was set at Grest for the accomplishment of a great tragedy with the fatality of a Greek play. "What is, is, and dreams have their end." Who had said that? Crespino Ferrer on Ischia. Julian had been travelling towards Grest, wondering, perhaps, how he should force an entrance into his own house and bring his contented enemies to their bitter reckoning. And lo! by the crazy invention of this great lout, Brute Bellingham, the perfect road had opened out. Henry Linchcombe with his new Office, Frances with her beauty, her high position and her child, were sitting quietly amongst their dreams in their most lordly mansion, and over the dark roads the avenger was drawing nearer with every revolution of the wheels. Nothing could hinder the designated end. Let him meddle, if he dared, and another way as unforeseen would open. But Elliot did not dare. He was no more than a word of conjunction in the whole grim story and must fall obediently into his place. He tore up the sheet of paper with its splutter of ink in front of him.

"I shall go to Grest," he said. "I shall do as Julian asks."

He was too burdened to realise what name he had used and to see the amazement which overspread Bellingham's face. But he was oddly conscious that the odour of musk and amber was heavy in the room.

Chapter Twenty-Six

JULIAN RETURNS TO GREST

"Sir James, the decanter is blushing for your dreams," said Henry Scoble.

"They were as white as a child's, full of ogres and big faces and strange fears," Elliot replied.

He hurriedly filled his glass with port and passed on the decanter to his neighbour. Could he have said anything more foolish, he wondered? But nobody was at the pains to take him up, not even Henry Scoble, who sat smiling and easy at the head of his table. Sir James had been pushed from his discretion by a mind at war with itself over a couple of trifles. On the one hand was the incredible speed with which supper had been served and eaten. Supper was a meal to be taken leisurely, the conversation, light but swift, making for good digestion. But tonight at Grest, it was over, so to say, before it had begun. Another minute and they would be joining the ladies in the great drawing-room. Yet, on the other hand, there had been no flurry, there had not even been that sprightliness of wit which wings a meal from the *hors d'oeuvres* to the sweet as fast as the passage of a bird. There had been country talk – lots of it. Henry Scoble, to be sure, had quoted a few lines from the Georgics, but they had not appreciably lightened the entertainment. The supper party had in fact dragged more than a little.

Elliot had had time to notice the pride of Henry Scoble diffusing about him the consciousness of his Ministerial office, the care with which Frances Scoble waited upon his words and his needs, and, above all, how the light of the candles on the table from mere white specks in the twilight had grown into golden spears now that darkness curtained the windows.

"Now, why in the world am I held in this contradiction?" – so his thoughts ran, but being on the whole naturally honest, he broke off his speculations. "Rubbish, my man! You're pompous and you're a coward. You're in terror of the moment when Henry Scoble will rise from his chair."

For all was set now. During supper he had heard a sound for which his ears had been alert – the creaking of wheels as a chaise came down the hill to the door. Brute Bellingham was talking loudly as was his way. Had any but himself heard? He was reminded most relevantly and most unhappily of the legend of a great Scotch family: that when the chieftain of the family was to die, the death-coach was heard winding down the glen behind the house. But no one except himself had been aware of that grim warning – unless – yes, unless one … For Frances Scoble dropped her napkin on the floor at that moment, and the butler, old Gurton, picked it up. She stooped too and her face was hid. As she raised her head again, it seemed to him that her face was white beneath its paint – the face of a woman who lived very near to fear, but kept it dungeoned in her soul. Yet she answered Brute Bellingham easily enough: "Without the new good bourgeois blood, and the new enterprise we bring into the country, how, my dear Brute, could you stand for a day?"

The moment of fear had passed; or had it ever been? Sir James leaned back in his chair. Was there anything more deceptive than the flicker of a candle across a woman's face? And the creaking of the wheels had ceased. And after all, Mr Robert Joyce was expected at the house. Indeed, Frances Scoble had had that expectation in her mind. For she spoke to Gurton: "If Mr Joyce has arrived and missed his supper, you will set a place for him."

"Very good, my Lady," said Gurton.

He went out of the room and the conversation flowed on. Now the door by which Gurton went out opened behind the back of Frances Scoble and to the left of Elliot, and in a few minutes he saw the door re-open and remain ajar. Elliot had a vision of the man, now growing old in service, standing with his hand upon the door-knob and steadying himself after some appalling catastrophe. Then the door opened wide. For a moment Gurton remained upon the threshold, surveying the table with its dishes, of delicate porcelain heaped high with fruit, golden oranges from overseas, red apples from the home orchard, candles glistening in the light; and the Linchcombe family with a few favoured friends gathered about it. He shut the door behind him silently. He was trained to his service, and the service must go on though the house fall. But Elliot watched his face as he advanced. Here was a man who had seen a ghost and was shaken by the chill of death. Yet he spoke without a tremor in his voice.

"Mr Joyce, my Lady, will meet you in the drawing-room. He has supped already."

That excuse was in itself a little perplexing, for, after supper, the port would be hopping from chair to chair about the table and the vintages at Grest Park were rich as princes. However, Frances Scoble was eager for reassurances. She had only heard Gurton's voice. She had had no glimpse of his face. And a moment afterwards she gave the signal to the ladies. There were five of them in all, a sister-in-law, and a niece of Henry Scoble, a cousin of her own and her great aunt, the stout old Lady Fritton, whom Elliot remembered to have met long ago at "The Golden Ox" in Naples. Brute Bellingham, who was nearest to the door, held it open, and as Frances Scoble passed out the last of her small flock, he said in what he hoped to be a whisper, "I shall persuade Henry to join you before the bottle's twice round the table. I beg you to wait," and with many sly nods and grimaces, "I've invented a surprise in your ladyship's honour."

"Idiot!"

Sir James almost uttered the exclamation aloud. But once again the sense of a tragedy impending which nothing could prevent, not even the stupidity of Brute Bellingham, caught and held him in a kind of admiration. For Frances Scoble faltered in her step, shot a swift glance of alarm at Brute Bellingham and suddenly broke into a laugh which had only amusement in it and disdain.

Brute Bellingham! Plots and alarms and subtleties were none of his intentions. Some new and childish game of cards perhaps. Some wild romp for a house-party!

Thus Elliot explained her laughter. It was the way of such tragedies that by their own wits the victims should be out-played. But at this point in his reflections the decanter, replenished, stood again before Sir James. It had started on its second round, and opposite to Sir James it stopped. For Henry, smiling, gracious, and a trifle condescending, said in answer to a word from Bellingham: "You shall have your way with us, Brute, tonight," and he stood up. "Gentlemen," and with a mocking submission, "I bow to a new master of Grest. Mine own house is not mine own," and with a bow he stood aside whilst Bellingham held open the door. Henry Scoble was a little heavier in the shoulders than he had been the last time that Elliot had seen him a year ago, but he was still the hard, strong animal with the stubborn red jaw and the blue eyes of his family, and he moved lightly and easily in his gold embroidered coat of scarlet satin, his yellow breeches and his pale grey silk stockings.

A wood fire was burning on the hearth in the drawing-room beneath the great Chinese mirror with the gold storks, and the ladies were gathered about it. But with a swirl of hoops and ribbons, they dissolved like a covey of the partridges to be shot on the morrow, as the men entered the room. A twitter of voices filled the air.

"Come, Brute!"

"I am positively swooning with suspense."

"Expound, or we die!"

It was Brute's hour. Sir James Elliot observed, not for the first time, how similar positions have their similar expressions. Brute Bellingham had the very smirk of an impresario titillating an audience with the promise of an incomparable new diva.

"Ladies and gentlemen, he began, "my friend Lord Linchcombe, though I protest I cannot endure his politics …" and he snatched a slip of paper out of his waistcoat pocket. Even Charlie Bassett, his confederate, could not put up with effrontery so blatant.

"Brute!" he cried, shocked to the centre, "you're not going to make a speech!"

"Just a few friendly thoughts strung together," said Brute modestly. "For instance—" and he glanced at his slip of notes.

A wail rose from the ladies, an imprecation from the men.

"In front of Lord Linchcombe, too!"

"The arrogance of the man!"

"No wonder the Whigs are in office these fifty years."

"Take his notes away, please! Then he'll be tongue-tied!"

Brute Bellingham drew himself up. He was offering to this ribald company the treasures of his mind, pearls of which each one had produced a corresponding bead of sweat upon his forehead. Very well! They should be deprived of them. He advanced.

Henry Scoble was standing with a smile of amusement upon his face sideways to the fire. Behind his shoulder at the corner of the mantelpiece, where no flame from the burning logs could betray her, stood Frances, so still in her pale blue satin gown that not even the diamonds on her breast gave out a single spark. To them Brute Bellingham made his bow.

"To grace this evening above all other evenings, I have brought to Grest for your pleasure a great singer."

Something rattled upon the floor at Henry Scoble's heels.

"A great singer! You have brought him, Brute?" said Henry warmly; and it was indeed a rare proof of Bellingham's goodwill that he, of all men, should have devised so delicate an entertainment. He stooped, picked up his wife's gold comfit box and handed it to her.

"The sweets, my dear, alas! are spilt beyond recovery;" and it occurred to Elliot, not for the first time that night, how the words which Henry used bore, beyond their plain meaning, an irony of which the speaker was quite unaware. But Elliot was not surprised. The pattern was drawn long since by destiny. Every sentence spoken, every movement made would now weave the tapestry. But Elliot was allowed little time for observation. The ladies broke in too noisily upon him. Their wailings were now raptures.

"A great singer? Who, dear Brute, who?"

"London's last idol," cried Robert Joyce, who thought it high time that some of the incense should mount to his nostrils.

"Oh! Not … Not …"

Prayerful clasped white hands were extended towards him.

"Yes," he said.

"Impossible!" cried the niece.

"I dare not ask," exclaimed the cousin.

Henry Scoble broke in upon these ecstasies.

"But, my dear Brute, I am moved by your kindness." He was without suspicion. An unexpected compliment had been paid to him. "Egad, I am moved. But so much generosity is not to be accepted. You must allow me to be the treasurer. I am told these fellows ask a fortune for a ballad."

"This one," replied Bellingham, "on the contrary will accept nothing. More! He will sing at no other house in England, but he will for your pleasure sing at Grest."

Probably not one of these country girls had seen Marelli or heard him. But the fame of his singing, the accounts of his beauty, the Stories of the romantic seclusion in which he lived had spread to every house where the London journals were read and young ladies wrote letters.

"It is he, then!" they cried.

"Yes, ladies," cried Brute Bellingham, with a flourish. "It is Marelli, the boy from the sea, as they call him," and he walked down the long room to the Library door.

The boy from the sea. In the shadow by the corner of the mantelpiece, Frances Scoble, as still and white as its marble, received the words like the stroke of a dagger in her heart. For a moment she felt neither pain, nor shock, nor shame, but a dull relief. Ever since she had seen – how long ago that was! – a medallion flaunted by some foolish woman who must be in the mode or perish, Frances Scoble had lived in torment with a smiling face. Every little happening which was unusual had been distorted into a menace. Even after she had fled from London to this country refuge she had known no peace. The very quiet had been no more than the hush of expectation. At night she had not slept until the whiteness of the morning had distilled its comfort in the room. By day she had walked under a descending hammer.

Now the delay was over. How had the trap been set? – she gave no thought to a speculation so futile. Was there a way out of it – even now, when the last seconds of the last minute were passing on? She could not find it. Wonderful things occurred, no doubt. A heart failed and an arm raised to strike fell limp. If only that should happen now! Suddenly she came to life with a spurt of rage. There was Henry, the poor fool, talking in his courtly condescending way.

"This is a kindness not easily to be repaid, Signor Marelli" – yes, he was in the room now – Julian! She could not see him from the spot at which she stood. All these foolish girls, these still more foolish hobbledehoys of little squires stood in the way; and Henry Scoble's voice went on: "It has been my misfortune that the pressure of the State has hindered me from hearing you. The burdens of Ministry! In your delightful art you are happily free of them. And my friends here are chiefly country mice. So that we shall be too much in your debt. But perhaps after you have sung … and the group parted and Frances saw him.

Chapter Twenty-Seven

AN OLD SONG IS SUNG AND AN OLD HIDING-PLACE DISCOVERED

He was dressed in a velvet coat of the colour of a dark rose, breeches and waistcoat of white satin, and white stockings. His hair was powdered and tied with a black ribbon. The bow of cambric at his throat and the ruffles at his wrists were edged with fine lace, but without extravagance, his buckles were of plain gold. If he shone, he had his glitter from the rustics. There was not a trace of the coxcombical flourish, against which he had confessed to Elliot that he must be ever on his guard. He was in his own home and at one with its grace and decoration, its painted ceilings, its mirrors, its deep carpets and delicate furniture. As she watched him, this stripling so endowed to match his great possessions, all Frances Scoble's hatred quickened into flame, and with a savage and most hateful joy she said to herself, "But marred – for all his life."

And still Henry talked. The pair of them were near now to the harpsichord and the candles on the top of its frame.

"After I have sung … ?"

Was Henry blind, she wondered? Couldn't he recognise in Julian's face the family, if not the boy? The same thought was for a second or so stirring in Elliot's mind, but only for a second. The pattern was already drawn. The copy was already a-weaving.

In its due time it should be woven.

"After you have sung, Signor, we must talk."

Frances Scoble saw the youth's eyes turn and rest on her husband's face. An inscrutable smile hovered about his lips, but like a good actor, who had so conned his part that he was always its master, he set his lips straight.

"As you say, we will talk after I have sung," he said quietly, his eyes still upon the eyes of Scoble.

And now Henry did wake to some disquiet. Was it Julian's face, the colour of his eyes, his bearing? Was it that he used no title when he addressed his host, yet was so tutored in his conduct that he had left his sword behind him in the Library? These Italian singers were famous for rustling about with their rapiers at their hips, even though from time to time they took a public caning in spite of them. But this lad – Marelli – knew that you left them outside the drawing-room of a country house. As Julian turned towards the harpsichord, his music in his hand, Henry Scoble's brow was furrowed, his eyes troubled. He shot a glance towards his wife, as if he had a sudden fear that she could answer him. Then he flung his head back and with a touch of impatience in his voice, which he tried in vain to hide: "I take it, Sir, that you have another name than Marelli?"

Julian turned with a polite bow.

"But Marelli is the name under which I sing."

He waited, but Henry Scoble could not press his question.

"We shall be beholden to you," said Henry, and he took his seat.

Under the instructions of one of the ladies, Gurton arranged the chairs in a semicircle a little way from the harpsichord with their backs to the high-curtained windows. And whilst the house-party spread itself upon them like an opened fan, Julian spoke to Sir James at the harpsichord.

"You will be kind enough to accompany these two songs for me, Sir James?" he said.

"Let me see them!"

"You will know them both."

At the corner of the mantelpiece Frances Scoble drew a chair towards her.

"This is a short song," said Marelli, standing behind the harpsichord between the lighted candles. "The words are by the Italian poet Metastasio, the music by the great master, Hasse. It is a song of spring."

Below him Sir James ran his fingers over the keys. Frances Scoble slipped silently into her chair. He sang with the Italian accent which he generally used, modifying his voice to the size and structure of the room; and in the clear sweet music his small audience heard the joy of the budding earth, the lilt and whirr of the lark into the pale blue, the bursting into leaf of the black, gaunt trees, and with it all a hint of tears nearby, because so much loveliness must waste so soon. When he had finished, the young ladies were drying their eyes and sniffing into their handkerchiefs, and the young gentlemen were damnably uncomfortable and hoping that the boy from the sea would sing them next a rousing sea-chanty with a recurrent line on which they could all let their tongues loose. But he followed it with the song of "Verdi Prati" from Handel's opera of *Alcina*, which Carestini had first refused to sing.

Julian told the story of this refusal and Handel's bullying him into consent and of the triumph which the singer secured, as though music were the only passion in his thoughts, so that even Frances lost the sharp edge of her terror and Henry Scoble was lulled quite out of his suspicions. Elliot, for his part, no longer reasoned. He was the looker-on, believing that each interruption, each effort to break the spell and avert the "doom to more than Troy", impending over this house, was a mere part of the ordained plan. But he observed with eyes less occupied than anyone elses in that great room. He saw the return of ease to Henry, the lessening fear of Frances Scoble and amongst a few unimportant trifles, a relaxation of the household's discipline. For within the room at the far end by the Library door, Gurton and two or three of the footmen had gathered, and behind their shoulders could be seen the mob-caps of a few of the upper women.

When the applause had died away, Julian laid his music sheets aside and said – it seemed to Elliot that his Italian accent had never given so harsh a rasp to the English tongue: "I will end, with your permission, my last concert in England," – with one protest the voices of the ladies threatened him with all the blame for their premature deaths if he adhered to so cruel a resolve.

"I shall positively go into a decline," cried one.

"It will be murder. I can smell the lilies about my bed," said another.

And in his gentlest voice, the singer answered

"Nay, madam, by your leave, for murder there is but one perfume – the musk and amber of revenge."

He turned to Sir James

"I have not the music to my hand, but, as Mr Bellingham says, I can, if you'll allow me, do the notes myself."

He bowed to Bellingham as Sir James rose. Bellingham returned the bow with a great grin, half friendliness, half pleasure that two-thirds of this odd caterwauling was over. But as Julian slipped into Elliot's seat at the harpsichord, the grin froze upon Bellingham's face. He half rose from his chair, but a chorus of indignation assailed him.

"The poor man must play at billiards at this hour."

"And he's not so clever with his cue neither, for all his practice."

Brute Bellingham flung up his hands.

"On your own heads be it, young ladies!" he cried, and he resumed his seat.

Julian ran his fingers lightly over the keys.

"I call the song 'Musk and Amber'," he said. "The title is not perhaps very appropriate to the theme, but it may be thought to suit the hour and the place."

He struck the few chords which prepared the song and Elliot's body stiffened from his head to his feet. He had never guessed how the reckoning, eight years old now, was to be presented. He knew now. He looked across the room at Henry Scoble and Frances in the shadows by the mantelpiece. Surely they knew as certainly as he did himself. But Henry lolled, a trifle bored, and hiding his boredom behind a smile. And Frances? Well, Frances had proved – nay, had admitted – that her ear was not to be trusted. She had not stirred. And then, without a trace of any accent, an English voice rang true across the room, singing English words on the clear note of a flute.

> "Boy Cupid with the bandaged eyes
> Draws tight his bow of pearl and jade.
> Swift from the string the arrow flies
> To wound the heart of youth and maid."

And the melody took a lilt:

"But in this odd world of sevens and sixes
Nothing is quite as it ought to be.
It is only my heart that the arrow transfixes
And never the maid's that was made for me."

The voice ceased but the fingers filled in the break between the verses, improvising with runs and shakes and chords, as though they were just garnishing the dish, and the voice rose again:

"I have her picture cut upon crystal,
Painted in exquisite colours and rare.
A pledge? If a pledge, it's a pledge that the tryst'll
Only be kept by one of the pair."

There was no change in the smiling face behind the harpsichord. The song was sung with a humorous sort of melancholy, as though the singer laughed at his solitary plight.

"She has eyes that are deeper and kinder than sapphires,
Her lips' dark velvet defies the rose.
Oh, I can't believe that other lads have fires
Fierce as the fire which destroys my repose."

Again the voice ceased, the fingers strayed carelessly over the keys. But at the door where the footmen and the maids were gathered there was a stir. Henry was leaning forward in his chair, bewildered, angry, afraid. Of the young people, some had heard that very song sung by the boy Julian when they themselves were children. All in that room were openly troubled except two. Trouble passed from one to the other like a contagion. But two remained apparently untouched by it, the youth smiling at the harpsichord and the silent woman in the corner by the fire. The voice rose for the third time, but now with a sigh of utter loneliness which certainly the boy had never known, and could never, if he had known, have conveyed into his song:

"And so I wander by forest and boulder
Hoping that one day in spite of my fears

I shall wake with a golden head at my shoulder
Instead of a pillow wet with my tears "

Julian's voice died away on a poignant fall which brought to the eyes of the young audience, with the tears, the picture of a wounded bird swerving in an arc to the ground. To most of them the air was still vibrating with the pain of the appeal, when the most unlooked for interruption swept like a tropic wave over a calm sea. Brute Bellingham crashed across the room and bending over the lid of the harpsichord cried: "Who in God's name are you?"

The boy's fingers ran lightly up the notes and executed a little ridiculous shake on a couple of treble notes. He looked up at Brute Bellingham, his eyes smiling, his voice very quiet and clear.

"I am Julian John Philip Challoner Carolus Scoble, Earl of Linchcombe, Viscount Terceira and Baron Hardley."

"What!"

Henry Scoble was now on his feet with a bellow of rage. But Brute Bellingham paid no heed to him. He was staring at Julian.

"By God you are, boy!" He swept round to Elliot who was standing at a little distance from the harpsichord. "You called him Julian in the inn at Winchester."

"I did?" exclaimed Elliot.

"You knew then," Bellingham continued. "I know now."

He struck a straight arm with a pointed finger over Julian's head.

"Look, all of you!"

And not a soul but looked, except the woman in the shadow who had no need to look. Even Henry Scoble must follow with his eyes that pointing finger.

By chance, perhaps, though Sir James Elliot would never admit that chance had anything to do with so much as a gesture in all this affair, the harpsichord had been set under a portrait of Julian's father in his youth, painted by Sir James Thornhill. It was a vivid picture of a stripling in a pale blue satin coat and wearing a powdered wig. Whilst Julian had sung, with Elliot as his accompanist at the keys, he had stood between the picture and his audience, masking it from their eyes. Only when he took Elliot's place had the picture been revealed, and so familiar a decoration it was upon those walls that only Brute

Bellingham's sharp eyes had seen and read its message. There it hung on the drawing-room wall in colours as fresh as though they had been painted the day before, and there beneath him at the harpsichord, sat his living replica, the same blue eyes, the same curve of jaw, the same delicate, straight nose, with this difference only noticeable now. Sorrow had given to the living face a droop to the corners of the lips and a shadow about the eyes.

"It's an imposture," shouted Henry Scoble, breathing hard. "An accidental likeness. There are always such for scoundrels to make their profit of. But Giovanni Ferrer, the Marelli—" in his rage and fear Henry Scoble was his own traitor, "will find no victims here …"

"Giovanni Ferrer lies at Naples in the high corner of the Campo Santo. You were present when he was buried, Henry Scoble, and you set my tombstone at his head," said Julian as he stood up at the side of the instrument.

"A cane!" Henry Scoble roared. "Who was it caned Senesino in the streets of London? Marelli shall find the same treatment here. You there, Grainger, Miles, Coates," and he swung round to the huddle of frightened servants by the Library door. "Get canes and whip this pretty rogue out of Grest. See to it Gurton!"

But whilst they stood muttering and mumbling in a confusion, Julian repeated Gurton's name.

"Come you here to me!" he added with a quiet authority, and even Henry Scoble's bluster was stilled.

In a complete silence Gurton walked across the room.

"Do you remember me?"

Gurton stood in front of Julian, looking at him, and without a word. He had no doubts to master, but he had a throat which worked and choked him. At last he began huskily: "My Lord, to see you again is honey in the mouth," and suddenly he dropped on his knee and seizing Julian's right hand pressed it against his forehead. "We have grieved for you, Admiral—"

Julian caught at the title. For the first time that night his poise and calm went by the board. He threw back his head and showed them all a tortured face.

"Admiral!" he cried aloud in anguish and then, dropping his left hand on Gurton's shoulder, he added in a voice broken between a laugh and a sob, "Yes, good friend of mine, old Admiral Timbertoes comes back to Grest for a night and a day."

Elliot was puzzled by that time-limit. It was new to him. It was to be put aside and understood at leisure. Meanwhile it was according to the pattern. Henry Scoble took some comfort from it. He waited. Julian raised Gurton to his feet.

"If any still doubt, I ask them to listen. Mr Bassett, you travelled with me yesterday in my chaise from Winchester to Mr Bellingham's house."

"Yes, I did."

"I was seldom out of your sight today."

"That's true."

"You drove with me tonight to Grest. We were taken straight from the hall into the Library."

Bassett nodded his head.

"But, by Gad, you knew your way," he said

"Aye and he knew of the big bookcase, too," added Brute Bellingham.

"Well then, let me tell you of my house and Mr Henry Scoble will correct me if I am wrong," continued Julian with a savage note creeping into his voice. "When I was a boy, I slept in the big bedroom fronting the east, on this floor, where my father slept before me, and Gurton in the closet at its side." He mounted, as it were, the stairs and described the long corridor and the rooms which opened out of it. Henry Scoble uttered a tittering scornful laugh.

"After all, Grest Park is not unknown," he interrupted. "And it would not be difficult for a stranger who took the trouble to make himself acquainted with its arrangements. I am not belittling Signor Marelli's ingenuity. On the contrary. It is of a very high quality since it can so easily corrupt our good Gurton's simplicity."

Henry Scoble had the trick of words. They went to his head like wine. They fed the passions in his mind. One violent phrase devised another still more violent, one bitter epigram sharpened the acrimony of the epigram to follow. That they missed their mark through their excess mattered not at all, so long as there were words and words like flails to beat an enemy down.

"With Gurton I shall deal in my own time. Admiral Timbertoes – yes, we all remember with a kindly smile the fancies of a young boy. But since the boy is dead, the least raw sentiment of decency might have left them in his grave with him. Meanwhile …"

Henry Scoble was snarling when Julian cut across his speech.

"Meanwhile my memory shall serve where no ingenuity could," he said. "In the long corridor above, by the side of the big staircase a door opens on to the south wing. Into that wing, a few paces from the corridor, a narrow stairway cut in the wall descends. It leads up to a big lumber-room in the roof, where all sorts of pieces of furniture, as they were discarded and replaced, were stored: pictures, mirrors, chairs, old cabinets, tapestries. In that room I used to play truant from my lessons." He turned to Elliot. "You caught me one morning when I was seeking refuge there with old short-sighted Dr Lanford at my heels."

Elliot could see as clearly as if it was all happening today, the boy as he stood on the lowest step in the narrow embrasure of the staircase with an impish grin on his face, a volume of Hakluyt's Principal Navigations under his arm and an appealing finger to his lips.

"I remember it as if it had happened this morning," said Elliot. "I was leaving Grest. Dr Lanford was hurrying up the big stairs, calling 'Julian! Julian!' one moment and moaning 'Oh, dear! Oh, dear!' the next."

There was a trace of that impish grin on Julian's face now, making a boy of him again.

"In my thoughts," said Elliot, "I was a boy again and played truant with you."

"In that bolt-hole I could never be found," Julian continued. "For across one corner a big cabinet stood making a small hiding-place behind it, with just room for a stool and a book and me. It was my private study and I decorated it not very politely with charcoal sketches, chiefly of a small boy with his fingers extended at the end of his nose, expressing his derision at an old tutor in horn-rimmed spectacles. I should be obliged if one or two of you gentlemen would look in that lumber-room now and report to us whether or no I am speaking the truth."

There could not have been a surer test. The cleverest magician of all the magicians since the days of Aladdin could not have found his way up to that lumber-room and scrawled his cartoons upon the walls since Julian had reached Grest. There was a pause, none the less, when he had done, for, in truth, no one now doubted the truth of Julian's claim, and all feared what the outcome was to be.

At last Brute Bellingham spoke up: "I'll go."

"And I," Charles Bassett added.

"Thank you!" said Julian. "You'll need one of the footmen to show you the way. Not you, Gurton. Your loyalty has made you suspect to Mr Scoble."

Bellingham and Bassett went out of the room. A footman lit three candles in the hall and led the way up to the lumber-room. In the drawing-room the rest of that unseasonable part waited. Elliot was seized with an uneasy notion that in the eight or nine years since the refuge had been used, the lumber-room might have been cleaned and the walls freshly painted. Failure in this test, just because it was so convincing if it were true, would, if it were false, offset all the rest. Sir James Elliot forgot the pattern which events must copy and waited in a dreadful expectation. The young ladies said nothing. If they had, they would have vowed they were ready to die, so terrible had become the suspense and the anxiety. But in truth they were exhilarated. Not one fumbled for her smelling-salts or felt her head swimming with the vapours. They were important. They were in the centre of great matters, they would have a theme to astonish their friends for the rest of life. Their one fear was lest they should be sent out of the room and they remained very quiet. Mr Henry Scoble flung himself back in his chair and gnawed the edge of his handkerchief between his teeth. How in the world had any slip occurred? The boy was to be led by – who was the fellow? – Traetta – young Traetta into proposing that he should steal away from the festival of San Januarius and go fishing in the bay. He was to meet his – friends, and Scoble's lips smiled grimly as in his thoughts he used the word – in the darkness of the arch under the Head of Naples, he was to be quietly knocked on the head, stripped of his buckles – yes, and the diamond brooch with which Frances had pinned his cloak, and dumped overboard into the water – a perfectly simple plan, which, according to Domenico, had been executed without a flaw – though, to be sure, it had cost a devil of a lot of money. What then had gone wrong?

But whilst he asked himself this question, the diamond brooch set his thoughts towards Frances. A devilish, good-looking woman she had been – nay, was so still, and passionate. Henry Sooble licked his lips over her passion. Yet he had always distrusted her a little over this – this removal of the boulder in his path. Yes, protest as she might, she had always seemed to be keeping something hidden from him. He turned sharply in his chair towards her. She shook her head, forbidding him to move. She sat apart, her hands upon her lap, her eyes staring from a face of stone.

There was a sound of voices in the passage. The two young men came into the room. Bassett shut the door and Bellingham stood beside him until the latch caught. Then Bellingham advanced until he was face to face with Julian. His face was very grave.

"It's as you say, Linchcombe."

He could have used no words more simple or spoken them with less emphasis. But no other words, no heavier emphasis were needed.

Chapter Twenty-Eight

AFTER EIGHT YEARS

Henry Scoble was the first to break the silence. Whether he thought to carry off the affair as a piece of impudence beneath his consideration or merely to gain a night for consultation with his wife, no one in the room was to know. He got up with a contemptuous flourish.

"Since my servants seem to have renounced their duties and the night is growing late—" he said, and he bowed to Lady Fritton, giving her the lead.

As that stout lady wheezed herself out of her armchair, Brute Bellingham stepped forward to help her.

"There are matters best left to the men," he said sententiously. He had gone openly over to Julian's side, and Henry Scoble flushed with anger. Henry Scoble was to be called to account now in his own house, it seemed, and he could hardly turn his back on the challenge.

"Come, girls," said Lady Fritton. "Very likely the men will bungle it no worse than we should."

She laid her arm lightly on Bellingham's and led the women towards the door. But as she came opposite to Julian, she put her escort aside and, moving close to him, asked in a kindly voice: "Boy, at dinner on the day of San Januarius, where did you sit?"

"Next to your Ladyship. There was an Italian lady on the other side of me. I had not much room," said Julian, and the impish smile shone for a second on his face. The old lady's heart warmed to him.

207

"And what was our position?"

"We were towards the end of the table. Opposite to us was an irreverent Monsignor with a sense of humour." The old lady nodded her head. "We were facing the window."

Lady Fritton smiled.

"That was the circumstance which I remember best of all," she said. "The sun of Naples may be all the poets say, but it can be a damnable grievance to an old woman."

She laid her plump hand with a charming motherliness upon Julian's shoulder and passed on to the door. Brute Bellingham held it open and she drove her reluctant party in front of her. At the door she turned and looked towards Frances Scoble, who had risen when the other women rose, but kept her place by the fire.

"I stay with my husband," said Frances Scoble.

"And indeed Lady Frances is gravely concerned," Julian added.

"Well!" Lady Fritton shrugged her shoulders helplessly. There came into her mind the moving words of the court-usher at the beginning of grave trials. She said very solemnly and quietly: "God send you all a good deliverance," and she went out.

It was odd, Julian thought, that she should use those words. It was the second time that he had heard them from the lips of a friend.

Brute Bellingham shut the door. Then he said: "Gurton!"

Gurton looked towards Julian, who nodded his head.

"Take the other servants with you!"

Brute Bellingham followed them to the Library door and closed that carefully after they had gone out. When he turned back into the room, Henry Scoble's rage burst out of him. Brute Bellingham was officiating; the little unimportant Tory squire with his handful of turnip fields, and at Grest, too. The impudence of it!

"Quite the Master of the Ceremonies, Mr Bellingham! Upon my word, Beau Nash must yield his place. Was there ever a more comical pretension!"

Then he swung round on Julian.

"Now, I suppose we come, Signor Marelli, to the real business of the evening. Well, what's the price of this cock and bull story? Come, out with it! A good stinging price, I'll be bound. Mud's up or down according to whom it's to spatter. What's your price, man? – I beg your pardon for using the word."

"The usual price of murder," Julian answered.

For a moment Henry stopped. For a moment he measured the slender frame of the youth in front of him with his eyes and compared it with his own. Then he laughed brutally and confidently.

"But you're alive, my good fellow."

"You must ask my half-sister why. She hated better than you did. You meant murder – just plain, straightforward murder – to satisfy your simple needs; place, land, money, opportunity."

"It's a lie," cried Henry.

"But Frances," Julian continued. He turned towards her. "If there's an Italian in this room, there the Italian stands." He had not raised his voice, he had not so much as lifted an arm to point her out or moved a step to approach her. But she shrank back against the wall and, as though she was blind, her hand sought for and gripped the edge of the mantelpiece.

"Frances Scoble wanted all you wanted. But she hated and she must have more. A blow on the head, a boy thrown into the water, oblivion, death! Not enough to satisfy the hatred of twelve years. She must maim – and the maimed boy, who could sing well enough for an Earl amongst his friends, must fail in that hard school, where only a rare few survive at a cost which makes survival worthless, and go down to die miserably in the gutter with his memories of Grest to bear him company."

"Calumny! Slander!" Frances Scoble cried in a sudden fierce voice, which in itself gave the lie to her words. There was no remorse in it, not even fear. Hatred made it shake like the flame of a candle in a wind. Regret that the last letter of her purpose had not been fulfilled made it bitter as salt.

"It is true," Elliot rejoined, and his voice was breaking with pain and self-reproach, "Lady Frances took me aside at Naples. She asked me, with a fear and an anxiety which I could not understand, whether it was possible that Julian had the making of a great singer. To my shame, I answered no. I no more understood the relief with which she listened than I had understood the dread which had prompted the question."

Julian's memories went back to a hut upon the hillside against which he had leaned and sung.

"Costanza Traetta was the better judge," he said with a smile which was meant to salve the reproach. He struck a bell on a small table and Gurton answered it.

"There is a portmanteau in my chaise," said Julian. "Here are the keys. You will find a roll of papers. Will you bring it to me?"

Gurton took the keys. The stables were built a hundred yards or so from the house, and the speed with which Gurton brought the roll to the drawing-room took everyone of them by surprise. Julian thanked him and when he had gone, he turned to Bellingham.

"There is the evidence here to prove every charge that I have made – the confessions of Domenico the courier, the Traetta family, Crespino Ferrer and his wife, the accounts of the monies received and paid by Fabricio Menico the attorney, on behalf of the Earl of Linchcombe – it is all here, their signatures attested by the Cavalier Durante and a summary of the investigation by Lelio Zanotti, one of the chief lawyers of Naples. I beg you to keep it in safety."

Brute Bellingham took the roll of papers gingerly. Indeed with its tape and its parchment and its seals, it looked a formidable charge.

"It smells damnably of the Law," he grumbled.

"It may never have to be used," said Julian consolingly. "It all depends on Henry Scoble."

Brute Bellingham's face wore at once a brighter look.

"I'm not a lawyer, God be praised," he said fervently. "Nor I hope a fire-eater either. I am just a plain countryman, and—"

"And there seems to be but the one way of settlement, with no more words than need be," said Julian, and he stepped lightly forward to Henry Scoble.

It seemed to Sir James Elliot that he had been waiting for this moment to come like an actor in the wings for his cue. He took his handkerchief from his pocket and flourished it, so that its perfume scented the air.

"The musk and amber of revenge, Henry Scoble," he said, and he whipped it sharply across Scoble's face.

Scoble stood stock still. He was as white as one of his sanguine complexion could well be, but his eyes gleamed with pleasure; and he behaved with a dignity quite in contrast with his outbursts of rage.

He turned towards Elliot as the oldest of his acquaintances present.

"Although you are against me, Sir James, I hope you will for a few necessary minutes serve me as my friend?"

Sir James hesitated. Violent encounters were not within his experience. He was the looker-on and had not the least wish to play even the smallest part in the cast, much less that of Charles his friend to Henry Scoble. But Julian added his entreaty.

"If you please, Sir James," and Elliot bowed.

"Mr Bellingham, will you oblige me?" Julian continued.

"At your service," Bellingham answered.

There was no question in any man's mind but that the quarrel, so vital to both the enemies, must be fought out to its end before he slept. Bellingham, once more Master of the Ceremonies, but this time on familiar ground, drew back the curtains and opened a pair of long windows. They gave upon the big portico above the Italian garden. The harvest moon was at the full, its great orb a golden red. There was not a cloud in the pale sky, nor a breath of wind in the garden. As far as the eye could reach the country slept in a light clear as the day, but more magical. The night was warm as a night in June.

"Candles will not be needed, Sir James?" Bellingham asked.

In the matter of candles, Sir James was an expert. His eyes had been too often distracted and dazzled in a hundred theatres by the ring of candles round the boxes for him now to disregard their danger.

"They would be the friends of chance," he agreed. Chance had nothing to do with the weaving of the pattern. So it must not spoil the copy. Since he had been cast for the part of Charles his friend, he must play it out honestly and fairly.

"Then will you come with me?" said Bellingham, and he lead Elliot into the Library.

Henry Scoble took off his coat and waistcoat and rolled back the shirtsleeve of his right arm. Julian followed his example, and when Henry saw the youth whom he was to fight made yet more slender and ethereal by the circumstance that he was dressed in white from his throat to the black edge of his shoes, he smiled with a contemptuous pleasure. This was certainly the best way of stifling the whole unchancy business. He would finish with Julian tonight. If there were trouble over the duel, he would plead his clergy and escape all punishment. He might have to postpone his entry into the Government, but not for long. There would be no doubt, too, some unpleasant gossip, but both his acres and his shoulders were broad enough to sustain and subdue it. As for those rolls of parchment which Brute Bellingham held – what value could they have if Julian were dead? They were mere imputations, forgeries made by a rogue. Whatever had been done, had been done in Italy. There was no law in England which could put him on his trial here or send him to Italy to stand upon it there. And there was no Scoble in Italy to raise a question. Besides he had little doubt that he could persuade Brute Bellingham to hand the evidence over to him, once Julian was silenced and underground. Brute Bellingham was poor even for a country squire – there were places and profits within his own patronage. The Earl of Linchcombe could deal with Brute Bellingham – so long as he had dealt with Julian first. And upon that point he was not in doubt; and for an odd reason. He knew very well – no one in the room better – that Julian was matched against him; but he could not get it out of his head that it was none the less one of those Italian singers whom he was going to fight – one of those *soprani* who, like Senesino, screamed with terror and ran off the stage amidst an uproar of laughter if a piece of canvas scenery fell upon their heads, or suffered themselves to be horsewhipped in the streets for an impertinence. Cowards, every man-jack amongst them, and here was one, with the accent of Italy and the high notes of a woman's voice when he sang, just waiting to be spitted at the end of his sword!

Bellingham and Elliot came back into the room, Bellingham now carrying two swords in their sheaths. They were followed by a third man, a short, dark, competent person who carried a case of instruments; and at the sight of him Henry Scoble frowned.

"I sent a messenger with a led horse to the village," said Bellingham. "He was fortunate enough to find Dr Conway at home and not yet gone to bed."

Dr Conway stepped forward.

"I know nothing of the dispute which has caused you to send for me. I understand only that it cannot be settled peaceably. My services are at your disposal."

"We all thank you, Dr Conway," said Henry Scoble.

Bellingham spread a cloth upon a table. He looked towards Julian, taking one of the swords from Elliot and resting it on the palms of his hands. The sheath was of white Cordovan leather, the hilt sparkled with gold.

"This is your sword?"

"Yes."

Bellingham drew the blade from the sheath. It was a rapier of fine blue steel, grooved and tapering to a point. He laid it upon the cloth. Elliot performed the same office for Henry Scoble.

"You all see that the two swords are of the same length," said Bellingham; and when all were satisfied, he wrapped the cloth around them.

"Now, gentlemen, will you be pleased to follow me?"

He led the way out into the moonlit portico. Some garden chairs were scattered about it, and a big, oblong Persian rug was stretched over the stone floor. Under Bellingham's directions, Bassett and Robert Joyce set aside the chairs and rolled away the rug. The portico was deep and long. In one corner Dr Conway opened his case and brought out his instruments and dressings. Brute Bellingham took up a position halfway between the windows and the edge of the platform and halfway between the side walls.

"Here, I think?" he said to Elliot.

"Yes."

"You will take up your positions, gentlemen." Henry Scoble upon Bellingham's right, Julian upon his left, took their places. He opened the cloth and the two enemies took their swords, measured their distance from each other, each one upright with his feet together. Bellingham held out a walking stick which Elliot handed to him, and over it the swords crossed. The moonlight rippled up and down the blades as they met.

"So, to it," said Bellingham. He drew the cane sharply away and stepped back.

Inside the drawing-room Frances Scoble drew close to the window. "Kill him!" she whispered, "kill him!" though there was no one to hear. During this last half-hour no one had remembered her.

Chapter Twenty-Nine

MUSK AND AMBER

Sir James Elliot had twice been flung out of his leisurely and quilted life; once when a boy in handcuffs had burst into tears in the lobby of his apartment in Venice; and now when the same boy was staking his life to avenge a crime and he himself was serving the criminal as his second. There was a difference, however, between the two occasions. In the first, a demand had been made upon him, swift and imperative. He had had to think and act for two; and it was astonishing to him to remember that he had not failed. Now he was a looker-on with a minor function and half of his mind was free to store away the contrast between the moonlit earth sleeping in the dew and the duel to the death in the moonlit porch. He heard the swords grate and hiss as they tried each other out; he saw their points circling like silver about each other within the compass of a curtain ring. But, himself a lamentable swordsman, his mind refused the intricacies of their movements. Idle questions assailed him. Which best nerved the arm and concentrated the eye? The passion to keep or the passion to recover? Did Julian mean to recover Grest and its titles and domains? He had spoken strange words to Gurton. Old Admiral Timbertoes had come back to his house of Grest for a night and a day. For only those few hours … ? And Sir James Elliot was freed from his speculations. Henry Scoble was pressing hard, breathing hard.

His lips were drawn back from his teeth in a grin, but a grin of surprise, of uneasiness. He wasn't fighting an Italian opera singer ready to sink, on a silken knee and bleat for mercy. He was fighting one of his own blood and there was no bearing him down by a show of ferocity. Julian might look fragile as a girl with a face to match, but the face was white and dry in the moonlight and his breath came easily. He was defending himself so far, on the watch for his moment, with a dexterity and suppleness given to him by months of practice intended for this one hour. He had no doubts, no qualms. He might have been in a fencing-school, but that his purpose was as an aura about him and his eyes had the blue steel of his sword. The end came swiftly. Julian's blade seemed to twine like a snake round Henry Scoble's, hold it in a lock and bear it down. Julian disengaged, lunged at his opponent's heart and the point of the sword shone beyond the back below the shoulder blades. Henry Scoble's sword rattled upon the stone floor of the porch, a fraction of a second before his body crashed. Julian wrenched out his rapier and stood back. Henry Scoble's body was convulsed, the knees drawn up to the chin in a spasm – could death be so ungainly, Elliot asked himself? – then it relaxed and lay still. For a few moments the surgeon bent over him, then he sat back on his heels and closed the dead man's eyes.

It was no longer Brute Bellingham who took control.

"Will you wait with him, Dr Conway?" said Julian. It was an order rather than a request. "I will send you help to carry him upstairs."

He turned upon his heel and with the other men behind him he walked back through the open window into the lighted drawing-room. As he reached the glass doors there was a flash of pale blue behind them. As he strode into the room he saw Frances Scoble leaning for support against the corner, her right arm outstretched against the wall to keep herself from falling, the other hanging at her side, rigid, with the palm of her hand pressed against the wall behind her. Her mouth was open, her face working in a spasm of grins, and every now and then a dreadful little laugh broke from her throat. Her eyes were bright with the madness of fear. Hatred and courage and disdain – there was no room in her now for any of these feelings. Fear possessed her from the soles of her feet to the hair which stirred upon her head. And indeed Julian, with his eyes blazing, his sword arm bare to the shoulder and his sword straight at his side dripping blood upon the carpet, made a figure pitiless enough.

But he was not aware of the sword which he held and there was no satisfaction in his voice.

"Frances, I have thought and thought and thought, how I could make you pay for your crime," he said, and he spoke as though there had been no answer to his thoughts but weariness. "But the crime was irreparable and there was no way. You have won, my good sister," and he made a movement with his sword, dismissing her. For a moment she did not understand. She stood clinging to the wall, awaiting the sword's red point. Then with the speed of an animal she ran, her shoulders bent, her hands clutching at her skirts. To the men who had seen her moving always with a high carriage, there was something shockingly ignoble in her panic. They could hear her sobbing in her terror as she ran. She tore the door open and left it open. They heard some cries of alarm and astonishment – for by this time all the servants were clustered in the hall – and then, as those noises ceased, the hurried tapping of her heels upon the stairs.

Bellingham puffed out his cheeks with a great sigh of relief.

"She has gone to her room."

Julian shook his head.

"To her boy's room, Brute," he corrected, with a queer smile on his face. "Listen!"

It was not long before the others heard for what Julian was listening – a key turned in a lock. Julian had a picture of Frances Scoble standing behind the locked door in her child's room, defending him – against no one. It is not to be wondered at if, with recollections of a hut above the Bay of Naples, where there were no doors to be locked, and no one to lock them, his smile was bitter.

He went out into the hall and called Gurton to him. "Take four of the men and a cloak. Go out by the door to the south porch. You will find Dr Conway there. You will carry Mr Scoble up to his room. Meanwhile, send the rest of the servants to their beds. You will bring Dr Conway to me when all is done."

"Very well, my Lord," Gurton answered, and Julian went back into the drawing-room and shut the door.

"I shall ask you gentlemen to be patient for a little while," he said, and only then did he become aware that he was still holding by the hilt his naked sword. The sheath lay upon the table by Henry Scoble's. He sheathed the sword and handed it with Scoble's sheath to Bellingham. "I shall ask Lady Fritton to join us. So we will observe the courtesies."

Bellingham carried the sheath and the sheathed sword into the Library. Julian rolled down his right sleeve and smoothed out the lace ruffle. He carefully straightened his cravat before a mirror, put on his white satin waistcoat and buttoned it, slipped on his embroidered velvet coat and carefully lifted the bag in which his hair was tied clear of it. In the mirror he saw the eyes of Sir James Elliot watching him with amazement. He turned round to him savagely: "Have you forgotten Ferrara, Sir James?" he cried. And the one reward for the students of my class?" Actually it was policy and not coxcombry which set him to the careful arrangement of his dress before the mirror. He had his plan worked out and clear to the last letter, but before he could inscribe the first letter, he must have the help of the ladies of the house. He was the more likely to get that if he presented himself to them with the customary deference of an ordered attire. Spick and span might win the day where the evidence of violence might lose it. He had hardly finished before Dr Conway and Gurton came down the stairs again.

"Will you sit down, Dr Conway? Gurton, I shall want you too," said Julian.

He passed through the hall which was empty now into the smaller drawing-room where the ladies were huddled and talking in whispers. They stopped as he came in and shrank even closer together. It was clear that already they knew of the dead body stretched on its bed in the darkness of the room upstairs.

"I ask for your counsel, Lady Fritton," he said with a bow. And to the others, "Her Ladyship will return to you in a little while."

The old lady had courage and knowledge born of her years and her keen intelligence. Reasonableness was never more needed than in these unreasonable and desperate surroundings. She had to calm the terrors of her younger companions. Therefore she must tread carefully the ways of the world.

"I shall be glad of your arm, my Lord," she said to Julian as she rose, and she laid her hand without a tremor in the crook of his elbow. There was a little movement of repulsion amongst the ladies she was leaving, but she turned to them at once with a quick reproof. "If you will wait, I will come back to you. Now," and after a moment's pause, "Julian."

Julian led her to a chair in the drawing-room and took his stand in front of them all. But there was no penitence nor appeal in either his attitude or his voice.

"There is one of two ways to be taken," he said gravely. "Each with its own consequences. I have thought of them both for years and I see no other. I have no doubt which I should choose, but the decision rests with you."

"Let us hear!" said Elliot.

"We can publish the truth – all of it. From the day of San Januarius in Naples eight years ago, until this minute, when Henry Scoble lies punished for his crime. What would happen to Frances Scoble beyond the universal horror and detestation in which she would be held, whether she could or would be tried in England for a crime for which the penalty is death in the country where it was committed, I don't know. What would happen to me, I do know," and his voice strengthened with just a hint of menace. "I should establish my title before my peers, I should plead my clergy, and I should go scot-free and justified."

A murmur of agreement, warm and hearty, followed upon his words.

"But there's Grest," he continued, and suddenly his voice broke upon the name, so that for a few seconds he must needs be silent; so deep was the love he bore to his home, so intolerable the renunciation which he had forced himself to the brink of making. "There's Grest," he resumed, and he spread out his hands as though with that gesture he embraced it all. "This big house should be noisy with children, its lands want young successors growing up on them amongst its people and its farms, with the love of them, the care for them sinking deeper and deeper in their bones with every hour of every day. Therefore ..." – and again he paused, and again he spoke, but in a louder voice so that all might take note and hold it against him if he went back upon his word – "Therefore, Grest is not for me. By a woman's hatred for a child who never did her conscious wrong, I am for life an outcast."

No one spoke at all. They were country people, moved by just the same deep, shy love of the soil as he was. They could understand his renunciation of it for the sake of it.

But how was it to be done? How was the secret to be kept? Julian turned to that unspoken question. He looked at Conway, the doctor.

"It depends upon you, Sir. Men die quickly, suddenly. A pleurisy, a fever, a heart unequal to its owner's ambitions – it is not for me to choose the malady."

Dr Conway sat, rather white and very still, with all the eyes of that small company upon him. He was an honest, competent, respectable man who had never till now swerved an inch from the code of his profession. But he was of that country. His father had doctored the villagers and the people at the great house before him, and his father's father before that. Better than them all, he understood the harm which would be done if the truth were known, the upset of all the traditions of the countryside, the arraignment, whether there was a criminal trial or no, of a great house. So many men saw only the worst. They would forget all that Grest had done to better the welfare of its tenants and improve its lands. In every alehouse, and farm, and cottage, the malicious, the cynic, the man or woman who knows that the world has gone out of its way to spite him, would have right of speech. The county would buzz, there would be mud thrown and not merely muddy words, as the young Linchcombe rode out in his red coat to the meet, or his mother drove past in her carriage. If this boy could forego so much, even to the punishment of Frances Scoble, how could he stand upon the nice letter of his calling? He nodded his head.

"I run with the pack, Lord Linchcombe."

"I thank you," said Julian, and now he turned his eyes towards Lady Fritton, and his face softened. The tears were running down her cheeks and she made no effort to check them. She lifted her head and tried to dry her eyes with a wisp of handkerchief.

"Can you answer for the ladies, do you think?" Julian asked.

She too was slow in answering.

"I never thought an old, dried-up woman could have so much water at the back of her eyes. Aye, boy, the women'll not talk. They have too much to lose if they do. I am much more afraid of the gentlemen in their cups." The old lady glared at Brute Bellingham and his friends. "These young sparks, with the port decanter swinging round the table, – no wonder they send the ladies out of the room lest we should learn the real art of gossiping – aye, and the proper round language to practise it."

The young gentlemen looked duly chastened and contrite. They understood that Lady Fritton had got to be angry with someone and they were content to be her whipping-boy. Moreover, there was a great deal of truth in what she said.

"But in this case," said Brute Bellingham, "we pledge our word and will keep it," and he added with the awkward manner of his kind when moved by a sentiment beyond the ordinary depth. "We shall none of us forget Lord Linchcombe for his own sake, apart from the debt we shall owe to him."

Charles Bassett gave a gruff assent. Robert Joyce actually clapped his hands and Julian turned to Gurton. But Gurton was flustered. Some of the house-servants knew, of course, that Mr Henry Scoble had been killed in a duel, and some of them that his young Lordship had returned from his grave. But they were in a confusion. It was the affair of the gentlemen and had better be left to them. They were for the most part sons and daughters of old servants and their loyalty could be trusted. In time, of course, there would be a little talk, but if nothing happened to bear it out, it would die away. He would do his best, as in duty bound, to carry out his Lordship's orders. Thus it was arranged.

Lady Fritton went off to the ladies and thence to Frances Scoble's room. There would be no shooting party in the morning and both Bassett and Joyce would return to their houses with the news of Henry Scoble's sudden illness. The doctor would come in the morning, and on the day after, Henry Scoble, Earl of Linchcombe, would die. Meanwhile, Frances and her son would keep their rooms.

"I shall sleep in my old room tonight," Julian said to the butler.

"My Lord, a fire is lit and your clothes laid out," Gurton replied. "I carried your portmanteau to that room as soon as your Lordship's chaise arrived."

"Thank you," said Julian, laying a hand upon the older man's shoulder with a smile. "I wondered how it was that you were so quick in bringing me that roll of papers."

"Ah! I had forgotten them!" Bellingham exclaimed and he went over to the corner of the room where he had laid them down. But Julian stopped him before he reached them.

"Brute, I shall be obliged if you will stay at Grest and dine with me tomorrow. Just you and Sir James."

"Of course – if you wish."

"I should like to spend the day quite alone," Julian continued in a quiet, even voice. "But at dinner I shall be very glad of your company. Will you keep the papers until then?"

Brute Bellingham carried the papers away to his bedroom and Sir James and Julian were left together in the big drawing-room. Of the two, Sir James Elliot looked the more troubled and unhappy. Julian watched him without a word for a minute or two, and then what Elliot had come to know as his impish grin broke over the boy's face.

"I know what you want, old friend," he cried, "but I can't give it you."

"And what's that?" asked the bewildered Sir James.

"A great big goblet of ratafia," said Julian.

Chapter Thirty

A DAY IN THE COUNTRY

Julian went away to that big room on the ground floor where he had slept as a boy. The same dark green curtains draped the windows, the same pictures hung upon the walls. A bright wood fire was burning on the hearth. The candles were lit. Gurton was waiting for him. Nothing had been changed except that now it was full of memories, whereas before it had been rich with hopes – hopes for a fine day, hopes of a new pony, hopes of a wooden leg and an admiral's epaulets. But there had been grim moments, even in those days, when a woman had bent over him and willed his dreams. He sat down upon the side of the bed and Gurton kneeled in front of him and unbuckled his shoes as he had done a hundred times.

"Gurton!"

"My Lord."

"Who has slept in my room since I went away?"

"No one, my Lord. Your Lordship slept here last."

"I am glad," said Julian and he uttered a little laugh of great pleasure as he stretched out the other foot. He was silent for a few moments and then again: "Gurton."

"My Lord."

"Is Wates still here?"

"The head keeper?"

"Yes."

Gurton thrust out a lower lip.

"He's here, my Lord, and just as holty-tolty and Lord of the Manor and damn-those-foxhounds as ever."

Julian laughed.

"I liked Wates, old friend."

Gurton admitted grudgingly.

"I'll not deny but what he had a proper respect for your Lordship."

"He was going to teach me to shoot flying the next year," said Julian.

But the next year Julian was in the warm upper room of the Conservatory of St. Onofrio and he was being taught to aim at high notes instead of high birds.

"'Tis all the fashion now, my Lord."

Again there was a pause and again Julian broke it.

"Wates shall give me a lesson tomorrow, Gurton." Gurton lifted a face eager with hope, but before he could speak Julian shook his head gently: "Only one lesson, old friend. I told you that I had come back to Grest for a night and a day. I was wrong. It's for two nights and a day, but that's all."

Gurton's head drooped and his fingers trembled over a very refractory buckle.

"I want Wates at eight o'clock, Gurton. My one day shall be a long one;" and as he turned on his side in his bed, he wondered whether, when he slept in this room as a boy, he had ever longed for a fine day on the morrow more eagerly than he did tonight.

Wates was ready at eight o'clock by the gun room door with a brown setter at his heels, a powder horn slung across his shoulder and a gun in his hand.

"It's a new gun, my Lord," he said as he touched his hat. "I thought as you might like as it were a gun that nobody had used."

Behind that gruff voice and weather-beaten face, there was a delicacy of thought which went to Julian's heart.

"That was kind of you, Wates."

"Just in the way of my dooty, my Lord. We'll take the home farm. We'll find a covey or two by the hedges."

The day was as fine a September morning as an Englishman abroad ever ached for. The sun was warm and there was a freshness in the air, and where there was shade the dew was still a veil of grey upon the grass. In the wheat fields the sheaves were golden and the apples were red on the orchard trees. Julian made no great figure in his first attempt at "shooting flying", firing for the most part under the birds as they went away and behind them as they went across him. But as the morning grew, he began under Wates' tuition to swing his gun and by mid-day he had eight to his bag.

"A bit o' practice, that's all your Lordship wants," said Wates. "Come out alone along o' me for a fortnight, my Lord—" he wheedled and shrugged his shoulders with a "Well, no doubt your Lordship knows best," when Julian shook his head.

They ate sandwiches together under a hedge and shared a bottle of Burgundy, and Wates cheered up a little.

"There be some wild duck down in the Low Pool and your Lordship should try your hand at 'em," he said. "I'll take you to a piece of good cover on the bank, then I'll walk round and put 'em up."

"Let's go!" cried Julian.

Wates loaded the gun with a vast deal of care.

"You'll get but the one shot, my Lord, and you'll have to be quick. They come up out of the water with a clatter as if all the shutters in the house were being slammed and they'll be off much quicker than they look to be. So choose your bird at once, and swing your gun right through from his tail to an inch or so beyond his long beak and fire on the swing."

He led Julian carefully to a clump of bushes at the edge of the pool, talking only in whispers and left him there. Towards the end of the pool the rushes were thick and Julian could see the ducks swimming, their backs a burnished blue in the sunlight. Wates was out of sight now, but he reappeared in a little while on the high ground beyond the rushes. The ducks began to swim towards Julian's hiding-place and as Wates came down to the shore, they streamed into the air like a cloud. Julian's heart was in his mouth, but he chose his bird and swung his gun as he had been told and to his delight he saw one duck close its wings, swoop out of the sky and plop into the pool like a stone. Julian had heard that noise before – yes, once, when a pair of handcuffs had been flung into the Grand Canal. Even after these months, he shivered as he thought of the Leads which roofed the Ducal Palace. There, but for the grace of

God and the courage of Columba Tadino, he might be eating his heart out now.

The best of the day was gone. As they walked back towards the house, Wates stopped at the stables.

"There's an old friend of yours here, my Lord," he said and held open the gate of the stable yard.

As Julian's heavy shoes rang upon the stones, an old grey pony pushed his head out of the upper opening of a loose box, looked at him and whinnied. Julian ran to it and stroked the pony's neck and the pony rubbed its forehead up and down its owner's waistcoat.

"That wasn't fair, Wates," he said with a break in his voice which he could not check. "Old Morley," that was the pony's name, for it was born on Morley's Farm – and he fondled the warm skin under its thick mane and smoothed gently the velvet nostrils. "It wasn't fair," Julian repeated as he turned away and the tears were in his throat and stinging his eyes.

"Well," Wates answered with a grunt. "We reckoned, Gurton and me, that if Old Morley couldn't keep your Lordship in your own home where you ought to be, nothing that we could say would do it."

Julian handed him back the gun.

"You make it difficult, Wates," he said as he shook hands with the keeper. "God knows, I've been tempted enough today."

He walked round to the east side of the house where the parish church stood, on a little knoll in the park, not fifty yards away. The door was unlocked. He pushed it open and going up the short aisle sat himself down in his proper place in the big pew facing the chancel steps.

It was very still. The walls of the chancel were lined with the marble tablets of Scobles, dead and buried beneath the stones. High up hung that of Philip Challoner Scoble, first Viscount Terceira, who had sailed with Drake to the Azores. Julian would have liked one day to bear that old sailor company, but it was not to be. His own place was in the Protestant corner of the Campo Santo at Naples, and he must keep it.

The shadows were beginning to creep into the small church when Julian shut the door behind him. The warmth had gone out of the sun although it still lay mellow on lawn and path. Julian's day was almost done.

He went to his room and dressed with care. He was in his own house, entertaining his friends, and seemliness was demanded. He awaited them in the big drawing-room. They dined in state, Sir James Elliot upon Julian's right, Brute Bellingham upon his left, and Julian at the head of the table. A fire was burning, the curtains drawn, the candles lit in the sconces, and the talk friendly and familiar. Julian made a good story of his first attempt to "shoot flying" and of his wild duck. But after the port had passed round the table twice, he said: "Brute, you have some papers of mine?"

Bellingham had brought them into the room and laid them upon the sideboard. He fetched them now to the table, but sat with his hands holding them down, as if he feared they would fly away.

"Publish them, boy!" he cried. "Say you came back and killed the rogue upstairs. Plead your clergy and stay at Grest. For, God's wounds! you're the best Linchcombe of the lot."

"I should be the worst if I obeyed you," said Julian. "Give!"

He gently took those confessions of Domenico and Ferrer, the Traettas and Fabricio Menico the attorney, all the evidence and proofs of the crime of Henry Scoble and his wife Frances from under Bellingham's hand. He walked with them to the fireplace and dropped them into the fire and stood over them, treading them down with his shoe, whilst the parchment curled over and grew brown and changed from brown to black. Not until they were nothing but flakes of white ashes scattered amongst the burning logs, did he turn away. Then he held out a hand to each of his friends.

"I shall be gone tomorrow before either of you is awake. But carry me, both of you, for a little while in your hearts."

And both of them, just before the day broke, heard the wheels of his chaise as it rolled away up the hill from the house.

Chapter Thirty-One

A HAVEN OF A SORT

From time to time during the next ten years, Sir James Elliot heard of the Marelli's progress through Europe. The singer never returned to England, but at Berlin and Hanover, at Vienna and Dresden, he was as familiar a figure and a voice as magnetic as in the cities of Italy. He passed three years in Russia, where he was said to have amassed a large fortune, a year after those between Florence, Milan, Naples and Turin; and then his voice was heard no more. Sir James Elliot understood from Julian's last words at Grest that he wished to cut himself off from all the memories and associations of his boyhood as utterly as he could; and with a melancholy submission accepted the separation. But Sir James was himself growing old. He was finding it more pleasant now to sit by his own fireside with his recollections, than to endure the long, dusty, lurching journeys and the vile inns of the Continent. The mode of the times, too, influenced him. The turgid librettos built upon ancient legends were fast losing their hold upon the sympathies of the public. Goldoni had pointed out a better way, and music was expectant of that great genius so soon to sweep the old style into oblivion, Amadeus Wolfgang Mozart. But Sir James wondered often what had become of Julian. He had loved the boy dearly and read his character well, and he could not easily imagine him retiring to some estate in Saxony or Northern Italy, or where you will, to enjoy his wealth in an idle seclusion.

Accident – or was it that the copy of the old pattern was not yet completely woven? – solved his problem.

Sir James roused himself with many reproaches from his lethargy five years after Julian had ceased to sing. He would make one last tour. He would go and hear these new Gods who were chasing from their thrones, Hasse and the Scarlattis, Jommelli and Porpora. Travelling southwards from Milan, he broke his journey at Lutria, the capital of a Duchy of some importance in those days. There was a church there, notable for its architecture, and an Opera House which burst into a short but brilliant season during the Carnival. It was early summer, however, when Elliot reached the town and the Opera House was closed. He put up at the Inn of the Lobster and called during the next morning upon the Maestro di Capella, one Orsino Romagno. Signor Romagno received the Baronet with great civility, showed him with pride his musical scores, his books on Church music and the organ in the church itself.

"All who love music know of your work in Lutria," said the Baronet, pompously, politely and not very truthfully.

Signor Romagno purred. But he must not take all the credit – oh no! A little perhaps was due to enthusiasm rather than to his talents which were no greater than those of other maestros. "I have, besides, every assistance that I ask for from the Chancellor of the Duchy," he added.

"He has a love of music?" asked Sir James.

Signor Romagno pondered.

"I cannot say that. What I ask for, I get. But I think that he has a grudge against music. But you will no doubt judge for yourself."

Sir James shook his head.

"I have not the honour of knowing him," he said and the maestro looked at him with surprise.

"His Excellency Giovanni Ferrer?" cried Signor Romagno, and Sir James jumped as if an early bee had stung him in the neck.

"Giovanni Ferrer?"

"The Marelli," replied Romagno. "He sang years ago during several carnivals. The Duke entertained him first as a singer, then as a friend. They talked affairs as well as music. Then the Duke persuaded him to take a place on his State Council and finally made him his Chancellor."

There had been such cases before. Stefani, the diplomat, had sung in Germany before he became the chief consultant of a great Prince. Was not Farinelli himself supposed to have exercised so much power in the politics of Spain that grandees humbly sought his favour? Elliot was glad that a like career had fallen to the lot of Julian. The ageing of a singer was at its best a melancholy business; and to one who had a grudge against music – Elliot thanked the maestro for the phrase – it would be a miserable one.

"And as a Chancellor?" Elliot asked, only half daring to put the question.

"He has all our votes," replied the maestro with a smile. "He is of a fair and liberal mind with a will of his own. There have been difficult hours in our little history, but His Excellency has not spared himself. He and His Grace are agreed and the State prospers."

Sir James walked back to the Inn of the Lobster, noting the comfortable aspect of the citizens with something of the pleasure he would have felt, had he been responsible for it himself. Over his solitary dinner the desire to renew his knowledge of Julian in his new dispensation got the better of his reserve. He persuaded himself without much difficulty that his manners would be faultier than a baronet's should be, if he did not pay his respects and announce his presence in the town. He seized paper and pen and wrote a letter. He made it easy for Julian to avoid him, if he would, by declaring that he was leaving for Florence in the morning. Then he sent the letter by hand to the Chancellery and waited, in a fever, for an answer. It came back by the same hand. Would Sir James take supper with him at ten at his private house?

Sir James made sure of the house before the light fell. It stood in the main square, a house of size and dignity with a big walled garden behind it.

At ten o'clock Julian made his apologies to Elliot for the lateness of the hour. He was now a man of thirty-five, his hair under its powder – for he still wore his own hair – was flecked at the temples and ears with grey and his face lined at the forehead and the mouth. But Elliot felt that some degree of contentment had smoothed out his life.

"I had to make the hour late," he said with the tone of one who had parted with Elliot the night before. "You see, here we are jammed in

229

between Piedmont and the Papal States, so we are often in trouble. Do you remember the desolation of Ferrara, Sir James?"

He took Elliot into the dining-room and so once more the pair sat down at the table together.

"I have shot a good many wild duck since I saw you last," said Julian with the grin which Elliot remembered. But he talked only of his little State and the life there. Elliot was careful to follow him with enquiries and comments. Grest was never mentioned by either of them until the moment of Elliot's departure. They stood together in the porch. A link-boy with a lighted torch was waiting in the square. The town was asleep. For the first time there was a note of constraint in Julian's voice

"So it's goodbye, old friend," he said. "You go tomorrow," and he laid his hand on Elliot's arm "I thank you for not talking tonight about the things of which we both were thinking. It was kind, and I shall ask from you another kindness." He spoke very gently, knowing that his words would hurt. But for his own salvation they had got to be spoken. "I shan't sleep tonight. Old Admiral Timbertoes will stump the Italian garden at Grest with his wife on his arm and scold his children for the noise they make and be laughed at by them for his pains, until the morning breaks. So when you come back North, will you, please, pass Lutria by? I don't want to find – do you remember that old song I sang as a boy? – a pillow wet with my tears."

Elliot could not speak. He followed the link-boy with the flaming torch. At the corner of the square, he turned. He saw the figure of Julian relieved against the lights of the hall. Then the door slowly closed.

THE END

SUNDAY, *September* 21*st*, 1941

A E W Mason

The Four Feathers

Harry Feversham is in love with the alluring Ethne Eustace. A dazzling engagement ball is held in their honour at her Irish country home. For Harry, it seems like life cannot get any better. But a mysterious package arrives for him and the contents turn out to be three white feathers. Publicly branded a coward, Harry suffers the ultimate humiliation when Ethne adds a fourth feather to his collection. Shunned from society, he sets out to regain his friends, fiancée and honour. He embarks on a deadly mission, which takes him from Ireland to England to Egypt, and which tests his courage to the limits and his will to survive.

The House of the Arrow

Messrs Forbisher and Haslitt are respected solicitors responsible for the estate of Marie Harlowe, who bequeaths her possessions to her young niece, Betty Harlowe. But when Marie dies, her will becomes hotly contested thanks to the shadowy figure that is Boris Waberski. He writes a series of desperate letters to Forbisher and Haslitt, laying claim to Marie Harlowe's assets and it's not long before Marie's niece stands accused of murder. In this famous mystery, the young woman faces poisonous blackmail and potential ruin. Only Inspector Hanaud is capable of exposing the villainous plot to discredit and destroy Betty Harlowe. But is she innocent?

'Inspired, a well-imagined, well-crafted detective story'
– *The New York Times*

A E W Mason

Musk and Amber

Julian Linchcombe is the remarkable heir to the Earl of Linchcombe's estate and he has the voice of an angel. When he is taken to the festival of San Januerius in Italy to witness a miracle, his uncle arranges for him to go sailing with a local fisherman. But Julian is soon lured into running away. A massive search gets underway to find the missing boy until eventually a body turns up broken and tangled in a fishing net. A sinister plot is uncovered involving fraud, kidnap and murder. Has Julian been stolen away for his voice? And who is dead?

The Prisoner in the Opal

An Englishwoman is brutally murdered in the South of France and an American goes missing. With the discovery of a body, a severed hand and an opal bracelet, Inspector Hanaud of the Sureté is called in to investigate. It's not long until allegations of devil worship begin to arise. Inspector Hanaud must race against time before a second violent murder is committed.

'One of the best by a detective ace' – *Herald Tribune*

A E W Mason

Running Water

The Brenva Glacier at Mont Blanc has always been a legend among mountaineers. When the talented John Lattery sets out one day to cross this sea of ice, no one thinks that it will be his last expedition. But, when Lattery fails to return, his long-time friend, Captain Chayne, is sent to search for the missing explorer. As his party engages in a heroic search and rescue mission, Chayne makes a sickening discovery.

The Watchers

It is 1758 and Lieutenant Clutterbuck, a tough but ebullient soldier, once stationed in the Scilly Isles, hosts a raucous party. During the high-spirited night-time revelry, a young boy appears. He tells the tale of Adam and Cullen Mayle, former acquaintances of Lieutenant Clutterbuck. This father and son duo turn out to be renowned for their thievery. But their days of stealing seem over when Cullen gets caught and disappears after mysterious men are seen watching the Mayle's house. Who are the watchers? And what happened to Cullen Mayle?

Printed in Great Britain
by Amazon